# World's End
## and the Sea Angle

# WORLD'S END AND THE SEA ANGLE

*Revised Version 2024*

**YANK SHI**

# Editor's Note of the First English Edition

World's End and the Sea Angle, by Yank Shi, is a very ambitious undertaking. In addition to being a novel about the courtship and long and happy, adventure-filled life of the main characters, Emily and David, it pushes right up against, past, philosophical, and space-time frontiers.

Much of the novel is written in the present time. But David time-travels back to a primitive era, and both Emily and David travel forward in time to an idyllic future. They use the Bermuda Triangle as a portal or space-time conduit for these trips.

They are adventurers and seekers of truth. Before their time travel, they journey throughout the United States and China, and go to Egypt, seeking out monuments and great works of art. They discuss what they see at length. In the process, they cover much of history. One of the nicest things in the novel, for me, is the philosophical dialogue that the two lovers have. These are long, intimate, leisurely, and probing, actually breaking new ground in thought as well as showing the depth of the relationship. These dialogues are key to the relationship between the two, and they also advance knowledge.

There are additional stories at the end, including one about Wuhan at the time the coronavirus struck, and another about worldwide nuclear war and what that feels like in the United States.

Despite the many characters, periods of history, and events covered in this book, it is consistently lyrical, descriptive, and probing about what life is about and what it should be about. My hat is off to the author for a complex piece of work done boldly and with a sense of poetry and grace.

# Foreword

The vast universe, the immensity, is amazing. Looking up at the sky, the stars dot it like jewels. The stars are shining and mysterious, like countless bright eyes overlooking the world.

Time is like a river, running ceaselessly, day and night. Every minute comes and goes in a hurry, and "This moment" is soon vanishing. "Today" quickly becomes "yesterday" and "this year" turns to "last year" in a flash.

Stars in the space converge into galaxies. Among the many galaxies, there is a galaxy called Milky Way, in which there is a solar system. In the solar system, there is the sun, with eight planets orbiting it. One of the eight planets is the Earth where we live.

Earth is surrounded by a blue ocean, set off by several brown and green land, and wrapped by a soft atmosphere. Most of the land is lush, fresh, and sunny. There are mountains, water, plants, animals, and human beings on it, so it's lively and colorful. Intelligent people accumulate knowledge, develop science and technology, and make life richer and more convenient. Artists show their talents and inspirations and create art treasures so that people can enjoy the beauty of vision, hearing, and soul.

Human beings on Earth have experienced numerous changes and developments since ancient times. Man and nature intersect and stand in harmony with each other. People meet and cooperate with each other to form a human society to create a human civilization and a better future. People are often opposed to each other due to different beliefs and ideas, and even occasionally have conflicts. They combine and divide, and combine again, composing human history.

The love between men and women is often full of joys and sorrows, twists and turns, and presents touching comedies and tragedies.

Everyone takes a certain space, some areas of activity in the universe, such as a country, a province, a city, a district, or a village in the world. Everyone is at a certain period in the long river of time. For example, a century, a year, a month, a day, a moment. A person is always in a coordinate range of time and space. The space-time coordinates of a person are always changing. The body is constantly moving, the location is inevitable to move, and time is always with him (or her), passing by in a hurry.

Human stories all involve some individual or a group of people. Everyone has his or her own specific story. With billions of people in the world, there are billions of stories. If we are interested in exploring and interviewing the parties, we will learn countless extraordinary and colorful life stories, including plenty of vivid and moving plots.

The story we are going to tell here is one of them. It consists of one main story that leads to several related ones. However, in the numerous human stories, we can only focus on a certain person or certain people, a certain period of time, and a certain region, and also rely on an observation perspective of the author.

Some of the plots in our story are beyond the normal time and area of ordinary people's activities, and the perspective is also kind of unusual. It makes readers feel a little unrealistic and absurd. For example, when it comes to ancient times, the future and the aliens, and when it comes to the modern people's crossing into the ancient times and the future, being immersed in the environment, like in dreams, seemingly true, but actually not.

People in different eras and in different regions have common humanity despite their different lifestyles, habits, and ideas. Ancient Chinese enlightenment education has the "Three Character Classics", which begins with the saying "Man is born good. Men's nature is close to each other; while his custom might be remote to others". There is much controversy about the saying "Man is born good", while "Men's nature is close to each other; while his custom might be remote to others" is widely recognized. In this sense, the East and the West, the ancient and modern, the aliens and the Earth people, despite their distinctive lifestyles, all have similar "human nature". The difference in space-time coordinates does not make them different and incompatible aliens or extremes. This understanding also runs throughout our story from beginning to end.

# Note

This is a book of fiction. Names, places, times, events, etc., are all products of the author's imagination and invention. Any resemblance to an actual person, place, or event is purely coincidental. The discourse in the writing about mankind, the world, and the universe is just personal outlooks, not achievements on rigorous scientific research, nor a reliable theoretical basis.

# Contents

# Chapter 1

## CAMPUS LOVERS

**The End of the 20th Century and the Beginning of the 21st Century AD**

In the state of Colorado in the United States of America, at the foot of the Rocky Mountains, there is a city that is not very big, called Boulder. In Boulder, there is a university, which is a good one, called the University of Colorado Boulder.

The university is close to several magnificent, steep peaks of the Rocky Mountains. The school buildings are built of red mountain stones. The high ranking of the university, the unique style of the campus, the mountainous environment, and the spectacular scenery of the Rocky Mountains attract a large number of in-state, out-of-state, and foreign students to the University.

One summer evening, David Polo, a biology graduate student, was walking alone in the schoolyard when he saw a girl sitting on the lawn. The girl was looking at a distance and seemed to be deep in thought and meditating. By her appearance, she looked like an East Asian girl, in a white shirt and with her long hair hanging down her back and down her chest. David was deeply moved by her elegant temperament, beautiful face, and slender figure. In the eyes of David, she was clearly an Eastern Venus. David was intoxicated in a perfect situation. Unable to leave, he stopped and looked infatuatedly at the goddess. A powerful force pulled him close to the goddess.

David began to chat with the girl, "Excuse me, can I know if you are from China, Japan, or South Korea?" The girl raised her head and looked at the strange man with a curious eye. She said, smiling and, unrestrained, "Then guess it." Her voice was soft and friendly. David looked at the girl's face carefully and noticed that the girl's eyes were rich in connotation as if they could talk. He asked: "Chinese?" The girl smiled and said, "Quite right." So, they began to talk.

The young man introduced himself, saying that his name was David Polo, a doctoral candidate in the Biology Department.

The girl said that she was called Jin Li, her English name was Emily. She was from China and is now a graduate student for a master's degree in the Department of Fine Arts. They talked about the university, Boulder, Colorado, and the Rocky Mountains. David felt that Emily was easy to communicate with, and Emily found David quite talkative.

Emily had a good feeling about David. She felt a strong energy and burning passion in David. David's face was well-contoured with bright eyes, a powerful trunk, and a height of at least 1.84 meters, reminding her of the images of men in ancient Greek sculptures, even a bit like Michelangelo's famous sculpture "David". David's extraordinary demeanor and free and easy conversation had left a deep impression on her.

Later, they met several more times in the school library and UMC (University Memorial Center). They talked more as if they were old friends. David said his parents, who were of Italian and Ireland origins, had lived in Virginia and now lived in Boulder, Colorado. His father worked in NCA (National Center for

Atmospheric Research). Emily told David she came from Yantai City, Shandong Province, China, actually from the coast of the Bohai Sea on the other side of the Pacific Ocean to the foot of the Rockies in the mid-western United States.

In their contacts and associations, the feelings of mutual love gradually grew and surged in their hearts. The face and figure of the other always flashed in one's brain. They were dealing with the daily curriculum and the trivial matters in front of them in inertia.

David found that he had virtually fallen in love with Emily, and also faintly perceived Emily's warmth towards him. But for this Eastern woman who he just acquainted with right here, he still felt some mysteriousness and could not read the girl's mind. In particular, Oriental women had a special reserve for emotion. Besides, he did not know if she already had a boyfriend. He did not want to reveal his thoughts to her at this time. If an unripe courtship was rejected, it would destroy the intimate friendship that had been established and ruined the nice spiritual paradise that the two were commonly managing.

One evening David and Emily met on the lawn where they had first met. They had a good talk. The content of the conversation became gradually unimportant, and the emotional exchange heated up. Both of them enjoyed the happiness and beauty of this emotional fusion between them. Emily closed her eyes as if to quietly appreciate it and contemplate. David also fell silent and looked at Emily, who was close at hand. David carefully examined Emily's face. He thought her features were pretty and perfectly arranged on her face, giving a sense of grace and beauty. He admired the Creator's magical design. Emily's face and the curved lines of her figure, limbs, waist, and chest were like an enchanting Oriental movement, beyond expression. David felt that the appreciation of nice things was an infinitely enjoyable and pleasing experience.

The passion in David's heart began to sprout and burn, just like the hot stirring magma under the earth's crust.

He found it hard for him to hold back his emotions, and difficult to suppress the strong gravity from Emily. But he was uncertain about the Oriental goddess in front of him and did not dare to act rashly. He held his breath and struggled to restrain himself. However, the raging, spurting magma suddenly broke the shell like a volcano eruption.

David almost involuntarily kissed Emily on her cheek. Emily opened her eyes and stared at him. David was a little perplexed, with a guilty sense of blasphemy, and a bit like a child who got into trouble, being at a loss. To his surprise, he saw that

Emily's face was calm at first, and then a gentle sunshine gradually appeared on it. Emily smiled so naturally and peacefully. David intuitively felt that this beautiful goddess was no longer reserved and had accepted his love.

Emily, like most women, had a natural sense of love for the opposite gender. She had long felt the love of David and was ready for David to break through the surface of the diaphragm and was even psychologically prepared and silently waiting for the moment to come. David bravely told Emily what he had long hidden in his mind: "I like you, Emily. I love you."

David looked at the face of the beautiful girl in front of him and saw the bright light in her eyes. How charming her eyes were! Emily deliberately avoided David's gaze, lowered her eyes slightly, then slowly raised her head and said softly and lovingly: "Me too." At this moment, the emotions of the two were mingled together like two surging waves. They hugged, forgetting about time, about the place, and others. It was as if there were only two of them in the world, and everything else was lost or insignificant. The first close physical contact between them was as natural as it should be. A magnet-like attraction brought the two together. This converging of their souls was sweet and mellow, which made them excited and intoxicated. They wondered in their minds who attached the gravitation and intoxication between human genders, which made them curious and fascinating.

David was so immersed in the happiness of love that he thanked the Creator for presenting him with such a goddess. David felt that the beauty of Eastern and Western women belonged to different aesthetic types. Oriental women had a different kind of tenderness and elegance. At this time, David had been completely overcome by the charm of this Asian woman. He devoted all his love to this Chinese girl. Whenever he thought of Emily, of her voice and smile, he felt as if a gentle and pleasant breeze was blowing in his heart, which made him merry and cheerful.

For Emily, David's sudden arrival made her happy. The young man was like a Prince Charming from the sky. She thought that she had met an ideal boyfriend, a lover who could be trusted, relied on, and be proud of. Every act, move, smile, and words of David were etched in her memory, like the close-up in a movie. David alone was concentrated, highlighted, and drawn, while others were shrinking, getting smaller, blurring, and downplaying.

David and Emily had almost the same feelings. Since falling in love, everything in the world seemed to have changed. In their eyes, all things seemed to be particularly lovely, not only flowers and trees but also pedestrians on the road, regardless of their age, gender, height, prettiness, or plainness. David and Emily infected the whole world with their own inner happiness. Their deep love for each other had kindled their love for the entire world and all the people.

This love was the noblest of human emotions.

David and Emily began to keep in close contact with each other. After school, they watched football games together, saw movies in the cinema, and attended concerts. Both indulged in the endless sweetness of their fresh love.

The dancing of the two at the party attracted many admiring eyes. They forgot all kinds of life trivia, and troubles of reality, while their souls sublimated to a transcendent realm.

In talking with Emily, David learned that Emily had lost her father at the age of six, and her father had died of liver cancer. Her mother later remarried. The lack of family warmth in adolescence and youth allowed her to develop a quiet and thoughtful character. She had a passion for Western fine art and knew a lot about the development of Western art. She liked oil paintings. She studied art at the Central Academy of Fine Arts in Beijing for four years, graduated with honors, and was retained as a teaching assistant after graduation. In the meantime, she applied for graduate school in the United States and was admitted to the Fine Arts

Department at the University of Colorado Boulder with some financial aid as a teaching assistant.

After about three months, David asked Emily to visit his parent's house to meet his father, McCarthy Polo, his mother Catherine, and younger sister Jessica. Emily readily accepted the invitation. The home of David's parents was at a fascinating location in Boulder. There were flowers and trees around, in a lush green, quiet, and elegant environment. Occasionally, wild deer appeared outside their backyard.

There was a feeling of a fictitious land with idyllic beauty.

David's parents liked Emily very much and hoped that she could come often later and told Emily that whatever difficulties she came across they would be happy to help. David's younger sister, Jessica, became friends with Emily in an instant. They talked cordially. It was getting late before they knew it. The family warmly invited Emily to join them for dinner at a Chinese restaurant. David's parents also called to invite David's uncle Timothy Polo to go with them. During the meal, Timothy said he had visited Beijing, Shanghai, and Dalian a year ago and talked a lot about what he had seen and heard there. Emily felt that the family of David's parents were sincere and kind, and she seemed to have found a warm home in a foreign country.

David and Emily's hobbies tended to be close to nature.

They enjoyed the natural environment of Colorado. They went touring in the Rocky Mountains, boating in the lake, picnicking and camping in the countryside on weekends and holidays, and went skiing in winter.

Beyond that, they preferred to explore life, the world, and the universe, with topics as boundless as the sea and the sky. Their discussions were serious, not a love affair episode. David discovered that Emily was an extraordinary woman. Her thinking was out of the ordinary and her speech was often rich in philosophy. She had a broad vision and a magnanimous mind. David himself was a student of biology and had a unique view of life, mankind, the Earth, and the universe. Whenever he talked about these, he found that Emily was particularly interested, with bright eyes, and being able to deliver extraordinary insights.

David said that he had a special interest in Chinese traditional culture. He had read the English versions of the four famous Chinese classics: Dream of the Red Mansions,

The Romance of the Three Kingdoms, Water Margin, and Journey to the West. He also had a general understanding of the theories of Lao Tzu (Laozi), Chuang Tzu (Zhuangzi), Confucius, and Mencius. He loved Peking Opera and Chinese martial arts. He studied Chinese martial arts in the United States. The coach was a martial arts master from China.

Speaking of literature and art, David was surprised to find that Emily was so familiar with Western literature and art. Needless to say, Emily's familiarity with Western art history, the number of Western literary classics she had read as well as her perception of them, were no less than those of him as a Westerner. Emily loved Shakespeare's plays, Charles Dickens, Honoré de Balzac, Leo Tolstoy's novels, and Lord Byron's poems. She often talked about Victor Hugo's Les Miserables, Stendhal's Red and Black, Romain Rolland's John Christopher, Sholohov's And Quiet Flows the Don, and so on.

The cultural gap between the East and the West is quite large. Each has its own spirit and charm. Some people say that the East is the East, and the West is the West. It seems that it is difficult to communicate in-depth and to achieve true understanding between the two sides. However, Easterners and Westerners are both human beings and should have a common humanity. The people of the East and West should communicate with each other, integrate with each other, understand each other, and adapt to each other. Anything is possible. Some Chinese pianists play Western classical music, showing their charm and transcendence in depth and detail, which makes Westerners greatly surprised. Some Americans blend in with the general public of China. They speak standard and authentic Chinese and have acquired Chinese customs and ways of thinking which have penetrated into their bones. Chinese people are left speechless in surprise.

The marriage between the Orientals and the Westerners is not uncommon. Sino-US marriage is even more commonplace. The convergence of the two sides is increasing, to learn from other's strong points to offset their own weaknesses. Many can produce beautiful, happy fruit.

The combination of David and Emily is a perfect example.

Emily's heart was stormy. She thought of the confluence of the Yangtze River and the Mississippi River in the vast ocean. David's heart was magnificent. He thought that the rock of the Rocky Mountains could attack the jade of Kunlun Mountain (from a Chinese idiom literally "Stones from other mountains can be used to attack jade").

David and Emily looked up at the sky and were filled with emotion. In the vast universe, in the long river of history, among the world's mortal beings, they did not know how many men and women met each other, got to know each other, joined hands, walked together, and became lifelong companions. Cupid blesses them and nature sings their praise. Youth is beautiful; love is sweet.

*Eastern and Western civilizations have different origins, with distinct characteristics and individual charms. However, the two are not insulated and mutually exclusive. The mutual exchange and integration of Eastern and Western cultures are completely possible, which will make the human civilization more brilliant and colorful.*

*Love between the two sexes of human beings is a a kind of sweet and noble emotion, which has no boundary and can transcend the racial boundary and cultural di.Iference.*

# Chapter 2

## HUMAN ORIGIN

David and Emily once talked about the origin of mankind, and their views were very close. The following is a conversation between them.

Emily: A picture painted by Paul Gauguin is entitled Where are we from? Who are we? Where are we going? Can you answer these questions, David?

David: There are divergent opinions on the origin of mankind. The theory of evolution still has an impact, although doctrines other than evolution continue to emerge. Different religions claim the source of human beings by divine creation.

Emily: I do not believe in the "creationism" of any religion, nor do I agree with the "theory of evolution" advocated by Charles Darwin that many scholars follow. It is said that some schools in some states of the country have stopped teaching evolution doctrine.

David: Yes. The main forces that negate evolution come from both new advances in scientific research and religions.

Emily: It seems as if it were an either/or. I don't think so.

David: The Achilles' heel of evolution is the lack of systematic and compelling evidence. Species can improve and change. But evolution from one species to another is still a corollary.

Emily: Evolution from the ape to the primitive is the key.

David: Archeologists have discovered a number of fossils to prove this transformation. However, these fossils only show that early human form is close to the ape, but could not prove the transformation from apes to humans. Molecular biology has confirmed the essential difference between human and anthropoid nuclei and the fact that the cells of apes cannot become those of human beings.

Emily: Except for the evolution from the apes to the human beings, the transformation of other species to different ones is like a myth. Can monkeys turn into orangutans? Can magpies become crows? Not to mention that fish become amphibians, amphibians become reptiles, and reptiles become mammals.

David: There is supposed to be a gradual change in a species transformation, and a large number of species in some gradual states. The physical evidence in this regard is insufficient.

Emily: Yes, there's always a clear line between apes and hominids with no distinct transition.

David: The DNA (deoxyribonucleic acid) theory and technology are rapidly developing today. People have made some interesting discoveries in the testing and analysis of individual DNA samples. The ancestors of many people in Asia and Europe can now be traced back to the original Neanderthals, and even to the assumed early humans in Africa. If the quest for ancestors through DNA can be further traced back to apes and earlier animals, it should be a significant breakthrough in the theory of human origin, a great victory for evolution. Unfortunately, today's DNA chase has not achieved such a goal.

Emily: Besides, why are there so many different species of life on Earth, and the number of species is declining?

David: Extinction of species is quite common. It is said that one species becomes extinct every hour. More than 99 percent of the 5 billion species that once existed on Earth do not exist now. The dinosaurs that once dominated the world are extinct.

Emily: Why are species only extinct with no emergence of new ones?

David: According to the theory of evolution, species can change into different ones. New species should continue to be produced. No reliable evidence of speciation has been found so far in Earth's long history. Actually, species can just depopulate, not yield any new ones, that is, just decrease, not increase in number. This shows the flaws of the evolution theory. It seems that the variation from one species to another is not that simple. Without the possibility of species transformation, we will have to exclude the possibility of biological progression from the low evolution level to the high one and go in the other direction.

Emily: You mean "divine?" Isn't that a road with a dead end?

David: I don't believe in any specific religious doctrine, nor should the Creator of humans be the God of any religion.

Emily: I feel that "Laotinye" (literally "old Heaven father"), "Zaohua" (Creator), and "Shangcang" (Master of Heaven) often mentioned by the Chinese people have some reason. This Laotinye has no specific lineage, no systematic doctrine, no fixed believers, and no churches or temples for preaching and worship, very abstract.

David: I agree. It sounds like a universal Creator and Master of all things. This is a kind of belief, not a religion.

Emily: People often talk about "Tian (Heaven)," and everyone understands the meaning of "Tian." For example, in the Chinese language, there are expressions like "created by Tian and Earth (tianzaodishe)," "ruled by Tian (tianjingdiyi)," "as natural as Tian (tian ran)," "justified by Tian (tianli)," "genius from Tian (titania)" and so on. But why must there be a "Tian?"

David: To build a house there should be a designer. The designer draws a blueprint for the design, and the house is built according to the blueprint. A house does not grow naturally as a tree does. In the case that a tree grows naturally, it should do so according to certain rules, not at random. A poplar sapling will not grow into a pine tree. It must have various characteristics of the poplar, namely, it is grown according to the poplar design blueprint. A seed, a sperm, or an egg contains specific life-password DNA, which is the core and necessary element of the blueprint for growth. Living creatures are born and grown in accordance with their specific blueprints of DNA.

Emily: Where does DNA come from?

David: Given by the Heaven. Heaven is what the Chinese call the Laotianye and Westerners call the Lord (in a broad sense).

Emily: Do you mean that human beings also grow according to some design?

David: Yes. Races and individuals have some differences, but they all belong to the category of the human species, not other animals.

Emily: So, people have not evolved from other animals and will not be transformed into other animals. Right?

David: That's right. However, the same species can be altered and improved, just as the architectural design blueprint can be adjusted and improved in the process of construction. However, the blueprint for building a house doesn't make a ship or a plane. Ships and planes have to be built according to the blueprints of ship building and aircraft manufacturing.

Emily: Who is the Creator (Laotianye) of all things anyway?

David: I do not know. But it is really great.

Emily: Humanity is its work, or it is the designer of human beings. Right?

David: Right.

Emily: Humans are wonderful creatures. They're a master-piece of the Creator.

David: For the complexity and abstruse of the human body and life, people nowadays are only qualified to "discover" and "explain" it. For this exquisite work of "humans," one can just act as a "researcher" to study it, an interpreter to "explain" it, or a repairman (doctor) to fix it.

Emily: Each organ, each muscle, each bone, each nerve, and their coordinated operation in the human body is arranged in an ingenious and reasonable way. The shapes of male and female bodies, the perfect fit of the two sexes can be said to be a wonderful masterpiece.

David: Other animals are great designs, too. For example, the eagle and the lion, their physiques and images are amazing. Who can create such images out of thin air? Is there any clever designer, even with the help of a computer or advanced artificial intelligence, can approach such a design level?

Emily: That's a good point. It's impossible for humans to have such a high level of design, impossible.

David: The designer can only be a super wise and intelligent master. We do not know what to call it. Let's call it "the Creator" for the time being.

Emily: The belief in the existence of a God, the Creator, should belong to theism.

David: That's right. In fact, both of us are believers of a Creator and should be counted as theists.

Emily: Yeah, I believe in Laotian even though I'm not religious.

David: Theists are not necessarily religious.

Emily: Is the function of reproduction and generation of the biological world designed by the Creator?

David: Yes. This design makes the biological male and female match, propagate the offspring, and pass from generation to generation. The Hormone is actually a mechanism in the design that leads to the reproduction of the organism, which makes biological sex differentiation, and the opposite sexes attract each other. If this mechanism is extracted from the two sexes, love, marriage, fertility, children and so on are hard to find in the world, and animals don't mate, stubble upon stubble, and grow endlessly.

Emily: Oh, my God! If there are no opposite sexes that attract each other in the world, the two of us will not be together.

David: Right, my darling. So, we will be strangers, or good friends at most.

At that moment, Emily looked at David affectionately and then jumped into David's arms. They hugged and kissed passionately.

Emily: Thank the Creator. With His help we could be together.

David: Just imagine, if there is no attraction between opposite sexes in the world, what kind of scenario it would be! All the good love, solemn pledge of love, reaching old age together, will no longer exist.

Emily: None of the touching and poignant love stories, love poems and love songs are there any longer. No one would write Romeo and Juliet, Dream of the Red Mansions. In Dream of the Red Mansions, if there is no plot of sincere love between Jia Baoyu and Jin Daiyu, as well as emotional entanglements involving Baoyu with women like Baochai, Qingwen, Miaoyu, Xiren, Xiangyun, and so on, stories about Sister Xifeng with Jiarui, You Sisters, etc., this book will become dull and uninteresting.

David: Quite right.

Emily: Another question. Are you saying that the fate of each of us is arranged by the Creator and everyone has one's own destiny?

David: In my opinion, that is not the case. The Creator designs humans. Everyone's experience and fate vary widely.

This is beyond the control of the Creator, just as a ship is built off of a certain blueprint, each ship's experience varies. Even for the same model, some sailed for two decades at sea, safe and sound. Some like Titanic came to an accident on its maiden voyage. The ship collided with an iceberg and sank to the bottom of the sea, killing more than 1,500 people in it. The accident should largely be attributed to the negligence in the voyage. It had little to do with the design of the ship. The Creator only determines the "innate," not the later "acquired." People also have the issue of "congenital"and "acquired." Men's destiny is different, depends largely on their acquired ability, their own efforts, the opportunity, and so on. One should not complain because of something unsatisfactory or difficult to handle.

Emily: That is reasonable. We come to this world. We have to go our own way by ourselves. That is to say we can make our own efforts to change our destiny.

David: Yes, to a large extent. The so-called "let it be" (tingtianyouming) or "resigned" (suiyuan) does not make much sense. They are often misleading.

Emily: Human effort is a decisive factor. Right? David: Absolutely.

> *The universe, the world, human beings and life are mysterious and abstruse. In particular, where does this advanced creature, human, come from? This important and mysterious subject has made countless wise men to compete to inquire and explore and put forward various theories with di.Iferent approaches.*

*However, to this day, there are still di.Iferent opinions and inconsistencies. Is there a Creator in the world? Who is this Creator? Up to now, it is still the biggest problem, an unsolved maze.*

# Chapter 3

## LOVE AFFAIRS

One day, when Emily was walking alone down a path near UMC, a tall white girl student came up to her and blocked her way.

The girl asked Emily straight, "Excuse me. If I'm not mistaken, you are Miss Emily Jin?"

Emily replied, "Yes, I'm Emily Jin."

The girl said, "I'm Audrey Ludwig, a classmate and friend of David Polo."

Emily: Nice to meet you.

Audrey: Nice to meet you, too. Let's have a talk, shall we?

Emily: Sure.

Audrey: Is it true that David fell in love with you? Emily: Yes.

Audrey: David is really a good man. He is the idol of many girls. You know what, I love him, too.

Emily: David is your boyfriend?

Audrey: You can say that. We've been in love for years. Emily: Oh, I see.

Audrey: I hope you should consider my relationship with David and know what to do.

Emily pondered for a moment and said, "David loves me and I love him too. If that hinders your relationship, I'm sorry, please forgive me."

"It's hard for me to forgive you," said Audrey, "Since David met you, he has distanced himself from me and made it clear that he wanted to break up with me, which I can't accept. You are also a woman. If you are in my shoes, can you accept that another woman suddenly coming out of nowhere and taking your love away from you?"

Emily: I'm sorry. I didn't know that. But feelings are nothing else. I can't let David not love me and I can't let myself not love David.

Audrey approached Emily and said, "Let me take a closer look at you. Ah, indeed a charming Oriental beauty. No wonder David is falling in love with you. It's you that made him swoon and lose his head."

Emily: David is a very sensible person.

Audrey : I think David will eventually understand that it was just a momentary impulse for him to choose you. Don't you feel that David doesn't match you? My ancestors are from the Netherlands, and I am a pure blonde. Please look at my eyes, my hair, and my face. David and I are a natural couple.

Emily had already noticed the eyes, hair, and face of the white woman in front of her eyes. That is indeed a Greek sculpture-like Western goddess. Then she said, "Yes, you are very beautiful. I would like to draw you in my picture."

Audrey said, "OK, I am willing to be your model."

Emily looked at her watch and said, "Parden me, please.

Time is up and I'm afraid I must go to class. Goodbye."

Emily talked to David about her encounter and conversation with Audrey. David said he and Audrey were classmates in the same major and had been dating for about two years, but not very intimate.

David had discovered that Emily should be his favorite and ideal partner since he met Emily. They seemed to have long been a bosom friend, easier to communicate in depth with each other. They seemed to be two musical instruments that had been tuned to chord, easier to resonate.

Deep in the soul, communication and integration between men and women are often inconceivable. Only the person concerned feels the most and experiences the most truly. Outsiders only see the surface and make some secular comments.

David and Emily had originally been far away from each other, so far apart that they were virtual strangers. Now it's just a coincidence that they were together. Not only that, they had been merging into each other and entering a beautiful state of infinite harmony, mutual understanding, even inseparable, as one. They were intertwined with each other, with feelings as deep as the sea. This beautiful state, regardless of race or nationality, pulls the seemingly distant souls together.

Another time, in the evening, when Emily met Audrey in the vicinity of UMC, Audrey looked red and excited. She came forward as soon as she saw Emily.

Audrey shouted at Emily, "Emily, listen, you just leave him for me. Leave him alone. You know who I'm talking about. He's mine, mine! Do you know?"

Emily smelled a strong smell of alcohol. It was obvious that Audrey drank too much wine this time and did not know what she was talking about.

Emily asked, "Did you drink some wine Audrey?"

Audrey said, "What business is that of yours? I do what I like to do. I love who I like. But I don't seize love away from others. What are you, Emily? A black-haired wench who would even bully me. Get out of here! Go back to China! David is mine, and always belongs to me!"

Emily said, "I love David. I haven't finished my school and I don't want to go back to China now."

Audrey had not expected that Emily would contradict her. In the face of this unrelenting love rival, she was even more angry. Her head was hot and her whole body was about to burst.

Audrey stared at Emily's face with a drunken eye and suddenly reached out her hand and slapped Emily on the cheek. Emily was in a trance. She saw Audrey fall on the side of the road and went asleep. She hastened to call David by phone and the two sent Audrey back to her bedroom.

The next day, Audrey called Emily and apologized for what she had done to her the day before.

Audrey said that she had drunk too much wine yesterday and was in a bad mood. She said that she should not have said and done things to Emily that were improper. She asked Emily to excuse her. Emily said she didn't care about it. She did not want to blame Audrey, for she could understand Audrey's mood at this time.

A few months later, Emily learned from David that Audrey had been suffering from severe depression, mostly because David had alienated her by falling in love with Emily.

Emily asked David to stop their communications, no longer contact, and no more meetings. David was very surprised. He asked Emily to explain what caused their relationship to drop from the boiling point to freezing, but Emily did not reply. Since then, she hadn't called David, nor had she answered phone calls from David.

David knew that Emily often went to UMC after class, and he went wandering around there. One day, sure enough, he met Emily who was drinking coffee in a small café in UMC.

As soon as David met Emily, he asked, "Why? Why? You should at least give me an answer, Emily."

Emily said, "I don't think our relationship is appropriate. You might consider some other options as well."

David asked, "What's wrong with us? Please tell me clearly."

"You don't have to ask," said Emily, looking at David's sincere face.

David asked, "Did I do anything wrong that hurt you?"

After a long silence, Emily stared at David and said, "David, you had been in love with Audrey for years, but you betrayed her. Can you guarantee that you won't change your mind and betray me in the future? Besides, you didn't tell me about your relationship with Audrey as soon as you knew me. I would not have joined it as a third party. Pardon me. I have an appointment now."

David asked, "Do you have a new boyfriend?"

Emily said, "It doesn't matter to you, David. Byebye!"

Emily stood up and left. David stared at Emily's back until her figure gradually disappeared into the crowd. After Emily had gone, David sat in the same place for a long time, not knowing when and how he left there to return to his residence.

Another time, David saw Emily walking with a young man who looked like a Chinese on campus, and they were chatting cordially.

David lost his soul when the happiness around him suddenly disappeared. He felt as if he had fallen from the clouds to the bottom of the valley, and returned from a dream to reality. He spent each day in boredom and bitterness. What puzzled him most was Emily's sudden change of attitude towards him. From the very beginning, he sensed Emily's genuine affection for him. Emily was thoughtful and independent. She was, by no means, a woman who was superficial and distracted. He was puzzled.

David was a strong man; he did not want to devote his main energy and attention to love affairs. He delved into the subject of biology, mankind, and the universe, which was a very different domain, a vast, mysterious, charming realm. The love between opposite sexes of young people in human life was just a tiny ripple or a dim light in the broad universe. David, however, as an ordinary man after all had all the emotions and desires of men besides the subject he was studying. He felt that the more he was buried in the professional topics, the more eager he was in need of an extra-curricular emotional harbor.

Sometimes, he realized how much he needed the love of the opposite sex and longed for true love. Love could even irrigate his fertile heart, nourish his intelligent mind, and help him to bear the fruit of wisdom.

In order to seek some relief from the loneliness of his amateur life, David tentatively returned to Audrey. They had been in love for some time in the past after all. Audrey couldn't believe it was true at first, but David was there, she could even touch him if she wished to. Audrey was more in love with her boyfriend who had been lost and recovered. Her condition gradually eased, as if snow and ice had melted, and winter turned to spring. But in her dealings with David, Audrey felt that David had changed. David seemed a little reticent, absent-minded, and often spoke out of tune. In particular, he was no longer as prone to surging emotions as usual. Audrey faintly felt his passiveness and indifference as she hugged and kissed him. They seemed to be separated by an impenetrable mist, and could never get close to each other. Over time, Audrey's such feelings grew. To her, this David looked and behaved nothing like the David who used to be. He was clearly a fake David. Was the true David gone, gone forever? Audrey was tired of this false love, and this fake David.

She finally broke up with David, who readily accepted it.

Their love had come to an end for the second time.

Then Audrey found her true love and fell into a new love river. The new boyfriend was called Jerry Hamilton, a young associate professor in the Department of Biology.

Audrey found an opportunity to tell Emily: "My David is no longer there. He is gone, gone forever and now I will return to you Your David."

David and Emily reunited. At this time Emily exposed the truth to David. Her being unfeeling to David before now was completely to alleviate Audrey's depression while her own heart endured great pain. She had always been deeply in love with David. People say that love is selfish, but she could not endure Audrey suffering from severe mental pain, which was caused by her joining in. When David asked about the man who was walking with Emily on campus, Emily said that it was her townsman, also from Yantai. He was a graduate student at the Department of Physics and had been married.

David said that since his acquaintance with Emily he had devoted his love to Emily alone. For any woman other than Emily, his spring of love seemed to be completely dried.

That was the situation after the rapprochement between him and Audrey. He knew it was unfair to Audrey, but after all, feelings were not rational. He was hard to hide, not good at disguise, and finally caused the breakup with Audrey again.

*The emotional entanglements between David, Emily, and Audrey are, from their own view, quite spectacular. Each of them plays a different role and tastes a different flavor.*

*At the same time, the world beyond the trio remains the same. Students still attend classes, do their homework. People are still running around for life. The sun still rises in the morning and sets in the evening. The sea still ebbs and flows. The rivers keep flowing day and night.*

*It is the norm for the affairs between men and women to be on and off, and love stories are happening all the time. Where there is a crowd of people, there are love stories, among which some are touching and some mediocre. David and Emily's love story is just one of them.*

# Chapter 4

## Deep Mountain Adventures

The Rocky Mountains are tall and majestic and are known as the "backbone" of North America. The main mountain range stretches southward from British Columbia, Canada, across the states of Idaho, Montana, Wyoming, Utah, and Colorado to New Mexico in the US, more than 4,800 kilometers north and south.

The Rocky Mountains are somewhat like the Kunlun Mountains in China. The Kunlun Mountains are known as China's first sacred mountains, and the ancestor of all mountains. It rises from the Pamirs Plateau in the west and crosses the two autonomous regions Xinjiang and Tibet, and two provinces Qinghai and Sichuan in China. The total length is about 2,500 kilometers.

The Rocky Mountains cover a vast area of western Colorado and are the main scenic spot of the state. Even in summer, one can see the tall, snow-capped peaks of the distant mountains.

The Rocky Mountains are not as reminiscent of bare stone mountains as its name suggests. Except for the higher peaks, the Rocky Mountains in Colorado are mostly covered with thick or sparse virgin forests. Most of the trees are cold- resistant conifers such as pine and cypress, while there are aspen trees in the lower areas. In autumn, these poplar trees display yellow, orange, red, and other bright colors, as if wearing beautiful and gorgeous festival dresses. Nature lovers like to drive to the mountains in autumn to see the yellow and red leaves and they keep doing it every year.

David and Emily loved nature. They studied and lived in Colorado, and had the opportunity to enjoy the natural beauty of the Rocky Mountains. They were a perfect match, both of them were keen on traveling and adventures.

On holidays, they liked to drive on the winding, ascending and descending mountain roads in western Colorado, sometimes stopped to walk in the mountains and forests, appreciating and enjoying the charm of nature. Their footprints covered a lot of areas in the Rocky Mountains of the state.

On one occasion, David and Emily came to a large, unfrequented forest, overlooking from the top of the mountain. Suddenly, they heard a bitter and desolate animal cry. They roamed in the distance and saw a wild deer on the opposite hillside. It was jammed between a big tree and a small tree close to it and was trying desperately to break free. The wild deer, impatient and repeatedly forced to move forward, but to no avail. Then, it appeared apparently exhausted, gasping, and howling loudly.

David and Emily walked through the sparse trees, through valleys and up hills, and reached far enough to come to the stranded deer and tried to rescue it. It was a young deer, large in size but not very experienced, hence this catastrophe. Emily noticed that the wild deer was young and beautiful. The tip of its left horn broke off. David and Emily pushed hard the back of the deer, but could not get rid of the shackles that had been added to it. They tried to pull the small tree that was holding the wild deer but did not help.

Then David found a stone that he used to cut the small tree at the lower part with the stone edge. The small tree was thick and hard to cut. It stood erect.

When David kept chopping and cutting the tree to a deeper dent, they pulled the small tree together and tried to break it to get the deer out. They tried their best to pull. The two were exhausted and out of breath, but the small tree was still hard to break. They had a brief break and then continued to pull the tree while David shouted "One, two, three!" They worked jointly. The small tree had a broken sound and bent a little bit, the distance between the small tree and the big tree increased. The wild deer made a great effort to get out of the trees. Finally, it went out and was free.

Both David and Emily had concentrated on pulling the small tree. When the small tree split and broke, they both fell back to the ground. Emily stood up, but her body was unstable, so with a slip of foot, she rolled down the steep slope. When David saw that his sweetheart was in distress, he couldn't control himself and jumped down the slope, following Emily, to be together with her, dead or alive. David stumbled over the steep hill and tumbled to the bottom of the valley. With his face scraped and his body slashed by branches and stones, he was bleeding. With no regard for himself, he hurried to find Emily, who had fallen to the bottom of the valley. Emily laid in a semi-comatose state on some decaying branches and leaves. She was wounded more than David because she fell completely involuntarily. Emily was covered with injuries, especially in her right leg, which was so painful that she couldn't move. David examined it carefully and estimated it to be a fracture of bone in the calf.

David and Emily were lying on the ground, recovering from the shock. They discussed what to do next. David tried to call for help, but there was no cell phone signal in the mountains. They realized that they were in trouble. Emily had to be rescued and treated as soon as possible. They must first find one of the mountain roads and go out of the woods. So David picked up Emily, carried her on his back and walked hard in the forest. In addition, the forest was located in the mountainous area, with unsmooth ground full of uphill and downhill slopes. David endured the pain of multiple wounds on his body, and the right leg of Emily with a broken bone was even more painful. Walking and walking, there seemed to be no end of the forest. David with Emily on his back had been walking in the forest for a long time. They had lost their way in the woods. It was late and night fell. They thought it was even harder to walk at night, and both were exhausted, hungry, and thirsty. They had no choice but to find a place to spend the night.

In the rescue of the wild deer, the two of them had a lot of sweat, and they were especially thirsty now. David placed Emily in a flat spot by a rock cliff, where she was lying, while David went to find water by himself. At the bottom of the valley David found a small stream. He gulped the water, the water of the mountain spring, clear and sweet. David thought that he had never drunk water this delicious in his life.

But how to make Emily drink the water? The creek was far away from Emily's perch, and the way was not easy. Since he could not let Emily come here, he had to bring the water to her. But with no container of water around, David closed both his hands tightly, forming a bowl shape to hold some water, to bring to Emily. Unexpectedly, he got a bump on the way, half of the water he held in his hands was lost. Then he accidentally fell down, and the water was scattered all over. In desperation, David came up with an idea, he sucked the water from the stream into his mouth, took a big full, then with the water in his mouth he walked to Emily's side, and sent it to her mouth. Emily drank it. It started to quench her thirst. David repeatedly brought water to Emily with his mouth and temporarily solved the drinking problem.

They agreed to spend the night here. David took some leaves from nearby, spread them on the ground as a makeshift bed, and covered themselves with leaves as temporary blankets. They talked for a while and then fell asleep. At night, Emily heard a rustling sound that woke her up from her dream. She saw a large snake faintly in the darkness, and it was crawling towards her and David. The snake may have smelled blood on both of them and came to feed. Emily woke David up and he saw the snake too. He calmly grabbed the snake's tail with his hand and controlled the snake with both hands. David had a lot of experience with snakes. He threw the snake into a ravine in the distance and went back to sleep with Emily as if nothing had happened.

The next morning, David and Emily woke up and felt better. This "open-air camping" had a distinctive flavour.

There was no food, but they could drink water. They drank water in the same way and continued walking in the mountain woods, hoping to get out of the primeval forest as soon as possible. They trudged strenuously in the mountain forest. The sun was right above them before they knew it.

They lay on the ground, resting. David was gasping in exhaustion.

Emily noticed among the wild grass a kind of wild vegetable that she was familiar with. When she was a child, she often went to the wild with her neighbor's children to collect and eat it. It was a kind of wild food. Emily asked David to pick some. David did and also collected some mushrooms. At this time, both of them were very hungry. They had a meal of salad with mushrooms and wild vegetables as their brunch.

They looked around at the dense forests. This was a real virgin forest, free from human disturbance and destruction. Everything was silent without even the sounds of human activities, such as car motor noises. There was almost no sound except the soft rustle of pine leaves under the breeze.

This kind of natural, tranquil atmosphere was often rare to experience, it was fascinating. They could not help talking about the virgin forest in front of them.

Emily: There are fewer and fewer environments like this on our planet.

David: This is really the original ecology.

Emily: Before humans emerged on Earth, although there once had been dinosaurs and glaciers, it was natural, peaceful, and beautiful, like the Garden of Eden. Since the advent of humanity, especially the industrial revolution in Europe, the tranquility and natural order of the Earth have been disrupted. The world was smothered, and a lot of living things were enslaved by human beings.

David: But we have built an unparalleled human civilization, bustling cities, and convenient transportation.

There are factories, schools, restaurants, dance halls, cinemas, opera houses, art galleries, etc. Walking in the streets of Paris, Vienna, or London, looking at the magnificent architecture, to appreciate the strong cultural atmosphere, people will be proud of the achievements of human civilization.

Emily: For us humans, the development of nature provides us with quite a lot of convenience. But the damage to the Earth's ecology is also quite serious. A century ago, humans multiplied violently, colonized everywhere, buildings and roads covered the Earth, grasslands and forests stepped back, and rivers and lakes sang lamentations. People destroy the original ecology everywhere, and produce a lot of garbage, waste gas and sewage, causing pollution of the Earth's air and water sources and imbalance of temperature.

The Earth seems to have been plagued by insects and worms. People began to yearn for the idyllic life in ancient times.

David: It's much better now. The folks of the global village have realized the seriousness of the matter and are paying more attention to the improvement of the ecological environment. In the European Industrial Revolution, the water of the Thames was once contaminated, and later the rivers were cleared. The Great Lakes (Superior, Michigan, Huron, Erie, and Ontario) between the United States and Canada were polluted by industrial development, and their governance has improved significantly. At present, the world's major countries have reached an agreement to control and reduce greenhouse gas emissions. The situation will improve, and I am optimistic about the future.

At that moment, David and Emily heard a roar in the sky. The sound grew from weak to strong, very harsh, and then turned into a loud shrill. Looking up, they saw a plane flying through the sky. They felt that the noise was very incongruous with the surrounding natural environment.

Their wonderful feelings about the original ecology were completely ruined.

David and Emily had a picnic and rested for a while, and their physical strength was recovered a bit. David picked up Emily and continued walking on the road. After a long trudge, there were still endless mountains and trees ahead.

While they were at a loss, Emily suddenly saw a wild deer coming towards them. The wild deer, not afraid of people, came up directly to them. It licked them with its tongue, to show its affection. David put Emily down. They looked at it closely and found that this was nothing but the beautiful wild deer that they had rescued yesterday! Emily gently touched it with her hand. The deer jumped about in excitement at the sight of its two rescuers.

When they were talking and didn't notice, the deer disappeared. David picked up Emily on his back and was ready to go on his way, but he felt a little dazed. Looking around, there was still boundless forest with no path. Where to go? Just then, they heard the call of the deer. Looking forward, they saw the wild deer standing in the distant forest, as if to call them to go there.

They went forward and the deer disappeared again. In a moment, the deer was calling in the distance, and they immediately went up. At this moment, what appeared in their eyes was a mountain road with cars running on it. David and Emily were so excited that they hugged the deer tightly and said goodbye to it. Emily could not help feeling that animals were so emotional, also knew how to be grateful. She said, "We helped the deer out, and it led us out of our dilemma."

All of a sudden, Emily's eyes began to blur. Then she saw a bright and beautiful scene. The soft sunlight presented a harmonious scene like the fuse and merge of water and milk. All creatures in the world were friendly and intimate, including people, other animals, and plants, singing and dancing in a sweet atmosphere. It's a fascinating realm, but it's fleeting. Emily saw the surrounding trees and the mountain road again.

On the road, David and Emily stopped a car, and the driver enthusiastically helped them contact the emergency services. A helicopter arrived quickly and took both of them to a hospital in Boulder. Emily's broken leg bone was connected, and David's wounds were stitched and sanitized.

They were released from the hospital a few days later. They recuperated at home. Then they drove back the car parked in the mountains for days.

*David and Emily love nature. They know that nature has nurtured everything in the world including human beings. Human life is closely related to nature. Human civilization should include a peaceful and beautiful environment, where people live in harmony with other living creatures and interact with each other positively. The progress of human civilization should not be made at the expense of natural ecology. The exploitation of nature and the maintenance of natural ecology are in a sharp conflict. Modern humans and their descendants should be kind and lenient to nature and other animals.*

# Chapter 5

## HUMAN SOCIETY

Emily used to meditate and fantasize alone. She thought of people and other creatures on Earth. She thought of the survival rule in the biological world – the natural selection.

In primitive forests, all kinds of plants, such as conifers, broadleaf trees, shrubs, climbers, and grass, are competing to get the sunlight, rain, and nutrition they need. Actually, they are competing for growth, fruiting, and multiplication.

Wild animals on the grassland compete to get the food and water they need. Herbivores eat grass, leaves, and fruit. Predators hunt and eat herbivores, which form a food chain.

The following scenes often appear in Emily's mind:

A strong cheetah was running extremely fast on the grassland, chasing a wild antelope that fled desparately. After the wild antelope was caught, it was bitten to death, torn, bled with its flesh swallowed.

A small elephant that fell behind the group because of an injury, walking alone with a limp in the wilderness, being in a poor situation already, was spotted by a hungry lion group that encircled it, divided it, and bit it.

A goat toddler out of the flock because of playfulness, was caught by a fierce goshawk that suddenly descended from the sky. The little goat was bleating in the air, with a helpless and desolate cry. It would not be able to escape the fate of being devoured by the eagle's family.

A kind-hearted person will inevitably have a sympathetic compassion for small and weak animals, and feels the cruelty of the jungle law.

But how about human beings treating other animals?

The bison used to live freely, enjoying the rich green grass and clear water on the prairie. After being enslaved by human beings, they become cattle. The ploughing cattle make great effort to cultivate the land, pull the cart, sweating all over.

They are whipped in the slightest snub, and slaughtered in old age and infirmity. Their flesh is cut and eaten, with skins peeled off and made into leather products.

The same is true of chickens, that have produced in their lifetimes countless nutritious eggs for human consumption, and they will be slaughtered and eaten in the end.

There is usually no lack of meat from animal carcasses on human dining tables.

One evening, David and Emily were walking on campus, chatting at the poolside, and they talked about human civilization.

Emily: David, what do you say about the differences between humans and other animals?

David: People and other animals are all works of the Creator. But people are a kind of advanced animal. The human mind is more developed, more intelligent, and has unlimited creativity. People have systematic and freely expressive languages, capable of precise thinking and effective communication. Humans can make and use a variety of simple and complex tools and equipment with high efficiency to make other animals too far behind to catch up. Moreover, human wisdom is still developing, and advanced artificial intelligence are widely used. Humans can create unparalleled human civilization on Earth.

Emily: Humans flaunt themselves to be civilized, but they are barbaric to other animals.

David: Civilization is uniquely human. Other animals, may have behaviors similar to those of human beings such as maternal love, sexual attraction, caring for family members, etc., which is a kind of natural instinct. Different species practice the jungle law. In the animal kingdom, animals at the high end of the food chain live by hunting other weak animals. If they do not do so, they and their children will starve to death. They are carnivores.

Emily: Humans are at the absolute top of the animal food chain. Humans are accustomed to enslaving, killing and eating other animals, not even with a blink of an eye.

David: But people can't compete with lions, tigers, elephants, or even packs of wolves or hounds unless they work in groups, with tools and weapons. It is human group co-operation that have placed mankind firmly at the head of all living things.

Emily: Human group cooperation is very important.

The widespread use of tools and the manufacture of powerful weapons by human beings are carried out in groups.

David: Yes. The so-called human society is just a cooperative group formed naturally among people. To be honest, everyone in this group uses everyone else. Whatever one eats, wears, or uses is not made or given by others?

Emily: Everyone is lucky to live in a big, all-inclusive, collaborative community.

David: Society is like a well-knit network that helps everyone through countless links. Individuals get all kinds of products and services from the society. They also provide society with their own contributions, go to work on a daily basis (some people work at home), work regularly, make some products, or render some service to benefit others, which is called social exchange and cooperation.

Emily: The organization and exchange in society is so natural that everyone is accustomed to it. Now, the society is getting more developed. The division of labor is getting more and more detailed. When a person is engaged in a profession or a job, he can exchange and cooperate with others in the society, so that he can get his own basic needs and even more than that. The people of society work together, help each other, coordinate with each other, so people can live better. In fact, such a simple truth is often ignored. Imagine, today, who can leave society and live independently?

David: If someone leaves the human society, naked, abandons everything from the society, and comes to a deserted island, to make a living, he will have to return to the ancient human Stone Age, sheltering in the cave, clothing with leaves or animal skins, picking wild fruit and catching wild animals for food. Robinson Crusoe drifted on a desert island. Fortunately, he had some supplies and tools he brought with him from the human society, and he had a partner named Friday as his assistant, otherwise his survival would have been even harder.

Emily: A true story gives us some enlightenment. In January 1995, US air force colonel Mike Couillard and his eight year old son, Matthew Couillard, suffered a stalled snowstorm in a skiing tour and was trapped in the Turkish mountains for ten days. Cold and hungry, with information barrier, they were isolated. They spent the night in a cave with frostbite on their hands and feet. How eager they were to get in touch with the community and get some help from the other people. Later, Mike was fortunate enough to encounter a group of local lumberjacks in front of some abandoned wooden houses. With their help, Mike was rescued with his son and returned to his home in Colorado Springs, Colorado.

David: Also, in April 2003, Aron Ralston, a Colorado young man, was trapped in the mountains in Utah for 127 hours. In a rock canyon, his right hand was pinned under a large rock that slid down and was hard to get off. If he had carried his cell phone at the moment, (unfortunately, he did not) he would have been saved sooner. His food, clothes, and supplies in his backpack helped him to prolong his life. He used his knife to cut off his hand so he was able to survive. Two passengers on the road presented him with some food, and the helicopter arrived timely to help him get to the hospital as soon as possible, allowing him to escape death.

Emily: Moreover, in our last adventure in the mountains, without your help, I would have died of thirst, hunger, snake bite, or leg injury. In addition, the passers-by enthusiastically helped us to contact the emergency ambulance, the helicopter arrived shortly, and the hospital helped us to cure our wounds, and so on. The society is indeed a warm family. This is our personal experience, with our deep understanding of it.

David: Once a man leaves the society, even if not far from it, not for long, without the help of people, will be dangerous, or in desperation. Anyone needs the society, and is inseparable from it.

Emily: In fact, some animals also have a kind of labor division and co-operation. Lions and hunting dogs hunt in groups and share their prey. Bees and ants work together, everyone does its specific job.

David: It is the nature of these animals that passed down from generation to generation, which is incomparable to the active, strict, and reasonable organization of human society, the multifarious allotment of duties, and the fine division of labor.

Emily: The superiority of human society is more than that. Human progress is inseparable from society in all aspects. Academic research and inventions and creations are often the continuation of the past, and can be achieved only when later generations step on the shoulders of their predecessors.

David: Today's high-tech computers, mobile phones, and the Internet are all based on previous theories and technologies and develop and improve step by step.

Emily: Any high-tech company is a collaboration of countless scientific and technological personnel, drawing on and using current and traditional scientific and technological achievements, innovating and launching new products and services.

David: Now the technology is developing rapidly and changing with each passing day. Human intellectual property rights have been accumulating. Besides, the prosperity and development of literature and art is also inseparable from society, I suppose?

Emily: Yeah. Great works of literature and art are brewed, fermented, and forged in human society. Their greatness depends on social feedback and popular acceptance. How can a successful work be achieved without competition among artists, criticism from critics and praise from admirers?

The exquisite works of art that have been handed down for thousands of years have all shocked the hearts of future generations with its superb vision, mind, and art.

David: Good point. There are hardly any "lonely artists" who are divorced from the society and enjoy themselves.

> *Humans on Earth make up the society. The full cooperation of human beings in society has enabled human beings to survive, to develop and progress continuously, and to create a highly developed human civilization, which is far superior to other creatures on Earth.*

*The jungle law among animals is primitive and inferior. It is contrary to the spirit of human civilization and should not be advocated in human society.*

# Chapter 6

## Global Travel

David's uncle, Timothy Polo, made some money in running a real estate business. A year ago, he died of heart attack. He had made a will before his death for David to inherit most of his fortune from him. Timothy was homosexual with no children of his own.

After David earned a Ph.D. in biology and Emily obtained her MFA (Master of Fine Arts) at University of Colorado in Boulder, they didn't immediately seek employment. They had a simple wedding, and seven months later Emily gave birth to a cute boy named Oliver. This Chinese-Western mixed-race child had big eyes, light brown curly hair, and a slightly higher nose, appearing totally like the image of a Western boy. Oliver was loved by everyone, especially his grandparents.

David and Emily were staying with David's parents at this time. The baby Oliver was taken care of by David's mother when he grew a little bigger. At the age of one or two Oliver looked quite like the angel painted by the great Renaissance painter, Raphael. His character and behavior were so nice that everybody liked to call him "little angel."

David and Emily couldn't resist their loneliness, set out on a journey to travel. Part of the legacy of David's uncle would be used for their living and travel expenses.

David and Emily had a good trip around the United States by car. They had been to all the major cities and famous scenic spots, and had seen the different landscapes and customs around the country. They liked the towering of Colorado's Rocky Mountains, the grandeur of Arizona's Grand Canyon, the charm of Wyoming's Yellowstone National Park, the shock of Niagara Water Falls in New York state, the naturalness of Florida's Everglades, and the spirit of the United States embodied by the Statue of Liberty in New York city.

David and Emily shared the same ambition to travel around the world. In their tour, they would focus on the world cultural heritage and mysterious traces.

Their global journey began with a visit to Mexico to study the remains of Mayan Civilization. The Mayan Civilization is regarded as the cradle of American Indian culture. Thousands of years ago, the Mayans had unrivalled mathematical attainments and unique writing system like puzzles. On the Yucatan Peninsula, there are nine magnificent pyramids. David and Emily went to the top of the tower, and thought about the glorious Mayan Civilization, the magnificent palace, the towering pyramids, and the bustling city and commerce. People were industrious, rich in life and advanced in culture. However, the Mayan Civilization suddenly and mysteriously declined. Archeologists believe that the Mayan Civilization was ruined by a bloody civil war for wealth and power. David and Emily realized that even the advanced civilization could be destroyed in the war of mankind.

Then David and Emily went from Mexico to Chile in South America, where they went to Easter Island in the south Pacific Ocean to look at the giant statues on the Island.

The boulder statues called Moai are scattered throughout the island. In Easter Island, there are about 887 known giant statues, of which 600 are neatly arranged by the sea. They range in sizes from 6 to 23 meters high and weigh 30 to 90 tons. They have peculiar images, each with a long forehead, a high nose, sunken eyes, and a pursed mouth. They look solemn and face the sea, and seem thoughtful.

It is estimated that the stones were carved from around 1100 to 1680 AD. How could such huge and heavy boulders be chipped out of quarries and how to make them into statues? What measures should have been taken to transport them to distant locations and to make them stand firmly upright? In the first few centuries, the inhabitants of the island had not mastered iron works. How incredible it was!

Looking at these mysterious megaliths and their majestic faces, David and Emily were troubled. With so advanced science and technology at present, there are still such mysterious puzzles to be deciphered in this world.

After the expedition to Easter Island, David and Emily flew from Chile in South America to Cairo, Egypt in Africa to visit and explore the pyramids there. It's said that the pyramids in Egypt are the tombs of the pharaohs, which is one of the seven wonders of the world. In the lower reaches of the Nile, there are about 80 pyramid relics scattered in various sizes. The tallest of them is the Pyramid of Khufu, built around 2690 BC. With a height of 146.5 meters and a length of 230 meters, the tower is made up of 2.3 million pieces of stone. There is no adhesive between the stones, and the stones are stacked and bitten together. In front of the pyramid of King Harvard lies a sphinx symbolizing the king's power and dignity. It was always puzzling how such an enormous and arduous project was undertaken by the ancients under the succinct technical conditions of the time.

David and Emily flew to Europe from Cairo after their visit to the pyramids in Egypt. They arrived in Italy first. In Rome and Milan in Italy, they saw the masterpieces of the three representatives of the Renaissance in art: Da Vinci's The Last Supper, Michelangelo's paintings on the Sistine zenith and Raphael's The School of Athens, which were the pinnacle of world classical paintings. David and Emily watched each painting for a long time, and the genius of the work was impressive. The great zeitgeist and the essence of the Renaissance created these masters and works. In Italy, David and Emily also enjoyed ancient Greek sculptures such as Laocoon and The Discus Thrower. In the past, they had only seen these famous works of art in pictures, but now they saw the original works. They were extremely excited and delighted.

From the collection of ancient Greek sculptures stored in Italy, David and Emily saw a highly developed ancient Greek civilization. The splendid Greek culture that the Greek civilization creators constructed with their exceptional intellect and wisdom still amaze the world!

In addition, David and Emily visited the Ancient Colosseum, where the aristocrats had fun, while countless slaves were killed in duels with humans and animals. The stark contrast between civilization and barbarism in ancient society had made David and Emily sigh with emotion.

Then David and Emily left Italy for France. In Paris, they ascended the Eiffel Tower. On the tower, they overlooked the city of Paris, pondering and talking. They talked about France, the country where the 1789 Revolution shocked the world, where there were militarist Napoleon, writer Balzac, and impressionist painter, Oscar-Claude Monet. This was really a great nation!

In Paris, David and Emily naturally visited the Louvre, a treasure trove of world art. The palace was dazzling with all kinds of exhibits, many of which were world-famous works of art that they were familiar with. There they saw the world's art treasures like the Greek Statue of Venus de Milo, Summer Se Reis, the Goddess of Victory. The most memorable was Leonardo Da Vinci's Mona Lisa. The work was well known, but it was extraordinary to see the original. Both David and Emily loved the romantic painter Delacroix's Freedom to Guide the People. They also liked impressionist and other modern art. France had led the world in contemporary art. David and Emily believed that in talking about Western classical sculpture, one could not do without ancient Greece, when discussing the Renaissance art, one could not be separated from Italy, in referring to modern art, one could not avoid France and the United States.

David and Emily also visited the famous Notre Dame, which was a masterpiece of gothic architecture completed in 1345, lasting for more than 180 years. The shape of the church was magnificent, the interior was spacious and well decorated. The church was famous for its collection of art from the 13th to the 17th century. The name of the church, Notre Dame, was reminiscent of Victor Hugo's novel Notre Dame de Paris and its characters, the beautiful Gypsy girl, Esmeralda, and the ugly and kind bell ringer, Quasimodo.

Unfortunately, nine years later after their visit (2019 AD), this world's architectural art treasure was hit by a fire.

The roof and spire of the church were burned. Full restoration was estimated to take ten years. At this time, David and Emily did not realize how lucky they were to be able to enjoy the original Notre Dame before its disaster.

After bidding farewell to Paris, David and Emily went to London, England. As soon as they stepped on the British Isles, they came to think of Shakespeare and his dramatic works such as Romeo and Juliet, Hamlet, and so on. They thought of Charles Dickens and his novels Great Expectations, David Copperfield, and so on. Emily especially liked Charlotte Bronte's Jane Eyre. She had also read Thomas Hardy's Tess of the D'urbervilles.

In the UK David and Emily visited Shakespeare's Tomb on the Avon River in Stratford. Walking along the river from the city center, with green trees on both sides, they paid a visit to admire the world literary giant in this permanent resting habitat.

David and Emily also visited Stonehenge in Salisbury during their stay in England. There, they saw 247 erected stones, each weighing about 50 tons. The placement of the giant stones consisted of two laps of boulders inside and outside. From the present point of view, the scale and engineering difficulty of Stonehenge was inconceivable for early humans. It was 700 years older than the oldest pyramids in Egypt, but there were still a lot of debates about who had built this magnificent Stonehenge. Scholars claimed that Stonehenge was as mysterious as the Egyptian pyramids.

The Stonehenge in the setting sun appeared incomparably mysterious, also looked particularly beautiful.

David and Emily ended their European trip to the last leg of their world tour, China. In Beijing, they visited the Forbidden City and ascended the Great Wall, marveling at the magnificence of these buildings.

Then, David and Emily traveled from Beijing to Sichuan to visit and study Sanxingdui relics. Sanxingdui Civilization was a mysterious one completely out of touch with the ancient Chinese culture. They visited the Sanxingdui Museum in Sichuan. The most amazing of the many treasures unearthed in Sanxingdui was the bronze statues, which were beautifully cast and had various forms. They were not only large in size, but also had prominent zygomatic faces, protruding eyeballs, with high noses, wide mouths and big ears, and perforations in their ears. They were not like Chinese or any people on Earth. Therefore, many people had speculated that Sanxingdui Civilization may have been the relics of aliens (E.T. extra-terrestrials) from other planets.

David and Emily associated a series of mysterious relics in the world with the Sanxingdui Civilization. In addition to the Mayan Civilization and the Sanxingdui Civilization, the mega-lithic statues on Easter Island, the Stonehenge in Salisbury, England, the Pyramids of Egypt, and the widespread news about UFO, the mysterious testimony of the crop circle, etc., made it difficult to avoid the speculation that Aliens appeared and acted on Earth.

*Mankind, as superior beings on Earth, have created splendid and brilliant human civilization. The levels of human science and technology, literature and art have been rising and fruitful. The material and spiritual life of mankind has changed dramatically. Human understanding of the world is also deepening.*

*In human history, there are still some unexplainable phenomena and things around the world. They should be related to the formation and operation of the universe and the possible involvement of Aliens on Earth.*

# Chapter 7

## ALIEN DESCENDANTS

That day during their visit to Sanxingdui Museum, David and Emily noticed that in the audience there was a man who looked quite special. The more they looked at him the closer they felt that the man resembled the bronze sculpture images in the exhibition. Compared with other people he had slightly higher nose, with wider mouth and bigger ears. After the visit, David and Emily followed the man, and got a chance to talk with him. The man was a cheerful person, easier acquainted with strangers, and quite voluble. He said he and his family lived in Langzhong, Sichuan Province. His surname was Gan and given name Ruida, a descendant of the ancient Sanxingdui Aliens. He had visited the Sanxingdui Museum many times. When he learned that David and Emily were from the United States he had a higher interest in conversation with them. Then they sat down at a teahouse and chatted over a cup of tea.

As David and Emily were interested in Mr. Gan's origin, he started to tell stories and family history of his ancestors, about which David and Emily were fascinated. It was said that his earliest ancestors had come from the outside world, probably one of the other planets about 5,000 years ago.

They settled in the middle of Sichuan Province, in the area of Guanghan. They founded a unique Sanxingdui Civilization, which lasted for nearly 2,000 years. The bronze statues unearthed in the ruins of Sanxingdui showed that these people were strange in appearance, unlike anyone else of the present. They were referred to as the Aliens or the Starry Nationality. The Aliens later mysteriously disappeared, but were not completely extinct. Their few descendants, living with the Han and other ethnic minorities, still carried on some unique blood lineage of the Aliens.

Gan Ruida also vividly told a love story of his ancestors:

## Around 1000 AD

## (THE NORTHERN SONG DYNASTY)

As time went by, a few of the descendants of the Alien people had been living in the Sanxingdui area of Sichuan for nearly 2,000 more years, reaching the Northern Song Dynasty. At that time, there was a young Alien man named Gan Sanlang, who was strong with good archery. He often rode on a horse and went hunting in the wild. Every day, Gan Sanlang went to the Duck River so that his horse could drink water. There, he often met a young girl of Han Nationality who was washing rice, vegetables, and clothes by the river. The girl was called Du Lanzi. Du Lanzi also noticed the exotic horseman. People said that the Aliens looked strange, but in Du Lanzi's eyes this young man was kind of handsome. Lanzi did not have the ordinary people's rejection to the Aliens, and even had some admiration for him in her heart.

Once the young man walked up to her and threw a hare and a pheasant of his prey to her side, saying, "Girl, take them for dinner." The girl said, "I don't want them, brother. Please take them back with you." Sanlang rode away without looking back.

Du Lanzi's heart thumped as she watched the young man riding away. It seemed that the young man also liked her. Since then, the figure of the young man riding a horse had always appeared in her mind, and the girl's dream of love began to sprout in her heart.

When the family of Lanzi learned that the prey was from a strange Alien, they blamed Lanzi for accepting the gift, and for her association with the Aliens.

Gan Sanlang and Du Lanzi often met at the Duck River. At the beginning, they just exchanged a few words. Later, they talked more and more, feeling very congenial to each other. In this way, the two young people became closer and closer. Every time they met, they seemed to have endless intimate words to say. Lanzi sometimes sewed the clothes torn in the woods for Sanlang, presented him with fruit and local produce, and wiped the sweat off his face with a towel. Sanlang sympathized with Lanzi for her hard work and offered to help her do some physical labor.

Gan Sanlang was generous and open-minded. Du Lanzi was gentle and kind. Gan Sanlang liked dancing, Du Lanzi liked singing. They both sang and danced when they were happy.

Gan Sanlang used to tell stories to Du Lanzi, who listened with great interest.

On a summer evening, Gan Sanlang and Du Lanzi, were lying on a meadow in the wild when Gan Sanlang told a story to Du Lanzi. Gan Sanlang pointed to the stars in the sky and said, "You know, Lanzi, my ancestors came down from a star in the sky. The star looks small, but it is in fact very big." Lanzi asked, "So, how did your ancestors come to Earth?" "It's a long story," said Sanlang, "The star where my forefathers lived once passed through the sky, getting so close to Earth that some people fell down, scattering here and there to the ground." Lanzi asked, "Were those people hurt?" Sanlang said, "Most of them were killed. Only some of them fell into pools or bushes and escaped. It was said that those who survived were 77. They had lived in the Sanxingdui area of Sichuan for more than 2,000 years and had flourished there. Later it declined for some reason. Only a few descendants survived by luck and lived here, from generation to generation, and have passed down to this day."

"There could be such a strange thing!" said Lanzi, "Sanlang, I also want to hear stories about your ancestors on that star in the sky." Sanlang said, "It is said that my ancestors lived well on that star, and there was everything there as we have here, land and sea, mountains and lakes, melons, apples, pears, peaches, and grains, you name it." Lanzi asked, "Is there affairs between men and women?" Sanlang answered, "Of course. Let me tell you a love story of the folks in the sky. This is a folklore. The people on that star also had love, marriage, children, and so on like the people on Earth. There was a farm girl named Sina, who was extremely beautiful and graceful. She fell in love with Wootan, a young guardian in the palace. Unexpectedly, Sina was chosen as a concubine by the King and recruited into the palace. Wootan was in great pain. When he was patrolling at night, he tried and succeeded in rescuing Sina from the palace. Both of them fled, going far away. The King was furious. He wanted and offered a reward for catching the two fugitives across the country. Unfortunately, Wootan and Sina were both captured. Wootan was crucified and Sina was put in jail. At that time, a rebel army captured the capital and the palace, the King fled abroad in panic. Sina took advantage of the chaos to escape from jail. The dying Wootan was saved from the cross by the rebels. Wootan and Sina were reunited.

They had a son and a daughter, leading a happy life." Lanzi was deeply moved by this story and said, "The heaven and the Earth are quite alike. I wish we could be as happy as the couple on the star. All shall be well, Jack shall have Jill."

It was no secret locally that Gan Sanlang and Du Lanzi were in love. People began to talk about it. Most people were not optimistic about their affairs. Although intermarriage was not uncommon at the time, yet the man was a fresh- looking descendant of an extraterrestrial. People often regard extraterrestrials as heterogeneous. In Du Lanzi's village, there was a young man named Linghu Jin who was already obsessing on Du Lanzi, stirred up some enmity, saying that Gan Sanlang was of a demon race, and the marriage with him would not only harm Lanzi but also affect the Du family.

The Gan family was entitled to the rich, while the Du family was poor. Sanlang's father thought it the loss of dignity for his son to marry Du Lanzi. The Du family was pure Han nationality, Chinese descendants. Du Lanzi's parents did not want their daughter to marry an Alien.

Gan Sanlang and Du Lanzi were deeply in love and almost inseparable. But their parents and most of the villagers were opposed to their ally. Patriarches of both sides claimed that they would sink the two together in a pond if they insisted on a marriage. Sinking in a pond was a local practice of punishment, a cruel lynching to the sinner who, with hands and feet tied up, and a large stone hang on the neck, was thrown into the pond and drowned.

Good Samaritan advised Gan Sanlang and Du Lanzi not be too persistent, otherwise no one could save them.

So Sanlang and Lanzi got into a great dilemma. Obviously, their marriage seemed impossible. They did not wish to succumb to social pressure, and were unwilling to sacrifice their lives for it either. Instead, they would choose to step on the only way out—to elope, to run away from the troubled place, to conceal their identities in another land, to get married and make a living.

Gan Sanlang and Du Lanzi met on a dark night by the Duck River. Before leaving, they knelt down on the river bank to worship their ancestors, parents, and relatives, and kissed the native land by the side of Duck River. Gan Sanlang left a note to his parents that he had placed under his parents' pillow. He wrote: "I have no alternative but to leave home. I am sorry that I can't live with my filial piety. I hope parents could take good care of yourselves and live well. Also, please tell the Du family that I will take good care of Lanzi." Du Lanzi was in tears and could not bear to leave her old grandmother and her kind parents, her kind-hearted folks, and the home village where she was born and raised.

Then they both rode on a horse, for over ten days, they traveled west by crossing mountains and rivers and reached the district of Xikang, west of Sichuan, where the Tibetans used to reside.

The local Tibetans were very friendly to them. They gave a lot of help to the two young people and taught them how to live in the new environment. Both of them changed their names. Gan Sanlang changed to Gaosan Dorje, Du Lanzi changed to Turan Dolma.

Gaosan Dorje and Turan Dolma became accustomed to eating Zanba (Tibetan staple food) and drinking butter tea. They raised a few sheep and a Tibetan mastiff. They also learned the Tibetan language and converted themselves to Tibetan Buddhists. Like the Tibetans, the two loved singing and dancing. Turan Dolma's voice was also like that of the Tibetans — loud, lyrical, with a unique feeling of echoing across a vast plateau. Gaosan Dorje used to dance in the Tibetan style when he was happy. His dance was skillful and vigorous, well received by local Tibetans.

They lived by hunting and gathering and selling herbs. When they were lucky, they could get cordyceps sinensis and ganoderma, and could sell them for good prices. The young couple were leading a happy life.

After some years, they had two sons and a daughter. The children were gorgeous, with clear-cut features on their faces, much like their father. The children of Gaosan Dorje and Turan Dolma were not only the half-breed of the Aliens and Han nationality, but also had some shade of Tibetan culture in them.

As Gaosan Dorje and Turan Dolma grew older, they missed their parents and relatives and home villages far away from them. Looking at the Jinsha River in front of them, they recalled the

Duck River near their home village where they met and fell in love with each other and where they embarked on the elopement to Xikang. So in their fifties they decided to return to their orinal home place with the whole family.

They came to the village in central Sichuan where they had once lived. But greeted them were desolate scorched Earth and deserted graves. There were ruins everywhere, overgrown with lush weeds.

They met Linghu Jin from the village of Du Lanzi. According to Linghu Jin there had been a plague here about 10 years ago. All the people in the Gan village died, and their ancestors and the entire Gan tribe were extinct. Many people in Du village also died. Lanzi's grandmother, who became blind due to crying too much for missing her granddaughter, passed away early. Lanzi's parents, looking for their daughter everywhere, had died of fatigue and anxiety.

Gaosan Dorje and Turan Dolma changed back to their original names Gan Sanlang and Du Lanzi. They rebuilt their home in their homeland. Their two sons formed families and gave birth to five grandsons for them. The Gan family tree was luxuriant again. According to the family tree records of the Gan family, five hundred years later, that was, in the middle of the Ming Dynasty, the Gan family became a scale and flourished again in Guanghan area in Sichuan province.

This was the only surviving branch of the Alien descendants. By the end of the Ming Dynasty, Zhang Xianzhong, a leader of a peasant uprising, led the army on a large scale slaughter of the Sichuan people. The descendants of the Gan family once again suffered an extinction. Fortunately a few escaped, and after more than a dozen of generations the Gans came down with the only branch of Gan Ruida family. Gan Ruida was both sad and somewhat smug about it, because in his generation, he was extremely lonely, but there were children and grandchildren around him, the Gans still had offsprings to follow them.

Gan Ruida said that he was now over 70 years old. Being a retired high school teacher of history, he focused on the research of Sanxingdui Civilization at home. He often went to Sanxingdui to pay homage to his ancestors and to examine unearthed relics. Gan Ruida believed that the reason why there were many sacrificial objects in the unearthed cultural relics in Sanxingdui was because the Aliens were missing their ancestors out of the globe and often carried out sacrificial activities. The protruding eyeballs in some of bronze facial statues were an exaggeration by non-representational methods. The expression was the Alien people missed their distant hometown and relatives so much that their eyes were sticking out.

Gan Ruida claimed to be descended from the Alien family. However, after dozens of generations of mixed breeding and genetic variation, the gene in the current Gan family had become very rare.

Gan's story evoked the intense interest of David and Emily in studying the Aliens. After returning to the United States, they still kept in touch with Gan Ruida and often exchanged information about Aliens with him.

Many people questioned whether Gan Ruida was really an Alien descendant and the realness and dependability about his family history. There was even a fundamental denial of the existence of Aliens.

In order to resolve this mystery, with the suggestion of David and Emily, Gan Ruida conducted a DNA ancestor test. The institution collected his saliva samples. Through a series of procedures such as professional inspection and comparison, it was found that his progenitor was abnormal. For more than 5, 000 years, there had been mixtures of Han and other ethnic minorities, but his older predecessors had been elusive. Most of China's ancestors could be traced to Western and Northern nationalities, such as Mongolian, Manchu, Korean, central Asian group, and even European and African nations. That was to say, the DNA of the male ancestors of Gan Ruida was significantly different from that of the ethnic groups in the world. Their origins were unclear with singular and strange DNA manifestations. This provided some support for the allegation that the Gan Ruida family belonged partly to Alien descendants.

> *The rumors about Aliens from other planets may seem absurd, but in fact they reflect the fact that the existence of Aliens on other planets is reasonable. The universe is broad and vast. Planets with living conditions suitable for the advanced living creatures, planets with human beings actually living on them will not just be the Earth, and no others. Human beings on Earth should not be shortsighted, self-respecting, and arrogant. One should understand that there is sky beyond our sky and there are people besides our people. It is entirely possible for Aliens to visit Earth, and the mains and descendants of Aliens on Earth deserve studying and confirming.*

# Chapter 8

## The Brief Life

After leaving Sichuan, David and Emily went to Yantai City, Shandong Province to see Emily's mother. Emily's mother was delighted to see her long-gone daughter. She also liked her son-in-law David, a handsome, open-minded white man. In Yantai, David and Emily also met Emily's brother, Jin Shuai, who worked in a foreign company in Yantai. He had a family and a daughter.

Emily had a certain attachment to Yantai, her hometown, although Yantai had changed greatly over the years, almost beyond recognition. David and Emily loved the sea. Every day they swam in the sea and watched the sea at the seaside.

During their stay in Yantai, David and Emily went to Yantai Yongan Cemetery together to pay a tribute to Emily's deceased father. Yantai Yongan Cemetery is large and magnificent. The entire cemetery is located on a hill. The archway-style front entrance leads to wide steps upwards, that are escorted on both sides by twelve Chinese zodiac animals, lifelike. Rows of graves and tombstones line the hillside in good order. The hills are green with pine trees and the cemetery is quiet and solemn.

In the Cemetery Emily worshipped her father in front of his tomb. In accordance with the local customs she burned some incense and paper money, offered a bouquet of flowers, bent on knees to kowtow for three times. David bowed to his father-in-law. Although Emily's father passed away many years ago, Emily always remembered the years when her father was alive, and cherished the memory of her father's love for her. Her father was taken away by illness in his thirties, and the love of Emily's father for her was too short. She remembered once when her father drew a beautiful picture for her with crayons in his sickbed. Emily liked the picture very much. It was amazing that beautiful images could be created with imagination and crayons. This was the beginning of Emily's study of drawing and painting. Emily began to learn to draw, and later was fascinated, as keen as mustard.

As David and Emily walked through the tombstones on the side roads, Emily was browsing the names and calculating the ages of the deceased by their birth-death dates. Some tombstones were marked with vacancy reserved for the spouse. Half of the couple was already here, while the other half was still alive, after the death, would reunite with the spouse in another world.

David and Emily were deeply affected by the atmosphere in the cemetery, and they talked to each other.

Emily: David, we can imagine how many people have died on this planet since there were human beings on it, and the vast majority of them have disappeared. As the saying goes, from the dirt, to the dirt. There is a huge army of the dead underground.

David: Yes. But the world's population is growing. More than 360,000 births and 150,000 deaths daily are reported world-wide. That's roughly 4 births and 2 deaths per second.

Emily: There are births and deaths every second. Life and death are common to all.

David: Actually, life is not far from death.

Emily: Look at the rows of dead people in the cemetery. We are very close to them. It is just that we are in the world of Yang, and they are in the underworld of Yin. We are separated from them by Yin and Yang.

David: The people in the world are heading for the underworld. We are in this marching procession ourselves.

Emily: I hope that we should be together after both of us die.

David: Of course. There are some good cemeteries in Boulder. When we die, we can rest there and be buried in the same tomb.

Emily: Great. It's a deal.

David and Emily were on their way back from the cemetery and had to walk on foot part of the way.

They saw rows of hibiscus flowers along the roadside.

They were especially familiar with this kind of flower. There was also hibiscus in Colorado, normally called Rose of Sharon, but it was not quite that big.

These hibiscus flowers grew lush, taller than people, and the light red flowers bloom vigorously. Bees were flying among the flowers, and in the distance, the shrills of cicadas could be heard that called up Emily's hometown crush. The sun was shining with no clouds in the sky. Emily wondered how beautiful the world was, how fascinating to live, and how precious every moment of one's life!

Emily couldn't help speaking to David, "I often feel very happy to live a life. How about you?"

David: Oh, yeah. Just like you. First of all, we should be content to have the privilege of a visit to this world.

One afternoon, David and Emily went to a bank in Yantai to exchange RMB for spending in China. After the exchange, Emily went to the restroom and David waited in the lobby. David noticed that a middle-aged lady pulled out a lot of cash from the bank and stacked it bundle by bundle in a handbag on the side table. At this moment, a fat man with a "sun hair(-style)" walked beside the lady and stamped on the lady's foot with his foot wearing a heavy leather shoe.

The lady screamed with pain, and the fat man apologized repeatedly: "I'm sorry, awfully sorry." saying that he didn't do it intentionally. David saw it clearly, that the fat man had just deliberately stepped on the lady's foot. At the same time, a thin man stepped forward and took the opportunity to grab the woman's bag and quickly walked out of the bank. David ran after the thin man who had picked up the bag. The thin man handed the bag to a man on a motorcycle in the street. David seized the motorcycle, stopped the man from riding off, and grabbed the bag from him.

The middle-aged lady who lost her handbag also ran out of the bank. David handed the bag to the lady, who thanked him repeatedly.

David watched the middle-aged lady take a taxi and leave, which let him rest assured.

Then David suddenly felt a sharp pain in his back. He was hit on his back by a stick, and someone stumbled at his feet. He was pushed violently and fell to the ground. He was kicked by some people with their feet. Among those people, David saw the fat man with the sun hair and the thin man who stole the bag. They groaned in their mouths, "Kill the nosy foreigner!" A crowd of pedestrians gathered in the street to watch them, but no one dared to help.

David suddenly turned over and stood, then snatched the stick from the fat man's hand. The gang members took out their daggers towards David, but David was not afraid. He beat the guys with the wooden stick so skillfully that they could hardly parry.

Emily came out of the bank to look for David, just as David had a good fight with the gang. She shouted for everyone to stop, or she would call the police. The fat man realised that the situation was not good for them, and signaled to his associates: "Withdraw!" The gang fled. The thin man was trampled under foot by David and could not move. David had learned Chinese martial arts in the United States. He had been taught by some Chinese experts.

The man who was trampled by David was begging for mercy. Emily saw that the man was a little familiar, and looked carefully, recognizing her high school classmate, Fang Hua.

Emily asked him, "Are you Fang Hua?"

The man got up from the ground and said, "Yes, you are Jin Li? Haven't you gone abroad?"

"I'm back in a travel and a visit to my relatives this time," said Emily, "How do you hang out with these people?"

Fang Hua said, "I can't help it. I've had a hard life, not as lucky as you."

Emily: What's happened to you? Fang Hua: It's a long story.

"I'd like to hear your story," Emily said.

David said, "Let's go to the seaside and sit for a while there where we can talk."

"This is my husband, David." Emily introduced David to Fang Hua.

Fang Hua said, "Your husband is really terrifying."

"As the Chinese saying goes, it takes a fight for people to get to know each other." said David.

The three of them came to the beach and sat on the stone bench where Fang Hua told his story:

More than a decade ago, Fang Hua, who studied in Yantai No. 1 High School, was a classmate of Emily. He was born with a good voice and was a top singer in the school. In his class, he was a commissary in charge of entertainment and in school, he was the backbone of the song and dance troupe. He was a cheerful, personable, well-liked young man. However, he said that he only admired Jin Li, but never had the courage to express his feelings to Jin Li, which was actually a kind of secret love.

Fang Hua's family was poor, and he often got the care and help from Jin Li. Fang Hua's parents had divorced early, then he lived together with his father. Unexpectedly, his father was cheated by someone, and jailed for illegal embezzlement of public funds. His mother remarried, but life was not comfortable for her, when his stepfather indulged in alcoholism, often imposed domestic violence on her. Fang Hua had been yearning to enter the Vocal Music Department of Central Music Institute in Beijing. Due to the trouble in his family, he was extremely short of money, so he had to give it up. His life was hopeless, and he had to sing for life in bars and nightclubs, barely surviving.

Fang Hua abandoned himself and began to play the game. He was infected with alcoholism and gambling addiction and ran up huge gambling debts overnight. The creditors ganged up on the debts, and he went into hiding. But to survive, he had to show up to earn some income. He was found by his creditors and beaten badly. He was forced to promise to pay the money within a week, otherwise he would be responsible for the consequences. The creditors threatened that once he did not pay, they would cut off one of his fingers, and if he failed to pay it again, they would chop another finger until all debts were paid off.

Fang Hua thought and thought, all hopes were destroyed. In his childhood, he was full of illusions and expectations for the future. Unfortunately, his parents were divorced, his father went to prison and the family was completely broken. He seemed to have been turned into a lonely orphan from being a favorite of his parents. A warm home, good dreams suddenly vanished into thin air. His alumni, Bingbing, had become a star in the domestic film and television circles. Jin Li, the girl she fell in love with secretly, was much better than him in their careers. She not only went to the top college in China but also had the honor of studying abroad. His own talent was unrecognized. He idled his time in vain, now had been caught in the mud and unable to extricate himself.

That night, Fang Hua smoked half a box of cigarettes and drank half a bottle of spirit by himself in the house.

Fang Hua was hot and dizzy. He staggered out of the house and headed for the sea in a daze.

Fang Hua felt that his life had come to an end. Thinking of his lofty ideal when he was young and his endless yearning for a better future, Fang Hua, in total despair, intended to throw himself into the water, bury himself in the sea, and sleep in the embrace of nature, so that he would get true peace. He was itching to jump, closing his eyes, and ready to step into another world in an instant.

Then several young men came up. A fat man with the "sun hair" said to him, "What are you doing, old chap? Don't be so mean to yourself when you're young. The coming days would be plenty."

"Leave me alone," said Fang. "Go ahead and mind your own business."

"My name is Jin Yushan, called Fat Jin the 3rd," said the fat man with the sun hair. "We're here to save you. Come with us. Let us know whatever is hard for you. There is no Flaming Mountain that you cannot pass."

"No one can help me out," said Fang.

Fat Jin the 3rd said: "No matter how big the thing may be our guys can still straighten it up for our fellow. Do you know?"

"Gambling debts," said Fang Hua.

Fat Jin the 3rd said, "Gambling debts? Gambling debt is a shit! No one would dare to ask for debt of guys in our group. Fuck! No one dare to lay a finger on you. Do you know? "

Fang Hua felt that these people were a bit unauthentic.

Then he asked, "What do you guys do? "

"We are Liangshan heroes ( robinhoods ), " said the fat man. "Since you have difficulties, please go to Liangshan." (Liangshan was the base for rebel heroes (robinhoods) against the imperial government in Song Dynasty in China. )

Fang Hua knew he was going "to board a pirate ship." Since he was now at the end of his rope, just let it be. It should be better than hiding all day long. Thus, Fang Hua was "forced into Liangshan" and joined the gang.

Fang Hua saw that these people ganged up with Jin Yushan were not like robin hoods, nor "Water Margin heroes." It was a gang of thieves and robbers, who claimed to rob the rich and aid the poor, but in fact they were robbing other people to enrich themselves. They ganged up to commit crimes, and had a high rate of success. They used guerilla tactics by taking a shot to change a place with traces hard to find. The civilians were afraid of them, and the public security system had a headache about them.

Fang Hua was promoted to "the Third Chair" after a trial period in the gang because of his sagacity and competence. He planned the activities and strategies of the gang with Fat Jin the 3rd. His nickname was "Wisedom-Star."

That day when they were robbing someone at the bank, "taking the fortune by wisdom," according to Fang Hua's stratagem, unexpectedly, they lost the "silver" that was already in their hands. Blame the damn foreigner's meddling that broke their good deeds, blocked their way of getting money. They stroke the foreigner violently. Unfortunately, that foreigner was strong at martial arts, beating them up and down in return, and even having captured one of the heroes, Fang Hua, alive.

Emily learned the sad experiences of her old classmate and expressed deep sympathy.

Emily had a good talk with her old classmate, Fang Hua.

They talked about life, ideals, and reality. They all thought that one's life was actually very short. They felt that the path of a person's life had to go by oneself, and there were inevitably bumps and setbacks on the way. It was important to make the right decisions at the critical moments in life. Then one should have a clear distinction between good and evil, and have a moral bottom line. One should not do things that benefit oneself at the expense of others, let alone committing crimes. Fang Hua felt the warmth of the world from Emily. His eyes filled with tears, he was determined to mend his ways, cheer up, and get up where he fell.

With the encouragement of Emily, Fang decided to buck up and start all over again. One should rise at the same place where one falls. He decided to turn himself in to the police, to abandon the darkness for the brightness.

Fang Hua went to the Police Headquarters to surrender the case, and also gave out their criminal gang to help crack the gang headed by Jin Yushan. He was given a lighter punishment and sentenced to two years in prison.

David and Emily went to the prison to see Fang Hua before leaving Yantai. Fang Hua said that he would never forget the help of David and Emily. When he came out of prison, he should be a good person and would start a new life.

*Life is short, life is impermanent. In the vast sea of people in the world, for a variety of reasons, each person's experience varies a lot from others.*

*Whether a person can make a correct decision at the crossroads or key moments of his life, choosing the right path determines a person's life, destiny and success or failure.*

*In human life, righteousness, goodness, and evil are distinct. One should perform good deeds and be virtuous. Don't let a slip of error bring life-long regret. A person who has lost his way should recover the bearings, return to the fold, and turn over a new leaf.*

# Chapter 9

## A Half-Breed Girl

Shandong Province looks like the silhouette of a camel's head facing east towards the Pacific Ocean in the map of China. The nose of and mouth of the camel are the area of Rongcheng County, (now Rongcheng City). Rongcheng is located in the easternmost part of Shandong Province, surrounded by the sea on three sides. It is rich in grain and seafood, a famous land of agriculture and fishery. Rongcheng has beautiful sceneries, with endless pine forests on the beach, fluctuating with the sea wind, like waves. However, living conditions in the rural areas of Rongcheng are poor. Like most rural areas of the country, it has a large gap with regard to the urban life of the cities.

In a small village in Rongcheng, a foreign wife was brought around. This was a big piece of news in the village. Not only the residents of the village but also those in the  nearby villages were intrigued to observe. This woman had a white complexion, a high nose, and a chiseled face. She spoke a foreign language that they did not understand, just like the foreign women in movies and TV programs.

More than a decade ago, when a village boy named Ding Zhiyang was working in a Chinese company in Milan, Italy, when he met a beautiful local woman, Anna Marino, who was then a nurse. Anna took good care of Zhiyang in the ward when he was hospitalized for some illness. Zhiyang was deeply touched and fell in love with Anna. Zhiyang proposed to Anna, who was moved by his sincere love. The two had a romantic relationship. Anna's parents and friends were not optimistic about their affairs. However, Anna was persistent and ardently in love with this young man from China, vowing not to marry anyone else in her life. Anna's parents had to comply with the wish of their only daughter. Anna and Zhiyang were married in Italy and lived a happy life. A year later Anna gave birth to a daughter named Deborah.

The girl was pretty, lively, and lovely.

Ding Zhiyang had been in a foreign country for a long time. He became homesick, often missing his home village where he had lived. Also, the endless pine trees on the beach, the amiable faces of his parents, and the simple and kind villagers often appeared in his mind. Ding Zhiyang insisted on returning home to Rongcheng, China with his wife and daughter. But he also worried that Anna and Deborah would not be accustomed to the simple life of rural China. He told Anna about his ambivalence. Anna said: "When I chose you, I chose the destination of my love. I will follow you wherever you go."

So, Ding Zhiyang traveled far back to his home village in Rongcheng with his wife and daughter. Anna was shocked by the simple and crude living conditions in the Chinese countryside with small houses, no A/C, no hot water, no shower, no flush toilet. The heating, lighting, and cooking utensils were very simple, which could not be compared to the life in Italy, and it was also much worse than those of the cities in China. Medium cities of China like Dalian and Yantai that they came through on their way to Rongcheng were quite prosperous, where the residents lived a relatively modern life. Compared with the countryside, that was simply a different world. However, Anna was not discouraged and did not regret it.

Anna bravely faced the challenge of her fate. Like the rural women in China, she took on the heavy farm work and household duties, contracted together with her husband a piece of farmland with the village to grow crops and vegetables, and set up a chicken farm to raise about 1000 chickens. She was often tired with pain in her back and sweating all over. Anna and her daughter, Deborah, learned the local language and gradually adapted to the daily life in the Chinese countryside, mingling themselves with the local villagers. Their family were leading a decent life, and after years of hard work, they had some savings in their hands. Besides, they got the subsidy from Anta's parents and opened a café in Yantai. The business of the café was good. One year later they bought a house in Yantai, and their whole family moved to Yantai.

Deborah was attending a primary school in Yantai. She was good at singing and dancing. She spoke standard and fluent Mandarin Chinese. She was a cute Chinese and Western mixed-race girl. Her Chinese name was Ding Beilei (Bud). As the name suggested, she was indeed like a flower bud.

Ding Beilei was cheerful, lively and talktive. After class, her hearty laughter could often be heard. Students liked to hear her telling foreign stories and customs, listen to her singing foreign songs. She also learned to skip ropes, flip, turn somersault, swim, and play in the sea with her classmates.

The mixed-race girl had fully integrated into the group of Chinese children, and they were very close to each other.

Ding Beilei had a best friend among her classmates, called Jin Qinger. Jin Qinger told her that her aunt married an American man. Her aunt and uncle were traveling around the world and had now arrived in Yantai. A few days ago, her aunt and uncle went to their house for a visit.

Qinger also liked singing, and she taught Beilei many Chinese songs. One of Beilei's favorite songs was "Let's Scull." Beilei had sung the song at the school's singalong. The song goes like this:

> Let's play on the oars
> The little boat pushed the waves away
> The beautiful white tower is reflected on the lake
> Surrounded by green trees and red walls
> The little boat drifted gently in the water
> There was a cool breeze

Jin Qinger said that she admired her aunt Jin Li, who she regareded as her idol. She said that her aunt was independent, thoughtful, discerning, and talented, and was a "woman of strong will." She said her uncle David was a handsome, strong, kind-hearted, and generous white man. They matched perfectly. Beilei said to Qinger, "Your aunt and uncle, as well as my dad and mom, are all allies of Chinese and Westerners. This kind of marriage will be more popular, and people will no longer feel strange about it."

However, as the Chinese saying goes, "a storm may arise from a clear sky." Something unexpected happened to Beilei. She was diagnosed with leukemia a year ago, and her condition was getting worse now. The hospital examined her for several times, drew up different treatment plans, and found that the only viable option to save her life was a bone marrow transplant. But finding a bone marrow match was particularly difficult. The attending doctor looked through the national bone marrow database and even contacted the relevant institutions in Taiwan but found no suitable match. Ding Beilei could only wait for the end of her short life. When Zhiyang and Anna saw that the child's face was pale, with tears in her eyes, unwilling to leave the world, their hearts seemed to be pierced by knives.

Beilei's teacher and classmates had visited her in the hospital ward many times and brought her flowers. They wished her a miracle in her fate and an early recovery. Beilei smiled and thanked everyone for their concern. Jin Qinger knew that people were just trying to comfort her. She knew that Beilei's days were numbered, and her eyes reddened with tears for her best friend Beilei's impending death.

Whenever Qinger had time, she would go to Beilei's ward to accompany and chat with her, so that Beilei did not feel lonely. She told stories to Beilei. She talked about the Monkey King's havoc in the Heavenly Palace, Wu Song fighting the tiger, the

White Snake and other household Chinese stories. Qinger said, "I really want to learn from the White Lady to go to Mount Emei to collect the Ganoderma lucidum to save your life. But the doctor says that the only way to save you is the right bone marrow. It seems that the bone marrow is the Ganoderma lucidum that can save you."

At this time, David and Emily were staying at a hotel in Yantai. They occasionally went to Anna's café to drink coffee.

They learned about this in a chat with Anna, owner of the café. They felt very sorry and sad for the misfortune of Anna's family. David suggested that he might go to the hospital to test if his bone marrow could match.

Coincidentally, David's bone marrow matched Beilei's perfectly. David decided to donate some of his bone marrow, so as to save the girl Beilei. Emily also fully supported him. Only she had some fears that this would make David suffer a lot and might affect David's health. David told Emily to be reassured that everything would be fine as long as he had her blessings.

So, David had a bone marrow extraction and transplant at the hospital. This foreigner from afar, cured the lovely mixed-race girl with his bone marrow donated generously. The red marrow fluid slowly flowed into the girl's body, bringing the dying girl back to the lovely world, to her parents and her caring teachers, classmates, and friends.

The warm sun shone on the vibrant Earth. The gentle sea wind blew on the quiet beach. The sea gulls were flying gaily up and down, singing hymns and songs in unison. A good fortune, a miracle happened on Earth. A beautiful and lovely life was saved, a dying girl was saved!

Zhiyang and Anna were very grateful to David. The girl Beilei regarded David and Emily as the parents for her rebirth.

After the bone marrow transplant, David needed to recuperate and recover for some time. Bone marrow extraction was not only a severe pain, but also a great physical expense for the donor. David's health gradually recovered and recuperated under the attentive care of Emily.

David and Emily often went to see Beilei in the hospital. Seeing the sick girl, who was gradually recovering, they felt very happy, as if she was their own daughter. Beilei talked and laughed, unrestrained, and sometimes sang to them.

The girl was discharged from the hospital that day, ready to be nursed at home. The family were in high spirits. They invited David, Emily, and Qinger to their home. Zhiyang and Anna had prepared delicious food for them. The two families gathered together and were intimate.

Emily was delighted to learn that her niece Qinger was Beilei's best friend. A close bond had been formed between the two families.

Beilei quipped that she had the blood of both the Chinese Han nationality and Italians in Europe. Now she had the bone marrow of an American as well.

David said that he was also of Italian descent. His great-grandfather came from Milan, Italy, and immigrated to the United States. He was an Italian American.

A bone marrow donation and a DNA test had brought the two families together who had been separated from each other. David and Emily often went to Anna and Zhiyang's café to gossip. Anna and Zhiyang used to go to chat with David and Emily in the hotel room as soon as they had leisure time.

Beilei proposed to go to their home village in Rongcheng that they left years ago to see her old classmates and friends. Ding Zhiyang and Anna planned to spare some time to go there with their daughter. They invited David, Emily, and Qinger to go with them and they readily agreed.

So, the six of them drove from Yantai to Rongcheng, passing through the fertile land of Jiaodong in the eastern part of

Shandong Peninsula. In Rongcheng, they saw the village and house where Zhiyang, Anna, and Beilei lived years ago. Seeing the simple housing, Zhiyang and Anna could not believe that their family had lived, worked for years under such conditions. They felt very familiar and excited to see everything here.

David and Emily admired Zhiyang and Anna very much for their hard work in pursuit of a better life. They regarded it as a love of life.

Nowadays, the village had changed a lot, with many new buildings being set up. Housing conditions were gradually improving.

Beibei was overjoyed to see her former classmates and friends. Beilei said she missed them badly, especially when she was in a critical condition. She had thought that she would never see them again in this life. Unexpectedly, she survived miraculously, as if in a dream. "They are my second parents." Beilei said, pointing to David and Emily. "They gave me a second life." The children thanked David and Emily and looked at them with an admiring eye.

They all went to the seaside. The sea here was even broader than that in Yantai. David and Emily looked at the vast expanse of the sea, the broad Pacific Ocean, and thought that on the other side of the ocean was the United States where they had their home, their son Oliver, their relatives, and friends. Although the two sides of the ocean were far apart, they felt very cordial to their loved ones and warm homes on both sides.

David and Emily stayed in Yantai for a few weeks and by saying goodbye to Emily's mother, brother, and sister-in- law and Qinger, Zhiyang, Anna, and Beilei, bid farewell to Yantai, aboarded the return plane, and returned to Colorado, thus ending their journey around the world.

*The harmonious relationship between human beings is reflected in the benevolence of the lover, following what is right, and enjoying pleasure in helping others, regarding people from all over the world as brothers and sisters, regardless of their race, region, gender, age, social status, etc. In particular, the kind of good deeds that take risks to save people from the fire and water, and their lofty spirit, that deserve people's praise, admiration, and emulation.*

*For a better life, to forge ahead with courage, not being afraid of difficulties and hardships, is a virtue and the model of people.*

# Chapter 10

## PREHISTORIC ADVENTURES

fter David and Emily returned to the United States, they still lived in the home of David's parents in Boulder, staying with David's parents and their three-year-old son.

The family of three generations was intimate and happy. David found a job in the laboratory of the Department of Biology at the University of Colorado, Boulder. Emily was engaged in art creation.

Two years later, David had reached the age of thirty- three. But he still remained a man of action and adventure. Being fascinated by the hot air balloon flying he was keen on learning to fly a hot air balloon himself and intended to take his whole family for a balloon ride.

David had mastered the basic principles and operation skills of hot air balloon. Flying a baloon was a different experience from driving a small plane in the air. In the balloon, he had a more stable point of view to enjoy the beautiful scenery below, and to experience the special charm of the high range rover.

One day David was flying a balloon over the city of Boulder and its suburbs. When he was preparing to return, he suddenly felt the balloon violently oscillating and difficult to control. He then decided to make an emergency landing, but he found that the balloon was driven eastward by a sudden west wind, and it kept rising, tossing, and turning like a fallen leaf driven by the autumn wind, completely involuntarily.

David saw that his balloon, carried dangerously by the high winds, swiftly sweeping over cities of Bloomfield, Thornton, and DIA (Denver International Airport, over the eastern plains of Colorado and into the state of Kansas. On the great plains of Kansas, winds were even stronger. The balloon went up and down in the air. David felt dizzy, sick, and helpless.

Moreover, misfortune never comes singly. There was a strong tornado on the plains of Kansas, approaching the balloon in which David was riding. David was a little panicked. Once the balloon was rolled up by a tornado, the consequences would be unimaginable. David kept praying that the tornado would pass by and let go of his balloon. He struggled to manipulate and tried to avoid the tornado. However, the tornado did not slant and headed right towards the balloon. The balloon was caught in as rapidly as the thunder. It spun so fast inside the tornado that David felt dizzy, giddy, and totally at the mercy of the wind. The balloon was completely detached from him and was torn into several pieces by the wind, making some squeaking sound. David's body was floating in the air. Under the power of the overwhelming force of nature, David felt himself so tiny and powerless. He closed his eyes tightly and gradually lost consciousness, drifting in the air with the wind. Finally, he passed out.

## Around 1,000,000 B.C

Not knowing how long afterwards, David woke up from a coma, and found himself out of the sky. The scene in front of him was kind of weird, not like the world today. It was surrounded by lush greenery, flowers, and trees. In particular, clusters of ferns and primeval trees covered the land, giant lizards sticking out their tongues in short intervals, giant birds with long tails flying around in the sky, as if they were living in the era of prehistory.

When David tried to stand up and walk on the ground, he suddenly found that he could not move. His body was stuck by a kind of glue and bound up by several translucent ropes. The translucent ropes formed a large network around him, which turned out to be a large spider web. When he fell from the sky, he was lucky enough to have this net buffer, so he would not fall to the ground. He was glad that his life was strong and had survived a great disaster.

David was elated over his luckiness when he saw a giant spider slowly approaching him. He realized that he had become a prey of the giant spider with his body firmly tied to the web. If he did not resist, he would be slaughtered and devoured by the monster. Instinctively, David thought of self- defense. He took a knife out of his pocket, which he would use to cut the balloon rope when necessary. He thrusted his knife into the round belly of the approaching huge spider, and a sticky liquid oozed from it. The spider shivered in pain and retreated. David took the opportunity to use the knife to cut off the thick and strong spider silk and broke free from the spider web.

David was free, and he curiously strolled in this wonderful and strange environment. What the hell was this place? He felt a little lost. He examined the plants, animals, and insects on the ground. He was surprised to find that most of them belonged to the early species of the earth about a million years ago. Was this the original garden of Eden that had never been disturbed by human beings? David came across some footprints similar to those of a man walking barefoot. He followed the footprints, hoping to find someone living here so that he could try to return home with their help. He was thinking that his wife and son at home should be worried about him at this time.

Just as David was indulged in thinking of his home and loved ones, he suddenly felt that he was seized by two strong hands from behind. Looking back, he was shocked.

There were two stout men, not very tall, like savages, with dark complexion, long hair, and a suede on the waist. David concluded that he had fallen into the hands of "savages." Although he had practiced martial arts and knew some kungfu, yet by this time he was exhausted and could hardly stand up to these tough "savages." The two "savages" uttered some sounds, which David did not understand. They escorted David to the riverbank. After walking for about half an hour, they came to a cave by the river. There were many "wild men" inside and outside the cave. They all looked up and down at David with curious eyes and made some hard-to-understand sounds in their mouths.

In a moment, David was brought into the cave to meet a female elderly. The elderly, not quite thirty years of age in appearance, with enhanced breasts and slender waist, dressed in leather, wearing feathers on her head, with long hair hanging down to her shoulders, was a beautiful and imposing figure of extraordinary temperament, who looked like the leader of the savages. A number of valiant guys waiting by her side, appearing obedient. When the leader asked David some questions, he did not understand, so she mumbled to the man close to her. The man politely let David rest in a hole. After a long while, David was invited to the banquet on the outfield of the cave.

There was no dining table on the site. Everyone sat on the ground together. Dishes were various wild fruit and vegetables at the front, drinks were coconut juice and water. Cups and plates were made of nut shells, clam shells and concave slates. The dinner was full of raw, bloody meat and offal. There were also raw fish and live insects, which David could not stomach. He saw that the diners were eating happily, with their mouthes, faces stained with red blood, just like the lions that were gnawing their prey. David was pretty hungry at this time. To satisfy his hunger, he could only pick up some pieces of wild beef with little blood and ate them as if they were underdone pink steaks in a restaurant.

Most of the utensils here were made of stone. There were stone axes, stone knives, stone spears, and so on. David thought this should be an early human Stone Age. It seemed to have been isolated for millions of years, so that the level of civilization had stagnated and was far behind the world today.

David thought again. No, the world was now an information developed global village, how could there be such an isolated corner for millions of years in the present world? It seemed that the people here were not "savages," but the "primitives" in human prehistoric times. David was shocked. Did he pass through a time-space channel to the primitive era of prehistoric times? In fact, David himself did not know that he was sent into the space-time tunnel by the tornado in a completely comatose state, and then he traversied back to the primitive era of humans about one million years ago, located in eastern Africa.

David was given temporary shelter in the primitive cave, living with the primitive people here. He gradually became familiar with the simple and vivid language of these primitive people, assisted by gestures, he could exchange daily information with them.

David had a lighter with him. He taught the primitive people here to ignite hay and dry branches to make a fire and to use the fire to make BBQ and various cooked foods. He also taught them how to get fire in the absence of a lighter. Cooked food was gaining ground. He also taught the primitive people here to make bows and arrows with bamboo and rattan, which improved the effectiveness of hunting. David taught the villagers to collect wild beans, wild potatoes, plant them in the ground, water them, weed them, and harvest them when they were ripe for eating. David also taught them to bundle the bamboo sticks together in a flat row to make a rafter, put it in the river for use as a boat, and use a pointed bamboo stick to fish in the water as a harpoon.

These measures helped the primitive people at the time improve their hunting methods and pioneered the original agriculture, fisheries, and so on, and thereby improved their living conditions and strengthened their ability to resist foreign invaders.

The primitive people here, especially the elderly woman, known as "Nava," liked this smart and handsome "gentile."

David also had a general understanding of the social structure of the tribe in his conversations with them. This was a social group of matriarchal clan. The tribal chief had the ultimate authority to lead and rule the entire clan. The tribal chief had multiple male sexual partners without a fixed spouse. The children only knew their mother and did not know their father. Nava ordered David to be one of her sexual partners. David declined, but Nava was not discouraged. She once forced David into her cave, cuddling and kissing. David said he had his own wife and children and should not accept another love.

Nava was puzzled and asked what was the problem if one already had a wife? David said that his society was monogamous. Nava was even more puzzled why monogamy.

Nava was not pleased with David's defiance of her will. She did not believe that she could not touch this man with a stone heart. She imprisoned David and persuaded him every day, but David still clung to her wife Emily and their child, unwilling to seek a new love. Later, David was cut off from food and water and forced to submit. The cramped cave where he was confined was sweltering, infested with flies and mosquito bites, harassment by snakes and scorpions. David was faced with the choice between yield and death. He felt that he could not hold on any longer. He upheld the Western values and wished to concede and condescend to save his life. He succumbed and survived in this situation.

The tribe headed by Nava was called "Giant Lizard Village," and the giant lizard was its tribal totem. The tribe in the north of the Giant Lizard Village was called "Giant Python Village," with the giant python as its tribal totem.

The leader of "Giant Python Village" was called "Kansha." She learned that the Giant Lizard Village thrived with the help of a captured gentile, and also let the handsome and gallant gentile be the "Village Husband."

The chief of the Giant Python Village Kansha, out of jealousy, launched a war against the Giant Lizard Village, demanding to hand over the gentile to her. Battles were fought, the Giant Python Village was not successful. Kansha ordered her fighters to set a trap in the ground to lure the villagers of Nava tribe into it. One day, at dusk, the Giant Python Village troops came to challenge again, and the Giant Lizard Village fighters came out to meet the enemy. Nava and two soldiers unfortunately fell into the trap and were captured alive.

Kansha forced Nava to surrender the gentile, and Nava swore to death not to submit. Under the command of Kansha, Nava was thrown from a height into the Nulu River in the deep valley. There were numerous ferocious crocodiles in the Nulu River, and those who fell into it would surely die.

At this time, David was hidden by Nava in a secret cave. He managed to escape from the cave and learned from the Giant Lizard villagers about the defeat of their Village and the death of their chief Nava. David was very sad. He sneaked into the virgin forest and secluded himself.

In the virgin forest, David had no difficulty in finding food and water. There were ripe fruit and nuts, ponds and streams everywhere. There were also protein-rich bird eggs and insects.

He gathered and used a lighter to light some fallen leaves or dry hay to make a fire and cook them.

When night fell, David spent the night in the hole of a big banyan tree and prepared a wooden stick for self-defence. Wild animals often haunt the forest and he had to be on guard against them. In the middle of the night, David was in pain all over his body. When he opened his eyes, he found that his body was covered with termites that were eating into him. David knew the termites well. He ran out of the hole in the tree, turning and jumping, trying to get rid of the termites. But those hateful termites were biting his skin and flesh firmly. David had to be impolite, he took out his lighter, with the flame to roast near the termites. The termites squirmed, some ran away, some were dying, and some were dead.

The next day David continued on his way, trudging through the woods all morning. At noon, he ate some fruit and two big bird eggs. He felt a little sleepy. Then he laid down on the grass, fell asleep, and had a dream. In the virgin forest, the plants were luxuriant, criss-crossing, and the beasts were rampant, especially large animals, dragging their large and bulky bodies and walking through the gaps between trees and weeds.

While sleeping, David suddenly felt some sharp objects touching his body. He had a feeling of his whole body being squeezed. When he woke up, he found himself being put into a pocket. It was dark inside, only part of the inner wall appeared pink and light green due to the illumination of external sunlight. There was also a smell of entrails in the narrow space, and he could see the soft walls of animal flesh all around him. David realized that it was too bad that he should be in the belly of a big beast or a giant worm. He had been swallowed, only to be digested. He took a sharp knife from his pocket without hesitation and thrust it into the flesh wall. He made a long cut in the wall with his sharp blade, and suddenly the glaring sunlight came in

and made him dizzy. He cut the opening even wider, emerged
from it, and stood up. In front of him was a huge python, which
was incomparably thick and long and enormous, writhing and
trembling in pain. The giant python died and became a big meal
of huge lizards and vultures. At this time, David felt a little scared
for himself. If he had not opened the snake's belly in time, he

would have been suffocated, digested, and excreted. In addition to the light wounds that the snake's teeth touched his body when it swallowed him, there was no major harm. This was a rare experience, but also a blessing in his own misfortune.

After walking in the forest for a while, David came out of it to the banks of the Nulu River. Here he saw a woman lying on the grass by the river bank. When he came closer, he found that it was Nava. He couldn't believe his eyes. As far as he knew, Nava had been thrown into the Nulu River at the bottom of the valley and drowned.

Nava saw David. With mixed feelings, she burst into tears. She clutched David as hard as she could and did not let go. She told David about her experience. Nava said that she was thrown into the Nulu River by people from the Giant Python Village but she did not drown. A hippopotamus in the river drove away several crocodiles that were approaching her and pushed her to the bank. It turned out that Nava used to feed the hippos in the river, and the hippos were very friendly to her.

David and Nava returned to the Giant Lizard Village together. The people in the village were very excited. They danced cheerfully and sang exciting songs. Primitive people liked singing and dancing, being good at expressing their straightforward feelings.

People of the Giant Lizard Village, under the leadship and guidance of Nava and David, were rebuilding their homes. They improved their life with fire and cooked food, hunted with bows and arrows, and fended off foreign attacks.

The strength of the tribe had soared.

David found that Nava was versatile. She not only had outstanding leadership skills but also was a good artist. Nava liked to draw pictures on the walls of the cave. She used red and black soft stones and plant stains to make various shapes on the flat gray rocks, such as bisons, wild deer, birds, rivers, the sun, the moon, and so on. The paintings were so vivid and powerful that they reminded David of the original frescoe pictures he had seen in books. Those were printed copies, while these paintings were genuine.

The life of Giant Lizard Village was rich and the villagers were happy and healthy. It was largely owing to David's contributions. David's growing prominence in the tribe, and the fact that he was favored and loved by the chief Nava, had inevitably incurred some people's envy, jealousy, and hatred for him. Two of Nava's sexual partners who felt disfavored colluded to get rid of the gentile. They tricked David into hunting in the south woods together, and found an opportunity to set out to push him into a deep cave.

However, David had already learned about this terrible "Scorpion Cave" from Nava. There were numerous scorpions, centipedes, lizards, and poisonous snakes in it. If a man fell into it, he would hardly have any chance to survive from death. David was on the defensive when he found out about the two men's bad intentions. David flashed their fists with flexible martial arts skills. Then he pulled out his sharp knife and made a shallow cut on one of the men's body. The knife mark oozed blood. The two people were frightened, with pale faces, fleeing away desparately.

The tribal chief, Nava, was furious about the incident.

The two perpetrators were ordered to be severely punished.

They were defamed as the untouchables, and sentenced to a year of hard labor, digging holes, building roads, and cleaning up trash. David pleaded to Nava for forgiveness for their first offense. Nava reluctantly agreed to halve their hard labor. Nava warned the other men that they would be punished the same way if they hatched a sinister plot.

David didn't forget his major (biology). He used the opportunity of prehistoric times to conduct some observation and research on animals and plants at that time. He often walked around to inspect various kinds of animals and plants there.

The African grassland was a paradise and hunting ground for large animals such as elephants, lions, cheetahs, and wilde beasts. They ran unhindered and slept in the shade after eating and drinking. When they saw David, they were only curious and did not intend to harm this bizarre animal that only walked on two legs. Here, David also saw animals such as ancient southern elephants, ancient rhinoceros, and saber-toothed tigers.

Sometimes, David walked farther, once he saw a pterosaur-like animal in the distance on the wasteland. If it was really a pterosaur, it would be a great discovery of archaeological and biological value. Pterosaurs, or winged lizards, were similar to dinosaurs. But pterosaurs lived much earlier on earth, about hundreds of millions of years ago. Could it be a new species derived from pterosaurs? David was concentrating on his thinking and slowly approaching the pterosaur-like creature when he heard a cry behind him. He looked back and saw a few bruisers, each holding a stone spear. They wanted David to go with them.

When David asked them where they were going, they made no answer. David had to go with them. He was escorted by these bruisers, who were humming some tune, talking and laughing as they went until they came to a large cave after about an hour. They told David to wait for a while outside.

One of the bruisers who escorted David went into the cave and reported to the chief that they had caught the gentile of the Giant Lizard Village. The chief was overjoyed and personally came out to meet him. It turned out that the chief was none other than the famous Kansha of the Giant Python Village. Kansha looked younger than Nava and appeared gorgeous and radiant.

Kansha held the whole village for a celebration of the admission of the gentile into their tribe. People in the village played music by knocking on clam shells, slabs of stone, blew conches (shell trumpets), and bamboo tubes. Kansha who was a top singer took the great opportunity to sing high- pitched songs. Men and women of the village danced and danced until late at night.

Kansha arranged for David to live in a cave next to her bedroom. David was given the title of "senior assistant" and "preferred partner" which David was reluctant to obey. Kansha did not compel, did not put pressure on him, she just let David think carefully and never miss a good opportunity.

David was inevitably depressed. He had settled down in the Giant Lizard Villageandhadgraduallybecomeaccustomed to living there. Nava's affection for him was profound, her care for him was meticulous. Now unfortunately, he was confined to a strange environment. He couldn't help missing Nava and the villagers of Giant Lizard Village. At this time, he found that he and Nava were not in an ordinary friendship, and it seemed difficult for him to give up.

David made it clear to Kansha that he hoped that Kansha could release him and let him go back to Giant Lizard Village. Kansha said that it would be OK, but David had to teach Giant Python Villagers how to make fire, make bows and arrows, grow crops, make bamboo rafts and fish.

So, David taught all these techniques to the Giant Python Village one by one according to the agreement. From this, Giant Python Village benefited a lot, with their lives improved and their military strength reinforced.

After that, however, Kansha never mentioned anything about David's return to his village. Every day, she talked with David, trying to get closer with each other, advising David to stay in Giant Python Village and take it as his home, no longer fantasizing with unrealistic ideas.

There were quite a few young girls in the Giant Python Village, who seemed to be only twelve or thirteen years old.

They were lively and cheerful. They often came to David, talking and laughing with him. The girls were well dressed, with styled thin furs or green leaves about their breasts and bosoms, a pretty flower in the hair, pink-red dyes on the cheeks and lips, and kinds of fresh perfume on their bodies and hair, comparable to the French perfumes. David discovered that primitives also loved beauty, despite their backward production, and their low living conditions.

The Giant Lizard Village learned that David was being held in the Giant Python Village. Time and again, Nava sent people to the Giant Python Village for negotiations, hoping that the Giant Python Village should return David to them. But Kansha declined.

Nava decided to attack the Giant Python Village to seize back David. The mighty army of Giant Lizard Village surrounded the Giant Python Village tightly. Although the Giant Python Village had mastered the bow and arrow technology, it was difficult to resist the Giant Python Village army that had developed earlier with more powful arm forces.

Kansha, chief of the Giant Python Village, knew that her army was in danger, and personally came forward to talk with Nava, chief of Giant Lizard Village.

As a condition of negotiation, Kansha promised to return David in exchange for the retreat of the troops from Giant Lizard Village.

David was released. He met with the leaders and villagers of the Giant Lizard Village. He felt affectionate to see Nava and the other folks.

In the negotiations, David also added a condition of peace, hoping that the two villages would no longer fight each other, but get along well, to establish relationship of mutual assistance and cooperation, and to share technology for development. Nava and Kansha shook hands and agreed to David's proposal. The two leaders swore an oath of peace to Heaven.

In this way, a crisis was resolved. The army of Giant Lizard Village withdrew. David returned to the Giant Lizard Village and

Nava's side. Since then, the two villages had been living in peace and friendship for generations.

After David returned from the Giant Python Village, Nava loved him even more deeply. In addition to being sincere, straightforward and fiery like the love of the other primitive people, Nava could sometimes talk to her lover in a delicate and subtle way, heart to heart, bill and coo, like the modern people. She often invited David to take a walk in the wild, to watch the waves in the river, and to collect wild flowers and fruits on the grassland. Nava could also hum a little tune like a love song. The romance and sentiment of the primitive people were no less than that of the modern people.

Under the guidance of David, these primitive people planted crops and raised livestock, and their life was greatly improved. Now they could eat delicious roasted wild beans, baked wild potatoes, BBQ, lamb kabobs, and beef stewed with wild potatoes, cooked fresh fish, shrimps, crabs, and clams.

Most area of Africa was hot in a year, with only rainy and dry seasons. In the rainy season, the water and grass were rich, the wild animals were active and prosperous. In the dry season, rain was scarce and rivers and ponds dried up. Fish and shrimps in the water died in large numbers.

The wild animals on the grassland lacked water and food. So did primitive humans. In the dry season, there was not enough prey and fruits and vegetables. However the water of the Nulu river was still inexhaustible, which was the river of life for early human beings and other creatures.

As time went by, David had lived in this primitive environment for nearly a year and gradually got used to the simple and primitive life here. But in his mind he was never completely separated from his family and the modern society he had lived in for decades.

One day, while David and Nava were out for a walk, they saw a big storm on the prairie. A tornado came out of the ground. The tornado's volume was growing rapidly, standing and swirling from the ground through the sky.

David thought it might be a chance for him to return home. He said to Nava, "Nava, I want to return to our land by the wind. Thank you for your kindness to me during this period of time. I am sorry to say goodbye to you now. " When Nava heard this, she was terrified and burst into tears. She tried to hold David and said, "I can't let you go. You have to stay!"

David said, "I have my own home over there, and my own wife and son." Nava said, "I am also your wife and will bear children for you." David said, "You are a good wife. I will not forget you. I wish you happiness!" Then he ran to the tornado, and wanted to go by the wind. Nava lunged forward and put her arms around David's waist and held it tightly. She kept saying, "I will follow you wherever you go." David was so moved by Nava's ardent and true feelings that he finally said, "Well, my darling, let us go and see the other world." The wind rolled them up together. The two of them rose higher and higher, hand in hand, flying in the sky, the environment as well as their hearts had reached a wonderful height and realm.

The tornado sent David and Nava into the time and space tunnel, where they felt dizzy, in a half-sleeping and half- awake state, across a million years, to the origin of David's traversing – the great Kansas plains. After they were out of the tunnel they were wrapped in a strong tornado, the two of them floating in the sky. Later, the wind gradually weakened, and the magical wind slowly placed them on the ground and implemented a soft landing. Somehow, the Creator was particularly kind to them this time and the end of the crossing went smoothly. Could it be that the Heaven was moved by the true love between the two lovers and offered them some help? Or was it their own will at work, which was combined with external forces to achieve their goals and fulfil their wishes.? Could the mind also help? Who knew it?

# 2013 AD

David and Nava made a soft landing on the great plains of Kansas in the US. The local good-hearted people gave them a ride to the city of Wichita where David rented a car in a renting com-pany with a credit card in his pocket, and replaced Nava's leather clothes. Otherwise, just the leather and fur coat would cause a lot of curiosity of the current people. They ate some food and drank some coffee in a fast food restaurant, then drove on the road and headed for Colorado.

David carried this special prehistoric traveler, Nava, to the modern world. Nava was amazed at what she saw on both sides of the road. David patiently introduced to her the housing, cars, highways, food, clothing, and so on. Because the ages were so far apart, Nava found all these too complicated and difficult to understand. She needed a process to become familiar with them and a kind of digest.

On the other side, Emily and her son Oliver had been immersed in the pain of losing their loved one, David. About a year ago, David was blown cast by high winds in a balloon to Kansas where he was rolled into the sky by a tornado without a trace. Emily had sought help from many sources, and the police dispatched a helicopter to hover at the wreck site several times, searching in vain. David was still missing.

That day Emily suddenly a phone call from David in Kansas, saying that he was driving home and expected to arrive in the afternoon. Emily could not believe it, she could hardly contain her joy and happiness, and she was in tears. She asked David where he had been in the past year. David said he would talk about it in detail later, and also mentioned that he had brought a distant relative who would live with them afterwards.

Emily's family was beaming with happiness. At about 5:30 p.m, David, who had been missing for a year, returned  home. Everyone embraced and greeted him. David introduced to them the lady who came together with him, "This is Nava, my friend and relative who I met in a distant land." Emily warmly greeted Nava, saying, "I am Emily, David's wife." David translated the words into a language that Nava could understand. Nava smiled and said something naturally which Emily did not understand. David translated it into English, "Nava said, great! Let's have David as our common husband and run the family jointly." Emily suspected that she had misunderstood the meaning and asked David to explain. David told Emily his experiences in the distant land. Emily's eyes were wide open, and the experiences were so wonderful and thrilling that it was incredible. David said, "During that period of time, thanks to the help of Nava I am still alive. Otherwise, I would not have lived to the present and come to reunite with everyone." Emily was grateful to Nava. David told Emily, "Nava loves me and wants to be my wife. They are not monogamous in their society. Well, do you think we can respect their customs?" Emily said cheerfully, "No problem. I can't thank Nava enough for helping you survive to this day. Let us live together." David relayed Emily's message to Nava. Nava hugged Emily tightly, then David and Oliver also joined in and the four of them embraced tightly.

Nava was warm, kind, frank, and bold. She was quite popular among people. Only, she needed some adjustment and to hone for some time to gradually adapt to the modern life. First of all, Nava needed to learn English and communicate freely with others. In addition, she needed to be accustomed to contemporary diet, clothing, transportation, entertainment, and so on.

Nava was dazzled by everything in the modern society. Civilized society, political system, interpersonal relationship, culture and education were complex, and high technology was widely applied, which was magical for her. The huge difference had left her, a woman from the original clan society more than one million years ago, a bit stunned because it felt unbearable. Her nerves were shocked, distracted, and even felt like they were being squeezed and overturned. Despite all the love and considerateness that David and Emily had shown to her, she still felt uncomfortable and unhappy.

There were too many unnatural elements in modern society for her, who was used to living in the natural environment. She was even a little disgusted by the surrounding artificial objects and matters after some time.

In addition, she lost her authority as a tribal leader, the feeling as the moon surrounded by a myriad of stars and being able to summon the wind and the rain. In the depth of her heart, there was inevitably some kind of grievance. Nava often missed the old days in her tribe and the natural environment where the prairie was beautiful, the birds flying over and the flowers were fragrant, and even the giant lizards, giant pythons, and giant spiders would bring up her endless memories. Nava had primitive human genes, differing much from the genes of today's human beings, which would inevitably cause her psychological imbalance and collision.

Once, David found Nava was in low spirits and asked her, "Are you missing the Giant Lizard Village again, Nava?" "Yeah, I spent most of my life there, you know." David asked, "Are you still worried about the residents of the Village? Are you afraid that the tribe will be in disorder after you left?" "I'm not worried about that." said Nava, "My sister, Naka, will take over the leadership from me. She will do it well." David said, "Right, I remember that time when the Giant Lizard Village was defeated and you were said to be killed, it was Naka who propped up the situation and led the whole village to tide over the difficulties and revitalize it. When you were back to the Village, she returned the title of tribe chief to you." Nava said, "Yes. With Naka succeeding me, I'm relieved. Only my current life let me have a kind of unspeakable feeling. Everything is impeccable. You and Emily are very kind to me, too. But my own state of mind is always difficult to adjust, unable to balance. David, I still love you deeply, and this love is eternal in my heart. I want to lie in your arms, close my eyes and fly to Heaven."

David noticed some tears dropping from Nava's eyes and gently wiped them off for her with a tissue.

After about half a year, Nava was suffering from depression. Coupled with several complications, she was hospitalized for several weeks and eventually died of exhaustion at the age of 29. This should count as aborted in nowadays, belonged to however normal life span in primitive society. The departure of Nava made David and Emily very sad. They set up a grave and a tombstone for Nava in the cemetery to commemorate her.

David and Emily often talked about David's crossing.

They knew that it was a great reverse journey from the present to the past. The age was about a million years ago in the early human era, around the Old Stone Age. The location was approximately in the African savannah, that was said to be the cradle of early humans. The Nulu River at that time might be the current Nile River, but this remains to be verified.

> *The journey to the distant ancient times reveals the living conditions, social organization, interpersonal relationship, and natural ecology of early human beings, so as to know the evolution and progress of human civilization and humanity.*

*Human genes may undergo some variation due to di.Iferences in external environment and time, but they are not fundamentally di.Iferent. Although there are many di.Iferences between primitive and modern people, their basic human nature should be the same.*

# Chapter 11

## Phantoms on Blue Canopy

### 2012 AD

Time was back to a year ago. As David flew a hot air balloon, he unfortunately encountered a tornado and disappeared with the balloon mysteriously. Emily lost her husband in a moment and she experienced severe pain in her heart. One day she found herself in the park, lying alone on the lawn, looking up at the sky.

Emily said to herself: "Why is my fate teasing me? David's disappearance is a mystery. How to get rid of the predicament in front of me? I beg some Supreme for pointing me out."

A heavy and deep voice came into Emily's ears, as if from the Heaven: "I am the Heavenly Wise Man. Here are the answers to your questions — it all depends on the destiny of David himself."

"What do you mean, Sir?" asked Emily, rather excited.

The Heavenly Wise Man: A man's fate depends on his self-cultivation and opportunities. The combination of the two is his "destiny."

Emily: My husband David is good at self-cultivation and does a lot of charitable deeds. Sometimes there had been difficulties for him, but they could luckily be smoothed over.

The Heavenly Wise Man: According to what you said, Madam, David should have a seventy percent chance of getting rid of the predicament.

Emily: Thank you, Sir. However, I am still worried that opportunity is difficult to control.

The Heavenly Wise Man: Good and hardworking people can seize the opportunity and escape safely.

Emily looked at the blue and deep sky and fell into meditation. She thought, how many secrets were hidden in this mysterious sky, and how many vicissitudes of the universe and human stories it had witnessed.

Emily: Why are the acts of the world and the people so unpredictable? There are always endless stories and dramas. Who is the editor of these stories and plays, and who is the director?

The Heavenly Wise Man: That's a good question. The Creator designs all the living creatures, but allows them to act and play independently. In addition, the fate of every soul depends on its destiny. To understand this, please view the canopy screen.

A flock of birds appeared on the sky, and they gathered more and more. Viewing from a distance, the dense flock of birds were blotting out the sun. Suddenly, the wind was raging, the clouds were dense, and the sky became dark.

Then it began to rain, and the raindrops beat the wings of the birds with craking sounds. The rain was getting heavier, and quickly became a downpour with lightning and thunder.

The extremely bright lightning flashed the birds that were struggling in the rain, and deafening thunderbolts burst in the air. The birds were scattered, some struggled and rushed above the clouds; some march forward courageously despite the wind and rain; some persevered and struggled; some were beaten by the storm in disorder, fell to the ground to be safe; some were struck by the thunder and lightning, crying, badly hurt, or died.

Emily understood that the scene in heaven was just a portrayal of human life. The Creator only provides the innate, regardless of the late acquired. Everyone's destiny depends on oneself as well as the opportunity.

Then, there were many people on the sky canopy, crowds upon crowds, with a mass of bobbing heads, thousands, even hundreds of millions, countless. Looking at the distance, it looked like an overwhelming ant colony, resembling all mortal beings.

These people had been moving forward, walking and walking. Some went ahead, and some fell behind. Most people were in the middle. It was a bit like a massive marathon walking race. Only the participants were not on the same broad and straight road, but each taking a different path, some of which were full of twists and turns, some were rugged and difficult, some were covered with thorns, some were muddy, some having evil animals blocking the way, and some were full of traps. There were easier paths, and they belonged to the fortunate few, to those who kept forging ahead and persevering. Some speculators, trying to find a shortcut, often ended in failure. Some lazy people, who were not enterprising, coveting for ease and comfort, became unfortunate laggards.

Then, on the sky screen appeared successively images of great figures from ancient to modern times, including great thinkers, philosophers, statesmen, militarists, scientists, writers, artists, musicians, entrepreneurs, and so on. These people are the vanguard of mankind, the cream of society.

Their names and achievements are well known throughout the world, and their great contributions and outstanding talents are admirable.

Emily asked: Can you tell me, Sir, what is the secret to success?

The Heavenly Wise Man: In my opinion, there is no secret to success. However, the following points should be kept in mind: First of all, there must be pursuits and goals. As the saying goes, "where there is a will, there is a way." It is difficult for a person without a big ambition to accomplish a great cause. At the same time, success belongs to hardworking people. As the saying goes, "diligence makes perfect." There is hardly a high-tech mogul who is not a super workaholic. In addition, the pursuer must have a certain talent and ability, and the aspiring person without any talent cannot become successful. Talents are not innate, and the type of major varies from person to person. Give full play to your strength, and you will be able to do your best. In addition, a person's environment, background also plays a big role. The Renaissance had created outstanding people of humanities. During the period of the Republic of China, some great scholars appeared, and the high-tech boom in the US brought up outstanding scientific and technological elites. In short, the four points of "pursuit," "diligence," "talent," and "opportunity" are indispensable. Success is possible when the four are all available.

Emily: That's right. Only most people do not possess all the four.

The Heavenly Wise Man: So, the successful persons for great causes are only a minority. The top-notch elite is even rarer.

Emily: As far as "pursuit" is concerned, people have different goals. Some are obsessed with political power, some are crazy about wealth accumulation, some yearn for scientific and technological creations, some are keen on academic achievements, and some strive to show extraordinary talents and skills.

The Heavenly Wise Man: People have different aspirations. So, there is the Chinese tale about the Eight Immortals crossing the sea, each showing one's special prowess, and the world is full of brilliance and are colorful.

Emily: But most people with varied goals don't aim equally high. They are not equally diligent, talented, and smooth sailing.

The Heavenly Wise Man: So, people's destinies and careers are different. Those who do not aim high enough but had achieved their targets can also be considered successful.

This type is common among ordinary people.

Emily: In addition to this, there is a little more to consult.

There were some demonic figures and traitors in the history of mankind who had also possessed the above four conditions.

They were successful in climbing to high positions, but they had done evil and harmed the world. How should that be explained?

The Heavenly Wise Man: The "success" of the wicked is temporary. History will eventually cleanse and drive them away. Therefore, in the long run, the conditions for success should also be added with the item of "virtue." Otherwise, there will be situations in which the wicked will succeed, and the evil will be in power.

Emily: Why are there always evil people in the world? In terms of my humble knowledge, human beings all over the world and in different times have similar human nature.

The Heavenly Wise Man: That's true. But there are both good and evil aspects in human nature. Good people do good to others and benefit the society while bad people hurt others and harm humanity. In fact, good people and evil people are just different manifestations of human nature.

Emily: Sir, your guidance is better than reading books for a decade. I realized what is the way of life.

The Heavenly Wise Man: This kind of discussion is somewhat abstract and mysterious.

Next, the blue canopy will play something like a video, to exemplify the fact to the world. As the saying goes, "By one leaf you know the autumn," "A glimpse at one spot and know the whole leopard."

This is the true story of an ordinary family. The experiences of these ordinary people show us a variety of reasons for the ups and downs of one's life.

Emily: That'll be great. I am ready to watch it.

Images began to appear on the canopy screen, as if showing a movie.

In the late period of the Republic of China, there was a pair of young lovers in Yantai.

Two figures appeared on the canopy. They surely looked like a good match. The male was called Ye Weishan and the female, Zhao Jiping. They used to be classmates in high school and their love for each other was keen and profound.

They once vowed a solemn pledge of eternal love even when the seas ran dry, and the rocks crumbled. Later, Ye Weishan joined the army and did a good job in the army. He was promoted to the rank of major. Zhao Jiping stayed at home in Yantai to take care of her five-year-old son, Ye Qiuming.

That year, the mainland changed color, and Ye Weishan went to the other side of the Strait with the army. This loving couple was dispelled by a ruthless political storm. From then on, there was no news of her husband, Ye Weishan, for decades. Zhao Jiping was a pretty woman, kind and virtuous. She worked in a weaving mill, working hard, struggling to make ends meet and taking care of her parents-in-law and son in her spare time.

Her son Ye Qiuming was growing up gradually. He was a studious, brilliant, handsome, and ambitious young man. He excelled in his studies in college. After graduation, he was assigned to teach at a college in Yantai. His outstanding performance made him popular among students.

His father, Ye Weishan, was a fan of Peking Opera before leaving home, where he kept many records of famous Peking

Opera artists. Ye Qiuming also liked to watch and listen to Peking Opera since he was a child. Ye Qiuming was infatuated with Bai Yunhong, a famous Peking opera star in Yantai. Bai Yunhong was very popular in Yantai for playing the role of Yang Guifei, the Imperial Concubine, the protagonist of "Drunken Imperial Concubine." In Ye Qiuming's eyes, Bai Yunhong not only sang superbly, her acting skills were impressive, but she also looked particularly beautiful. Ye Qiuming began to pursue Bai Yunhong. Once after watching the show, he waited at the door of the theater. When Bai Yunhong was walking on the way home, Ye Qiuming stepped forward bravely and talked to her. He said he liked Peking Opera very much as well as Bai's singing and acting skills. He was willing to make friends with her. Bai Yunhong saw that this young man not only loved Peking Opera as her fan, but also was sincere and honest, not as impetuous, and shallow as some young people in society at that time. She agreed to make friends with him. She gave Ye Qiuming a business card and also wrote down Ye Qiuming's name and correspondence address. Ye Qiuming was very happy.

Since then, Ye Qiuming and Bai Yunhong became more and more intimate. Bai Yunhong told Ye Qiuming that she graduated in Yantai No. 1 Middle School. She liked recreational activities while at school. Her mother had been an actress of Peking Opera. So, she was also good at singing Peking Opera. She was determined to apply for the Theatre Academy. But because her uncle resided in Hong Kong, she failed for the application. At that time, overseas relations were regarded as a political stain that affected one's future, so she entered the Peking Opera Troupe. In the troupe, she studied hard and made great progress in singing and acting, and soon became the leading actress of the troupe. Bai Yunhong was a person with a personality. She also fell in deep love with Ye Qiuming. She and Ye Qiuming used to walking and chatting on the seashore, where she always bore in mind the feeling of Ye Qiuming holding her hands and hugging her.

In the mid-1960s, a piercing political turmoil swept across mainland China and became more and more intense. Due to her "bad family origin" (her father was a capitalist) and being a relative of the enemy, Qiuming's mother Zhao Jiping became a pariah and suffered from discrimination and insult.

The image of Zhao Jiping appeared on the canopy. Zhao Jiping was now a woman in her forties. She wore a sign on her front that read: "A family members of fugitive counter- revolutionaries, a bigoted capitalist daughter of bitch." She was dragged to the stage to be criticized. Jiping was full of bitterness on her face and bowed her head. When the criticism became fierce somebody pulled her hair, and spit on her face.

Ye Qiuming worked in the college for less than a year when he encountered the "unprecedented political catastrophe." He was regarded as belonging to one of the "Five Black Classes" (landlord, rich peasant, counter revolutionary, bad element, and rightist) known as "son of a dog," or euphemistically "a child who can be educated." He was reduced to the bottom of society, suffering from cold eyes everywhere. He felt that his future was hopeless.

Bai Yunhong was under heavy pressure in the troupe.

The relationship with Ye Qiuming became a major political stain on her own. She was therefore unable to play the main role in the revolutionary model opera. However, she was also a very strong person, and she actively demanded progress in politics. The troupe leadership clearly told her that the troupe's military propaganda team had gone to Ye Qiuming's work unit for an investigation and said that Ye Qiuming had a negative political background and was not reliable politically. Bai Yunhong should carefully consider her own future. The troupe was an important propaganda position for the revolution, and it must be a pure class team. Under the political pressure at that time, she decided her own future in an extremely painful choice.

The image of Bai Yunhong appeared on the canopy screen. She ran to the beach alone, looking at the surging sea waves, her heart struggled and cramped, and she was unwilling to make a decision to break up with her lover.

After saying goodbye to Ye Qiuming, Bai Yunhong was distressed and regretted it. She often stared at the pedestrians on the street from her upstairs window, hoping that her lover of the past would reappear in front of her.

Ye Qiuming's first love was frustrated. He once lamented his fate and regretted that he had been born in the wrong family and at the wrong time. He was emotionally pained to give up his first love, but he understood his girlfriend's choice. He silently bore the arrangement of his destiny, silently bore the present wailing wind and weeping rain.

A few years later, Ye Qiuming married Shen Huijuan, a female worker who didn't care about his unfavorable class origin. They loved each other and lived a hard life of ordinary people.

The world was changing and the political atmosphere of the mainland was gradually loose. Ye Qiuming became a graduate student at a prestigious university. His wife, Shen Huijuan, was not only a typical good wife and kind mother, but also had a long-term vision and a broad mind. She worked in a factory and took care of her two young children. She gave her husband her full support in his studies and progress. Ye Qiuming had been studying in the graduate school in a distant city for several years, and Shen Huijuan assumed all household duties in the family. Ye then went to the United States for further studies, which was inseparable from Shen Huijuan's support.

The image of Shen Huijuan, a virtuous wife and loving mother, appeared on the canopy screen. She went to work by bike, and after work, she bought vegetables, grain, and coal, carried by a bike. At home, she did laundry, cooking, taking care of the young children and elderly parents-in-law, with a yearning for a better life in the future.

One year after Ye Qiuming left China, Shen Huijuan and her two children went to the United States.

Ye Qiuming's mother, Zhao Jiping, had been hoping that her husband, Ye Weishan, would come back to reunite with the family ever since he left. There was a fig tree in the courtyard. It was planted by Weishan in the early years and was now flourishing with lush foliage. After Weishan was gone, Jiping's mother-in-law often said that when the fig tree bore fruit, Weishan should be back. Weishan liked to eat figs. Jiping was looking forward to the fig fruit every year. Days, months, years, almost four decards passed. The fig tree bore fruit every year, still she did not see her husband returned. Wrinkles appeared on her face and white hair on her head. However, she was still looking forward, looking forward to the return of her loved one.

One day, Zhao Jiping finally got the news of Ye Weishan. Mr. Zheng, a veteran of the National Army, returning home from across the Strait, brought a message to her. Mr. Zheng said Ye Weishan asked him to bring a vocal message, wishing his parents He did not know that his parents had already passed away by then, Jiping and his son Qiuming to live happily in good health. Ye Weishan had formed another family there. Mr. Zheng also brought a photo of Ye Weishan. Zhao Jiping looked carefully at Ye Weishan on the photo. Although he was close to 70 years old, he was still hale and hearty. Zhao Jiping was silent for a long while, then said to Mr. Zheng, "He is still alive, and I am contented. I wish him safe and sound and have a happy life in his old age." Mr. Zheng said he was a friend of Ye Weishan. Ye Weishan told him that he was going to return to Yantai for a visit the following year. Ye's current wife was sick and hospitalized, and he himself could not leave for the time being.

Mr. Zheng, the veteran who came back from the other side of the Strait to visit his family, told of his own sad story. In fact, he was also unfortunate. His wife, who was looking forward to the reunion with her husband, finally lost her hope after years of waiting in vain. She had remarried. Zheng's home town was in Qingdao, Shandong province. Zheng stayed in Qingdao for less than a day before he rushed to Yantai to visit his friend Ye Weishan's family. The separation of the two sides of the Strait for decades had created many family tragedies, which had caused many families to break up with husbands, wives, and children scattered.

In less than a year after Mr. Zheng's visit, Zhao Jiping passed away. Ye Qiuming was deeply saddened by the death of his mother. The old woman's life was really unfortunate. She bore the burden of humiliation and bitterness for decades. However, she had never been able to reunite with her departing husband.

Old woman Zhao Jiping appeared on the sky screen. Her face was engraved with the endless vicissitudes of life.

The figure of the old woman gradually faded away, and the hard life of a good woman came to an end.

Ye Qiuming returned to China to deal with his mother's funeral. He brought her mother's casket to the United States and buried it in a cemetery. In this way, he could come to his mother at any time, and his wife and children could also come to see his mother.

The next year, Ye Qiuming's father, Ye Weishan, came to the United States from Taiwan. He went to Colorado alone to see his son, daughter-in-law, and grandsons, and also to worship the soul of his deceased wife. Qiuming had taken his father's remarriage to heart and was indifferent to him. His father, who was in his seventies, came to his son's side after a tiring long journey. When they met, they couldn't help crying. The close blood kinship kept the father and son together. Qiuming's father asked about Jiping's life when she was alive and wanted to know every detail of it. He learned that his wife had been waiting for him for decades, and she had suffered innumerable hardships and bitterness. Ye Weishan felt that his heart was being pierced by a knife. Ye Weishan went to the cemetery with his son to see his wife, Jiping, who rested there. The old man screamed at his wife's tomb, sometimes bursting into tears, sometimes wringing his own chest.

After returning home, Qiuming urged his father to take care of his own health. Ye Weishan knew that his son did not understand his remarriage. He took the initiative to tell the story. He said that he had been looking forward to reuniting with Jiping and the family. Many people advised him to remarry and form a new family with a partner. Many mainland veterans had done so because they felt hopeless about returning home. However, he was still unswerving and still looking forward to the day when the situation would change. Romantically, he used to stare at the bright moon in the sky, hoping that Jiping was also looking at the moon at the same time. He had once asked the geese flying in the sky to send a message for him reuniting with his family, only to wake up to the cold reality of family separation.

At this time, a woman named Zheng Yufei took the initiative to woo him for love, struggling to pursue. This woman admired military heroes since childhood, with the French god of war, Napoleon Bonaparte, and the National Army general, Sun Liren, as her idols, and the National Army officer, Ye Weishan, as her dream lover. The woman suffered from a congenital incurable disease which was closely related to the patient's psychology. According to the doctor, her days were numbered. If Ye could obey her wishes and marry her, she would be able to live for a few more years. In addition, Zheng Yufei was the niece of Mr. Zheng. Mr. Zheng was a close friend of Ye Weishan for many years. Zheng sought mercy to Ye, let Zheng Yufei live several more years, he even knelt down to Ye Weishan for the request. Ye Weishan had to reluctantly agree to this, but he had a condition, it should only be a nominal marriage, not registered as a legal couple. In this way, they hid it from Zheng Yufei and held a wedding for them. Yufei's condition improved, and everyone was happy. After less than two years, Yufei's condition deteriorated again. When Mr. Zheng returned to the mainland to visit relatives there, Zheng Yufei was hospitalized. Shortly after Mr. Zheng returned from the mainland, Zheng Yufei suddenly passed away. After listening to his father's recounting, Ye Qiuming resolved his misunderstanding of his father. Ye Weishan regreted his obliged remarriage. He said that if Jiping did not learn about his remarriage she would not have gone so soon.

Later, Qiuming's father immigrated to the United States, settled in Colorado, to spend his remaining years in the US. He came here to be close to the place where Jiping lay in rest, where it was more convenient for him to visit her once in a while. After a few years Qiuming's father died in the United States. Qiuming buried the ashes of his father in the same tomb with his mother. After decades of expectations, his father and mother finally reunited in the underground world.

On the blue canopy appeared the tomb of Qiuming's parents, Ye Weishan and Zhao Jiping. The tombstone bore their names and dates of birth and death. In front of the tombstone, there was a bouquet of flowers presented by Qiuming's family. The environment of the cemetery was elegant. The old couple were willing to rest in the sky and not be disturbed by the world.

Ye Qiuming got two master's degrees in the United States, worked hard with his wife to start a company, which was quite successful. They had lived in the United States for more than 30 years. Now, Ye Qiuming and his wife, Shen Huijuan, were old and retired at home. Seeing the sons and grandchildren around them, the two sons were doing well in succeeding the business, the grandchildren were lively and lovely, and their hearts were infinitely comforting.

Ye Qiuming learned from one of his friends in Yantai that Bai Yunhong, his first girl friend more than 50 years ago, was now over 70 years old. She had not been comfortable these years. For decades, she had been climbing on her road, and had a successful official career. She was supposed to be satisfied with what she had achieved. However, she had some inner conflicts, although she had a family, husband and children, yet she was not really happy.

Past events were like smoke, but some events were eventually unforgettable. She felt that she owed a debt of love and could not repay it. Ye Qiuming's shadow had been lingering in her heart and she could not get rid of it.

She realized that her original decision had hurt her true lover and herself so much, and she always felt a sense of guilt.

The passage of time did not wash and dilute her memories of the past. Ye Qiuming's young, handsome, and sincere image appeared in her mind from time to time. Every scene when they fell in love seemed to be vivid in her mind. She had not expected that her decision at that time would become the trauma of her lifetime. She climbed hard on the political road to a higher position. What did that mean to her? Besides, she had seen so many ugly deeds and dirty faces in officialdom and celebrity circles, and she had been immersed in it. She felt sad and sick for her environment and for herself. She resolutely spurned the aims and principles of her own pursuit for the better part of her life, changed course, and became deeply religious. This ran counter to the ideology she had espoused for decades. Several times a week, she went to the church to listen to teachings, to worship God, to confess her life's sins and missteps.

What appeared on the canopy at this time was the image of the old woman, Bai Yunhong. She worshipped God devoutly in the church and was seeking some spiritual relief.

The story on the canopy screen was over. Emily was still immersed in the story. She found tears in her eyes. She lamented the unfortunate experience of the main characters in the story. The old Zhao Jiping in the story was a good friend of her mother. She had met the old woman a couple of times in Yantai, who was very kind and humble. As for the guy, Ye Qiuming, she also had heard about him. Ye had studied in the Fine Arts Department of University of Colorado in Boulder where he earned a master's degree, but it was many years earlier than her. Some professors in the Art Department said Ye was impressive and very talented.

The Heavenly Wise Man: Madam, who in the story do you think are winners and losers?

Emily: In my opinion, Ye Qiuming can be counted as a winner. He is diligent and successful in his academic career. After numerous twists and turns, he finally achieved his goal.

Ye Qiuming's mother, Zhao Jiping, had no lofty goals and ideals. She was kind and had undergone all kinds of hardships. She only wanted to reunite with her husband who had been separated from her for decades. This simple and normal wish was never fulfilled.

Ye Qiuming's wife, Shen Huijuan, could be regarded as a successful woman. Her goal was to work with her husband, to aim high, to improve the social status of themselves and to gain happiness for their family. She achieved the goal as she had hoped.

Ye Qiuming's first girlfriend, Bai Yunhong, should be said to be a loser. She abandoned her favorite boyfriend in pursuit of her own political career. However, in her later years, she deviated from her official career that she had set foot on and turned to another direction. When she was young, she emotionally hurt herself and others, and she felt uneasy inside. She had given up her efforts and repented for her wrong doings in her late years.

Ye Qiuming's father, Ye Weishan, had pursued the achievements and glory of the military service in his early years, and he was successful in this respect. For objective reasons, he separated himself from his beloved wife who deeply loved him for decades. The desire to reunite with his wife in his lifetime had fallen through. Poor opportunities had cast his family on the failure.

The Heavenly Wise Man: Madam, you've got the point. It seems that you have grasped the meaning of the journey of life in mind and have enhanced your savvy.

Emily: Thank you for your praise, Sir.

*The journey of life is varied. Subjective will and effort combined with objective opportunity. Circumstances create different colors of life.*

*One should live a life of meaningfulness, happiness, and beauty. However, man's fate is not predestined, fortune is also difficult to control. Aspiration, diligence, ability, opportunity, and goodness are quite important. As the saying goes, "young idler, an old beggar." Life is limited and short. Don't waste good times but cherish precious years.*

# Chapter 12

## TRAVERSING TIME AND SPACE

### 2013 AD

David's character was inherently challenging. He discovered that Darwin's theory of evolution was based on some unreliable facts and unstable arguments, being quite biased, on which David had written a number of papers to comment, which were pretty influential in academia.

David acted like he was out of the ordinary. For example, as a standard Western man he fell in love with an Oriental woman and regarded Emily as the apple of his eye. He was decisive and resolute, but his heart was chivalrous and tender. His love and care for Emily deeply moved her.

It was not long after the global travel and David's prehistoric traverse before he became lonely and began planning his next adventure. He and Emily agreed to challenge the daunting Bermuda Triangle. Emily, too, was not a quitter.

Since David was interested, why was she not? There are few wrestles in one's life time. It is a great pleasure to fight the devil.

David and Emily came to Miami, in the southern end of Florida, and lived there for a period of time.

They found the place very distinctive, with large areas of marshes and swamps, and the natural scenery was very attractive. There were numerous wild crocodiles and waterfowls in the swamp. The sky was pure blue, dotted with snow-white clouds in the daytime or orange-red clouds at sunset. In some streets of Miami, cats walked, chickens roamed, roosters perched on trees. Seagulls by the seaside were not afraid of people, they hovered overhead and sometimes rushed down to grab food on the outdoor dinner table.

When people talked about Bermuda Triangle on the sea off the east coast they often got scared.

The Bermuda Triangle is located in the southeastern part of the Florida Peninsula and specifically refers to a triangle in the Atlantic Ocean formed by the three-point link between the Bermuda Islands, Miami, and San Juan in Puerto Rico, with an area of 3.9 million square kilometers.

Due to the overlapping of tragic events in the Bermuda Sea, people have given this sea area nicknames like "Devil Triangle," "Bad Sea," "Magic Sea," "Graveyard of Ships," and so on.

The earliest information about the bizarre events in the Bermuda Triangle can be tracked to Columbus's record of Bermuda. In a voyage in 1502, Columbus encountered amazing scary danger in the waters of the Bermuda Triangle.

One evening, the sea was beautiful and the sky clear. The sea was as calm as a mirror, reflecting the dazzling sunlight. With water and sky linking up, the endless sea and sky, made people refreshed and cheerful.

Just as Columbus and his crew indulged in the fascinating beauty of the sea, things changed. Suddenly, the sky became dark, and the wind was raging. The hill-like sea waves rushed to the fleet. The water that was as flat as a mirror a moment ago rolled up a wave of tens of meters high, like a blocking wall hitting the deck. The splashing waves crashed into the ship bridge and made a terrible noise. The ship was in a critical condition, tossing erratically about and swaying in the wind and waves. What was even more incredible was that all the navigation instruments on the ship were out of action in an instant. Because the direction was unclear, the ship seemed to be a dislocated wild horse, no longer obeying the crew's control, and they had to let it drift.

Columbus was lucky that the ship did not sink after days and nights of turbulence. To his surprise, the storm that had descended from the sky came to a screeching halt.

Columbus wrote this in details in his nautical diary. In his letter to the King of Spain, he talked about this unforgettable experience – "At that time, the waves rolled over, for eight or nine days, we could not see the sun and the stars... I have seen various storms in my life, but never have I encountered such a long and violent storm."

According to statistics, during the period from 1800 to 1976, there were 143 missing ships and planes in the Bermuda Triangle area. What a terrible number! The equivalent was that every year, on average, almost a ship or an airplane disappeared there.

In fact, the actual number of missing vessels and planes in the Bermuda Triangle was far more than that, because many missing military aircraft and ships were not registered.

There had been more bizarre events in the Devil's Triangle in Bermuda.

It is said that a former Soviet submarine sailed underwater in the waters of Bermuda a moment ago and was able to float in the Indian Ocean in a minute, even more shocking was the fact that in the voyage that spanned almost half of the Earth, all 93 crew members in the submarine were suddenly senescent for 5 to 20 years. Immediately after the incident, the Soviet military and scientific community began investigating the submarine and all its personnel. The researchers believed: "The submarine had entered an accelerating time tunnel.

There was no other reasonable explanation."

Another story was that in the Caribbean in 1954, two Americans piloted a balloon in a balloon race with 50 other contestants across the ocean. At that time, the weather was fine and the view clear. Suddenly, in front of the crowd, the balloon mysteriously disappeared. In 1990, decades after its disappearance, the balloon suddenly appeared on the sea surface of Cuba. The Cuban government was so nervous that it mistakenly believed that the United States had sent secret weapons to attack. The big balloon was forced to land on the sea by a Cuban aircraft, and the two pilots were taken to a secret Cuban naval base for trial. It was confirmed that they had mysteriously disappeared during a balloon race in 1954. Investigators believed the balloon entered the time tunnel. "It may be just a moment for them, but it's been 36 years on Earth, quite a difference." Therefore, they had entered a magical tunnel slower than the time on Earth.

David and Emily felt all these were extremely weird and magical but they were somewhat dubious about the rumors associated with Bermuda and the time tunnel.

For the dangerous rhetoric Bermuda devil, David and Emily felt very excited, it had increasingly aroused their morale to challenge in spite of danger and hardships.

Looking out over the Bermuda Triangle from the east seaside of Florida, David and Emily were full of passion and confidence. They would "go deep into the mountains, while knowing well that there are tigers in there."

David and Emily rented a small plane locally, and after a period of flight training, they both got their flight licenses.

They began to fly at sea, hovering over the waters of Bermuda many times. The sea area was sometimes sunny and beautiful, sometimes cloudy, and stormy. It was as if the Sea God there was born with a strange temper. David and Emily had honed their skills in different weather conditions and had mastered techniques of flying up and down, swirling around with ease. Their plane soared through the air, through the clouds, sometimes flying low, close to the sea, then they could even see the swimming fish in the sea water.

The two of them talked and laughed on the plane, shouting and singing.

Emily sang "My Heart Will Go On," the theme song of the film Titanic:

> Every night in my dreams
> I see you, I feel you
> That is how I know you go on
> And spaces between us
> Far across the distance
> And spaces between us
> You have come to show you go on
> Near, far, wherever you are
> I believe that the heart does go on
> Once more, you opened the door
> And you're here in my heart
> And my heart will go on and on

The story of David and Emily, the young couple who bravely challenged the Bermuda Triangle, was reported in local newspapers and national media. People were eager to learn about the latest news about their adventures.

Day by day, nothing weird happened to them. In the Bermuda Triangle, they had been flying over and over again. David and Emily adapted to flying in different weather conditions and felt well. Now they not only "touched the tiger's bottom, but also rode on the back of the tiger," swaggering. They assumed the victors' posture, and felt that it was time for them to put an end to it, to beat a retreat.

One day, they set off for a last flight to bid farewell to Bermuda. The plane touched down in the middle of the Triangle. Early that day it was sunny and clear, when suddenly, it turned to blustery, with a murky sky over a dark earth. The sea surface in Bermuda was swirling with some countercurrent, and a stream of water became bluish, spinning rapidly at sea, forming a huge whirlpool which was wide and deep, like a bottomless pit, ghastly. The compass and the navigator on the plane had failed, and they were completely disoriented. The small plane was like a wild horse, hard to control, spinning round with the whirlpool.

They tried low-altitude flight, but no avail. They struggled to rise again, when they heard a clatter and the tail was broken. The plane seemed overburdened, uncontrolable. The wind was like a huge powerful hand that was tearing the little plane in anger until it was torn to shreds. Then they saw that the left wing was broken, the fuselage twisted, and the broken plane plunged into the big hole surrounded by monstrous waves.

David and Emily thought that this time they would be completely over, so they closed their eyes and were ready for death. The demon of Bermuda had devoured innumerable human lives, and they were merely adding a little "2" to the large number.

What puzzled David and Emily, however, was that they didn't feel like they were sinking to the bottom of the ocean or into a big fish's stomach. It was clear that they were still alive, and that around them was not water, but an indescribable space. David and Emily felt a little bit adrift, and their bodies seemed weightless. Yeah, it was like astronauts in a spaceship.

They could faintly hear around a whooshing sound, as well as see the rapid changing of environment and color.

They wondered where they were. They asked each other, puzzling, if this was what people sometimes referred to as the "tunnel of time and space?" The thought frightened, confused, overwhelmed, and aroused their curiosity. Where would this "time tunnel" take them? If they could not help it, they would have to let it go.

In the state of weightlessness, the two swayed in the strange space. They waited with trepidation for the arrival of an unknown future.

The two, now weary and drowsy, entered into their dreams for they had struggled hard with the wind in the air earlier of the day.

David and Emily had actually entered a time-space tunnel that would pass through into the remote future. The tunnel neither accelerated nor decelerated. That was to say, no matter how many years had passed outside the time-space tunnel, or how many years ahead of time, the age of the travelers in the tunnel would remain the same when they got out of the tunnel as before they entered it. People called this time-space tunnel a "preservation tunnel."

In this traverse, once David and Emily walked out of the time tunnel, they would find that the world had elapsed over a thousand years, but their age had not changed. This was incredible. They would step into the distant future more than a thousand years in advance.

> *Einstein points out in his general theory of relativity that space and time overlap in our universe. The space-time structure bends under the action of a strong gravitational field. When the speed exceeds the light speed one can travel through time and space.*
>
> *David and Emily fell into a time-space tunnel to the future in Bermuda, and they involuntarily traversed through time and space to an unknown world.*
>
> *It is inevitable for people to think of a number of black holes entrances in the troubled Bermuda Triangle that are associated with the disasters. Ships and planes that have been missing there over the years are likely to have fallen into them, mostly with no return.*

# Chapter 13

## THE WONDERLAND

### 3013 AD

David and Emily, driven by an invisible force, passed through a long time-space tunnel to the other end of it.

They awoke from their dreams and saw a wonderful world before their eyes. They looked around and were stunned by the scene there. This place was so beautiful, the sky was blue, with a touch of white clouds. The air was especially fresh.

The picturesque scenery was crystal clear, glittering, and translucent. Everywhere they saw lush woods, green grass, flowers in full bloom, birds singing merrily, fish swimming in clear water. The scenes before them were just like beautiful landscape paintings.

David and Emily walked in the wonderland with a curious eye and a merry mood. They ate some breakfast and had a cup of coffee in a restaurant. The restaurant did not charge them. The waiter looked at the young couple with a curious eye, almost regarding them as Aliens from another planet. When the waiter gently asked them where they came from, they could only be embarrassed to say, from somewhere far, far away.

The people here were kind, courteous and friendly, as if everyone had received a good education.

People's clothes were very different from those they wore.

Those clothes were hot-proof, cold-proof and water-proof, light and comfortable, decent and nice.

David and Emily found a house at a hillside overlooking the sea. The style of the house was chic, good-looking, and magnificent. The indoor equipment was advanced, the degree of automation was extremely high. Temperature, humidity, light, pleasing effect, and so on were automaticaly regulated and computer controlled. Some soft, relaxing, and melodious music was playing indoors. The change of tunes, the adjustment of volume, responded to vocal commands. There were fine paintings on the walls. The interior decorations were exquisite and the style elegant.

Indoor air was clean and replaced automatically. Utensils and walls were free of dust and grease. All kinds of chores in the house were borne by cute and clever robots. Meals were cooked by a smart cooking machine, dishes were delicious. It was worth mentioning that, at this time, people no longer ate the meat of animal carcass, but various alternatives instead.

The taste and nutrition were far better than the animal meat in the past. What amazed them most was that there was no rent for the house and all the houses were free of charge.

David and Emily learned that it was already in the 31st Century AD. They were in a region somewhat like the previous Australia. But at this time the continent was a completely beautiful oasis, without the wasteland in most part of it as before. People can still see kangaroos jumping on the grass and koalas perching on trees, full of Australian flavor.

David and Emily found their own jobs, teaching ancient history and ancient art history at the university. They found that they were curious old antiques here. The age that they had lived in was ancient time for the people of this age. They had interviews and lectures from time to time, and people were especially curious to learn about things in the ancient society from them.

They made an intimate friend with one of their colleagues, Prof. Robert James, who taught world history and archaeology in the university. Professor James often invited David and Emily to his house. This historian and scientist was very kind to the two young people from ancient times.

The information provided by David and Emily was of great value to the factual research of ancient history. The professor, in particular, enjoyed very much in listening to their stories of the ancient world, which to him were fascinating anecdotes. David and Emily also learned about the current local customs and practices from Professor James.

The surface pattern of the Earth had changed a lot at this time. The deserts, the plateaux, the barren land, and the frozen regions on the south and north poles were now being cultivated into good living and tourist environments. Maritime cities were built at sea. Underwater castles were built on the sea floor. The whole Earth was like a beautiful garden with charming sceneries. The fresh water on the Earth was used effectively, and inexhaustible.

The production efficiency here was extremely high and the social wealth extremely rich. Money and credit cards were already abolished and no longer in circulation. All required supplies were available on the internet. The delivery was very fast when one placed an order. People's spiritual and material life were rich. They had truly realized the fond dream of "each person does his best, and takes what he needs" that the ancient people had been longing for.

Natural energy was widely used in industry, and no smoke, no waste gas and no noise production had been achieved.

Production automation and intelligence replaced most of the mechanical and manual labor. Business management, even enterprise planning, new product development and design were heavily intelligent.

In this society, people loved work. For them, work was a pleasure, happiness, and pastime.

As a result of the great improvement of material and spiritual life, the number of people engaged in material production had decreased, and the number of people engaged in culture and entertainment had increased significantly. People pursue high-quality spiritual life and enjoyment.

Literature, fine arts, music, drama and film here had reached a pretty high level. David and Emily were fascinated, and soon they were infatuated with them.

Urban traffic was so convenient that the autopilot carrier was always on call, that could send people to wherever they wished to go in the city. There was no need to have a car and a garage in the house. There were no traffic jams, no hustle and streams of people busily coming and going on the street, no noise. Leisurely pedestrians were like strolling in a park, relaxed and happy.

The medical conditions here were excellent, having eliminated any health problems. Human organ regeneration to enhance vitality, and nanomedical technology were effective in preventing human aging. Life expectancy was significantly extended. A hundred years old looked like fifty, and two hundred years was not regarded as old.

Since every living creature in the world has life and death, the life span of a person can only be extended to a certain extent, instead of immortality.

This is a highly developed human society with a high degree of civilization beyond common sense. In this society, there were harmony, friendship, mutual assistance, and compassion among people and personal and public ethics were generally high.

People's life here was extremely relaxed, happy, elegant, and beautiful. The realm was like a fairyland in mythology or fairy tales. People's feeling was not inferior to that of the princes and princesses in the legendary. Its elegance was unspeakable and beyond description.

David and Emily soon became familiar with and accustomed to the life of the place and loved everything around them. Not only did they feel that their quality of life had improved greatly, but also their own life value had been enhanced significantly. They had a good time here and were reluctant to leave.

However, David and Emily sometimes inevitably missed their dear ones like parents, brother, sister, son, and friends who stayed in their original era. They talked about their thoughts with Professor James. Professor James was very sympathetic, but he had no choice but to say, "Your relatives, including your son, should have long passed away by now. It has been more than one thousand years since you left them."

This society had no state, no army.

Weapons of mass destruction had long been destroyed and extinct, which could only be seen in the historical museums.

The court solved all kinds of legal issues. The police assisted law enforcement and maintained public order.

In this society, on the spiritual level, love between men and women occupies an important position. Generally speaking, the relationship between men and women tends to be pluralistic.

Men and women fell in love with each other, hand in hand to finish the way of life. That was still the mainstream.

Artificial intelligence in selection was applied to reproduce and optimize embryos. Children were healthier, wiser, and more talented.

Since the society did not need much labor, the need for pioneering elites, optimized fertility, and singlism led to a slowdown in population growth. The world's population then had apparently shrunk than a thousand years ago, totaling to no more than two billion.

Some people had advocated sexual freedom, multiple sex, and family abolition. However, this proposition and behavior led to the dilution of pure love. It was not accepted by the whole society. The tide was receding.

Robot sex partners, developed from sexual love dolls, had been in fashion for a period of time.

Male and female robot sexual partners looked as if they were real human beings.

Male robot sexual partners were extraordinarily handsome, ardent, physically fit, and vigorous. Female robot partners were extremely beautiful, gorgeous, charming, and sexy.

But after all, they were artificial products, could mainly meet the sexual demand of people. They could never replace human beings.

In any case, a certain degree of division or polarization appeared between love and sex in the relationship between men and women.

Later, it was found that this division led to the degradation of human nature. The value and dignity of human beings were derogated.

The combination of men and women, after all, was not just for sex.

Behavior of sex without love was not different from that of animals. To put it better, it was almost the same as visiting brothels.

The most typical example of animal ruthlessness of sex with no love is that female mantis often eats its male partner during mating. As heartless as this!

People realize that the most precious thing between men and women is to love each other, to cherish the kind of pure and persistent love.

Love is the essence of human civilization. It is beautiful. Love is the eternal theme of literature, the bright colors of paintings and the dulcet melodies of music.

In a sincere love, the heating of love converts to a boiling of sex; the convergence of sex is sublimated to a perforation of love, thus achieving a high level of human beauty.

As the saying goes, one day a couple hundred days grace. Children are the crystallization of love.

The case of love without sex appears normally in some old couples. It is pure love.

Hand in hand, a couple stepped into the dream of living to a ripe old age in conjugal bliss. This is a wonderful life.

The gender division of human beings, the integration of men and women, and the production of future generations are all arrangements of the Creator. People should conform to the Creator's will and be comfortable with Heaven.

In this era, Aliens from other planets and their decendents on Earth were very common.

Science and technology were highly developed here. Space travel had become a common place that it was easy for civilians to travel to other planets.

The solar system was full of human space stations, like fancy hotels. It was very convenient to have transportation in space.

David and Emily took a trip to three planets in the solar system during the summer vacation, and they soon became addicted.

People in space would be homesick when they left Earth for a long while. Earth people meeting in space were very cordial, really like "folk seeing folk with tears." At this time, the Earth people had a wider field of vision. They realized how narrow their view was of focusing just on a country, or a local area in the past. Today, the concept of love and passion for the Earth should surpass patriotism and "motherland" was an outdated concept.

Overlooking the Earth from space, seeing this beautiful and spectacular blue sphere, one would be intoxicated. Getting closer, one could also distinguish between land and sea. White clouds were floating on the surface of the atmosphere, with blue sea and brown green continental plates, contrasting side by side.

Compared to other planets in the solar system Earth is really a good place. It is magnificent, with mountains and rivers, air and fields, forests and ranches, tall buildings from the ground, and transportations to everywhere. It is rich in gold and silver, brass and iron, cereals and fruits, cows and horses, pigs and sheep, fish and turtles, shrimps and crabs, tigers and leopards, coyotes and wolves, everything.

In this society, truth, goodness, and beauty occupy the overwhelming superiority. Although false, evil, and ugliness always exist, they are not tolerated by the society.

Is this the world that people always yearned for and pursue? Yes, it can be called the paradise world, or the Wonderland.

*The utmost truth, goodness and beauty are the ideal realms for human pursuit, where the society is highly developed, prosperous, reasonable, and civilized, where the material and spiritual wealth are extremely rich, where science and technology progress, life is convenient, with comfortable environment. There is a high degree of harmony between people, between human and nature. Love between men and women is pure and eternal. The friendliness of people in the world is warm and mellow. The sun is shining everywhere, orioles singing and swallows darting, like a paradise on Earth.*

# Chapter 14

## BEAUTY GARDEN ROMANCE

In the neighborhood of David and Emily's home, there was a young man named George Walsh who fell in love with Emily, and was hard on courting her. George said to Emily some words that she thought were out of line. He admired the beauty of Emily, as well as her intelligence and kindness. He expressed admiration and affection for Emily, proposed datings and intimacy with her. In the ancient society of David and Emily before they came here, this should be counted as "sexual harassment." After all, Emily was a married woman.

David was very upset when he learned about it. He went to see George about the matter. George told him that he loved Emily, and there was nothing wrong with it. George also said that his love for Emily was sincere and pure, and would eventually affect Emily. David and George had a heated debate. David proposed to fight George for the settlement of the dispute and let George prepare a pistol. He was to emulate the Russian poet, Alexander Pushkin, to settle the dispute with a rival in a duel.

David didn't expect that George would sue him in court. To the even greater surprise of David and Emily was that the judge ruled the case in favor of George. According to the judgement, it was not lawful for David to threaten to harm other's and his own lives in a barbarous way of dueling. George's pursuit of Emily was a proper act, not beyond the rules allowed by the law. Emily had the right to choose between David and George for her favorite life partner.

Emily politely declined George's love, saying that her favorite person was still David. George stopped his pursuit of Emily.

David and Emily noted that the law at this time was more rational and humane in the treatment of relationship between men and women, married and unmarried.

One day, George talked to David about the matter again.

George: David, I'd like to know, how deep is your love for Emily? How firm is it?

David: Deep as the sea, firm as the rock. George: Really?

David: That's true.

George: I want to see the truth. You can stand any test? David: Of course.

George: Then you can go to the Beauty Garden. I have a password here. Take it with you and type it and your own info on the keyboard at the gate of the Beauty Garden. Then you can enter the garden. But you can't bring a mobile phone with you, otherwise you can't get in.

David: No problem.

David came to the Beauty Garden alone with curiosity. Originally, he only wanted to stay here for a short while, so he didn't tell Emily about it. The Beauty Garden looked like an ancient European castle. This exquisite building was perched on the high slope of the sea surrounded by mist, like a fairyland against the sea, magnificent and mysterious. It was simply a place where fairies lived. David entered the password and his own info on the keyboard at the door and the door opened automatically. David stepped into the court. Looking up, he saw nobody around. The Beauty Garden was full of lush green, pretty flowers, small bridges, and winding paths. There were also fish in the water, butterflies, and bees among flowers, melodious chirping of birds and singing of cicadas. It was like a gorgeous and elegant royal garden.

In this fascinating environment, a beautiful girl appeared. She was smiling, warm and friendly. She greeted David and said, "My name is Wilda Wika, I'm the master here. Welcome to the Beauty Garden. Nice to meet you, Mr. David Polo." David replied, "Nice to meet you too, Miss Wilda Wika."

The voice of the girl who he met for the first time was sweet, crisp, and quite charming.

Wilda led David around the courtyard and into the palace. The facilities and decorations in the palace were magnificent, comparable to the royal palace in fairy tales. Wilda gave a signal, and a maid brought them two cups of high-grade coffee. They sat on comfortable sofas and started chatting. Wilda was elegant, graceful, and easy-going, talked and laughed, as if she was an old intimate friend of David's.

This completely relieved David of the formality of first meeting, and their conversation was surprisingly smooth and pleasant.

In a face-to-face conversation, David noticed that Wilda had an incomparablly beautiful face and body. David found that Wilda's eyes were very moving, with long lashes like two bays of crystal clear water, sparkling. Wilda's mouth and nose were elegantly contoured, with soft lips and delicate and even white teeth. The five facial features were balanced and harmonized on the whole face, like the beautiful movement of the scale, coupled with some gorgeous and appropriate jewelry set off, appeared more glamorous which was almost perfect. Wilda's figure was even more delicate and moving.

The curves of her waist, shoulders, chest, and hips were elegant and sexy, eye-catching and breath-taking. David was thinking that the design of each part of the woman seemed to focus on and to have selected the best solution in countless beautiful forms in the world. The eyes were the most beautiful eyes, the neck was the most beautiful neck... Wilda's image was simply a godsend stroke of an artistic genius.

After drinking some coffee, David felt both excited and dazed. The beautiful shapes and objects in front of him stimulated his senses, just like the strong wine pouring into his face that made him unbearable. All things that greet his eyes were reversed, sometimes clearly visible and sometimes blurred. David was intoxicated and addicted and he collapsed on the sofa.

Wilda got up, came to David and sat down beside him. She gently touched David's curly hair, and her smiling face was close to his. Her gentle, considerate, and pleasant attitude warmed David's heart. David felt trapped in the sea of love and was unable to extricate himself. In a moment, David regained a little consciousness, looked fresh again. He kept watching Wilda beside him, enjoying this world beauty. He smelled a strange fragrance of this beautiful woman, which was noble, intoxicating, charming, and inviting.

David was seduced by the beauty before his eyes. This, he thought, should be what George called "the test" for testing his loyalty to Emily. David urged himself to resist any temptation and never give in.

As she drew closer to David, her hair brushed his face and her soft, prominent breasts touched his chest. Her beautiful lips with slight lipstick were just two inches away from his. Her lips were like delicious food, tempting the hungry stomach, making him swallow saliva. The snow white and delicate skin of the beauty was attractive for him to touch. Even the erotic words "dongti" (fascinating carcass) and "suxiong" (soft and white breasts) in Chinese were far from enough to describe this beauty, and even seemed somewhat vulgar. David was in agony, sweating and gasping. This temptation was such a powerful magnetic force, that no physical man like a small iron scrap could resist. David floated in the sea of love, struggling, sometimes wheezing, sometimes swilling, and ventually helplessly pushed the boat down the river and gave up resistance.

Almost unconsciously, David put his arms around Wilda's waist and pressed his lips against her sweet lips. They hugged each other tightly. David wildly kissed the most beautiful woman on her face and body. He knew that he had lost his mind completely. The flood of emotion overwhelmed everything.

David realized that he was completely defeated in resisting the temptation of women. He had totally lost. Now he let go of everything for a moment of joy. He was full of interest and intoxicated. In his middle age, he was joyous to spend his honeymoon with the peerless beauty, Wilda. They made love frequently and had sex day and night.

They enjoyed the fun of life and thanked God for His generous gift. David thought he was in love with the most beautiful woman in the world, and the most beautiful woman in the world was in love with him. He did not decline the favor from the God of fortune.

These days, David and Wilda got along closely. Their love was vigorous, almost crazy. This rare high-pitched romance touched David's heart, rendering him immense ecstasy. In this way, David enjoyed the "good wine" in his mouth, drank and drunk, drunk and drank, leading a drunken life, muddleheaded. David felt as if he had been soaked in some good wine and was willing to enjoy the intoxication and charm of it.

He clearly realized his degeneration, but could not extricate himself. He seemed to be willing to spend more time in the Garden and could not bear to give up. It was like people who were addicted to drugs felt that they couldn't extricate themselves from the euphoria of drug addiction. However, he could not completely forget Emily. While he was infatuated with Wilda, he was also subjected to the condemnation of conscience, and his heart ached faintly.

Every day, the image of incomparable beauty Wilda filled David 's eyes and mind: her pretty face and figure, her graceful manner, her pleasant words, her lingering tenderness and sweetness. David fully enjoyed the endless pleasant feminine beauty. Gradually this beauty lost its original freshness. He seemed to be starting to feel a bit of "aesthetic fatigue." Courting couldn't last forever. After all, love in the ivory tower had to be implemented into daily life and family trivia.

David found that Wilda was a natural goddess of beauty. She was beautiful and charming, with all kinds of flirtations, but it seemed that she was out of touch with the mundane affairs. She was quite ignorant and disdainful of everyday trifles and daily necessities. In the field of knowledge, she was even more superficial and ignorant, belonging to the kind of hollow beauty.

At this time, David realized more and more Emily's value and beauty. It was a kind of beauty that permeated from the heart to the outside, completely different from Wilda's simple external beauty. David noticed that Wilda's love for him, though fierce, was different from that of Emily's. Emily's emotions were more earthly and natural, more like those from the bottom of her heart and deep in her soul. In addition, David was most fond of intelligent female beauty. In his mind, wisdom was beautiful, and wisdom was an indispensable quality of beauty.

David missed Emily even more. He and Emily had been deeply in love, vowing never to give up. Now he had turned his back on Emily and fallen into a situation in which it was difficult for him to extricate himself. He felt deeply ashamed of himself, thinking of his wife Emily. David grabbed his hair with his hand and pounded his chest with his fist. Tears came out unconsciously out of his eyes.

Once David carefully observed Wilda's eyes, which were beautiful, but lacked in connotation. David felt that Emily's eyes were kind of profound and almost bottomless. The inside was rich and shining with wisdom, revealing endless emotions and thoughts. In contrast, Wilda's eyes were like two shallow water bays, which could be penetrated to the bottom at a glance.

David and Emily had been deeply attached to each other, and they regarded each other as their treasure, heart and soul. Wilda struck David as something of a soothing tenderness, combined with seductive flirtation and lewdness.

The intersection with Wilda's body was not the feeling of physical and mental integration or even soul intersection and fusion while it was with Emily.

David noticed increasingly a fact that Wilda seemed to have no soul, being just a gorgeous intelligent work of human body. David didn't want to think about it further. It would be a ridiculous and terrible fact. However, contrary to his expectations, David found that Wilda had a lot of eccentric behaviors.

Wilda didn't seem to be earthly. She never dined with David, only occasionally drinking some coffee with him. She hardly ever went to the bathroom. Once Wilda accidentally hurt her index finger, but there was no bleeding. The wound showed no muscle, but some artificial material. In addition, her response to the same context had always been identical, even the tone and pause were exactly the same, just like repeating the preset procedure every time. David also noticed that Wilda went regularly into a secret room that no one else could enter, saying that she would go there to eat something, and stayed indoor for about half an hour each time. She normally wore a tired face, acted slowly before she entered the room, and her face was glowing, fast and agile when she came out of the room, as if full of power.

David finally woke up in pain. It turned out that these days he had been communicating with a highly intelligent robot and was manipulated by the robot, which controled his reason and emotion. He was mercilessly fooled, his stupidity and absurdity would be laughed at by the world. What was more painful was what his wife should think about it. David felt ashamed and unable to face the world.

David decided to leave the Beauty Garden. He typed the required exit password on the keyboard at the gate, as George had instructed. The door opened automatically and David walked out of the Beauty Garden.

As soon as David left the Beauty Garden, he went to see George. When he met George, he said, "You are not friendly enough, guy. You've made me miserable!"

George: You said that your love for Emily was as deep as the sea, and as strong as the rock. How about it? Could you resist the beautiful woman in the Beauty Garden?

David: No. I couldn't. I was defeated. I was broken down, broken down completely.

George: As the saying goes, a hero could be subdued by a beauty. It's almost impossible for a man to keep still when a young woman sits on his lap. I have also been to Beauty Garden and was defeated thoroughly. As far as I know, there are hardly any men who enter the Beauty Garden without losing. The sexually apathetic were provoked, and the sexually incompetent were stimulated, eager to try. The intelligent design of these beauties focuses on the best form of each part of the beautiful woman, with also the most elegant demeanour, decent manners, pleasant personality, charming attraction, combining together to create the most beautiful and attractive female image in the world. You know, the beverage that the beauty let you drink is actually aphrodisiac, and the fragrance on her body also contained a springing agent. Who, as a man, can be indifferent to gentle feminine charms?

David: God has set the gravitation between men and women. In some cases, it is simply irresistible. Artificial intelligence imitates God, but it's just superficial, like the skin or fur. A robot beauty has no soul. Besides, why do people set up the Beauty Garden?

George: This is the laboratory for some scientists to test the research results of artificial intelligence, human sex, love between men and women, etc.

David: These scientists shouldn't experiment with people.

George: No other animal in these areas can replace people. Many people voluntarily act as guinea pigs.

David: You hid the truth about the Beauty Garden and played tricks on me, George. I became a lab rat there.

George: OK, OK, David. I solemnly apologize to you for that. But how would you explain to Emily your affairs in the Beauty Garden? You left home for a few days without saying goodbye. Emily was so anxious that she searched everywhere for you. She came to me to look for you. I told her that you went to the Beauty Garden. She was even more anxious and was going crazy.

David: Now I have to confess to her for my sin and ask her to forgive me.

George: Do you think she will forgive you?

David: I'm not sure. I was deeply involved in the Beauty Garden. I feel sorry for my family.

George: There's no other way. Go home quickly and plead guilty to Emily.

David returned to the side of his wife, Emily, and told her the truth about what had happened in the past few days. He begged her to forgive him. Emily said, "I could understand you last time when you brought Nava back from prehistoric times. You could not be alive without her help. This time is different, you betrayed my love, empathized with another love, and fooled around with a robot for days. I can't forgive you, David. Let's break up." "No, no!" replied David, "We can never be separated. Our souls are intertwined. I just stumbled for a while. And I regret it. I'm back now, aren't I? Besides, Wilda is not a real person, but a robot with no feelings and no soul. I beg you, Emily! Let's stay together." Emily said, "I am forgiving you for the time being for the sake of the baby in my belly. This kind of thing must not happen again." David said, "I will swear by Heaven, that if I do it again, Heaven will destroy me, and the devil will take the hindmost. What did you say, Emily? Are you pregnant again? Really?" Emily said, "Could there be any fake? The hospital has an examination report." David said, "Great, great! We are going to have a baby born in the Wonderland!"

In this fabulous region and era, David and Emily's second child was born. It was a healthy and lovely girl, named Sophia.

The child was born like a typical Chinese girl with black hair and dark color eyes. David and Emily loved the girl as much as a pearl in their palm. Now that they had a daughter, that could somewhat make up for the pain in the loss of their son Oliver, though they could never forget him.

*Human beings are the magical works of the Creator. Human feelings, human love are the nature of people. Advanced artificial intelligence will be highly developed in the future, and it can create very real people who can pass o.If as real, but it cannot create a person's mind and soul, and it cannot create people with both physical and spiritual beauty. Robots can never have the true feelings and true love of human beings, and can never replace a living real person. Artificial intelligence products are inevitably dwarfed by the works of the Creator.*

# Chapter 15

## THE ACADEMY OF ATHENS

In a conversation with Emily, professor Robert James said, "Emily, for your being inquisitive and thoughtful, I would like to guide you into a special realm, to see the past and the present, to expand your horizon and open your mind. What do you think?" When Emily learned this, she said repeatedly, "Great, great! That'll be wonderful." "I have been teaching and studying world history for many years," said professor James, "with half of my life's efforts, and cooperation with some artificial intelligence specialists I have created an intelligent expo or institute named the Academy of Athens." Emily said, "a famous Renaissance painting by Raphael is also called the Academy of Athens." Professor James said, "I just borrowed this title to show the historical facts of the world. "Athena" in the academy is not the goddess of wisdom in ancient Greek mythology. She leads the Academy of Athens. When you get there, she'll introduce to you the collections in the academy and guide you in participating in some smart projects."

Emily asked, "Please tell me the address of the Academy of Athens, I will go there by myself." The professor pointed to the mountain in front of them and said: "It's simply in this very mountain in the depths of clouds, whose whereabout is not known." which is a sentence from an ancient Chinese poem. Emily had no idea what to do, but after a second thought, it became clear that the professor did not want to reveal the academy's location for reasons of confidentiality. She thought, "I will go to the mountains to look for it myself." Emily thanked the professor and said goodbye to him.

Emily told David about this and sent their daughter to the nursery, then she walked to the rugged green mountains.

The mountains were lush and thickly wooded. Beside the occasional deep and beautiful bird song there was a mysterious silence. Emily walked along the path in the woods, looking around, hoping to find what professor James had said about the Academy of Athens. After a long walk, there were still no buildings. The paths in the woods were winding and diverging. She was dazed and evidently got lost. In the distance she could hear the bleak howl of wolves, see the cobras sticking out their tongues in the grass, and the owls in the trees gazing at her. Emily shivered, but her mind remained calm. She thought, "Professor James won't hurt me. He's a good man. Perhaps he is testing my sincerity and perseverance."

Just then, a tall man with a serious look came forward and asked Emily, "Are you Mrs. Emily Polo?" Emily replied, "It's me." The tall man said, "Please follow me." Emily followed him to a steep hill. The tall man said, "Open, XYXY!" A gate opened automatically on the hillside. They went in and the door closed automatically. "This is so much like the thief's den in the story of Alibaba," thought Emily, "except that the secret code to open the door in Alibaba's story is Open Sesame."

When they entered the cave, Emily found that it was spacious and softly lit, unlike the thief's cave that Alibaba entered, and there was no treasure in it. Emily followed the tall man to an office. Sitting inside was a dignified and beautiful lady. The lady's eyes were sharp, she was graceful and radiant. The tall man said to Emily, "This is Athena, our supervisor here." Athena gestured to the tall man to retreat.

There were only Athena and Emily in the room.

Athena, looking at the somewhat prim Emily with a smile, said, "Thank you, madam, for your visit to this academy. Please forgive me if you are not well cared for during your stay here." Emily said, "Thank you very much for having me here. I am honored." Athena patted Emily on the shoulder and said, "Don't be formal, madam. Let's just talk casually, shall we?" Emily replied with a smile, "That would be the best."

Athena began to say: "This school was founded by Professor Robert James. It is not only a museum of history, including all the nodes and secrets of human history, but also a comprehensive school of wisdom, all important achievement of human knowledge are stored and displayed here."

Emily chimed in: There must be a lot of visitors, right?

Athena: Not really. Because admission to the academy for study is strictly screened. Admitted applicants must be people who are diligent, eager to learn, good at independent thinking, and knowledgeable, and must be people of integrity and determination.

Emily: My husband David Polo is such a person. Can he come here?

Athena: Not yet. Although he is a very good person, yet in the Beauty Garden he stumbled, that cast into a slight flaw. It will take time for him to cultivate his morality and pass some tests.

Emily: I'm sure he'll be able to stand up to the test and get away with it.

Athena: I hope so. This is no ordinary museum or college. It contains a treasure trove of human knowledge and the most confidential secrets of human history. Some can be made public, and some should not at present, but at a more appropriate time in the future.

Emily: That makes sense.

Athena: This time Professor James recommends you as a visitor to the academy. I will show you any items and people in history which you might be interested in.

Emily: The historical period I'm most familiar with is more than one thousand years ago, that is, the twentieth and the twenty-first century AD. After that it is a blank for me.

Athena: No problem. We can trace back to ancient times. A lot of things happened in the world in those years. It was a turbulent age. Please follow me, madam.

Emily followed Athena through the long corridor, turned round and round, and went to a hall, where there was a large number of lifelike characters and artifacts. Emily felt very familiar with the people and things of ancient times and the environment and atmosphere of that era, although for today's people, it was nothing but ancient ruins and artifacts, out of curiosity or subject research, occasionally came to have a look.

In Emily's casual glance, the image of familiar characters came to her mind. Emily couldn't help remembering the turbulent years when ambitious and formidable persons rushed to the stage and performed. The tragic war, the cold blood and killing of the tyrants, and the suffering of the people, all these were disclosed here. Emily recognized some familiar faces among the tyrants on display in the hall.

Their hands were stained with the blood of the people. One by one, they were nailed to the shaming column of history.

There were also countless good people, including some well- known figures of that era, all lifelike with bright eyes.

"You can talk to any of them," Athena said. Emily was taken aback, thinking that these people had passed away a thousand years ago, and had already become ghosts, she asked, "Can the ghosts talk?" Athena said, "You may wish to give it a try."

Emily pondered for a moment, reminiscing about the absurd years and squandering time she and her elders lived through. There were heavy feelings in her heart. She felt a bit depressed and unable to talk. She thought now that she was living in the present, her past memories should be buried in the past forever. She dismissed the idea of talking to them. She whispered to Athena, "Let's go and look elsewhere."

Athena asked Emily if there was anything else she wanted to see. Emily said, "Actually, I'm most interested in heaven and earth and the universe." Athena said, "In this field, the academy is rich in resources, all-encompassing, simply a place of exceptional charm." Emily was in high spirits and said repeatedly, "Great! I would love that."

The two came to the Astronomical Geography Museum, which was a wide hall. At the top of the hall is a simulated sky. They saw stars twinkling and shifting in the sky. The earth was a vast expanse of endless vicissitudes. The great changes of the universe were unfolding here in the form of compression of time and space. In a short time, viewers can see hundreds of billions of years of evolution. The universe, the earth from birth to death, the infinite vast space, and long-time panoramic view were all displayed in the finite time and space. This was the realm that Emily has always yearned for and dreams of. Emily was so fascinated and engrossed that she absorbed knowledge like a sponge. She had studied hard for half of her life about the macro world, and now she understood it in an instant. She could not restrain the spontaneous pleasure in her heart. It is a kind of pleasure in seeking knowledge and going upwards. It is unmatched by some people's desire for profit or power. It is incomparable, unreachable for them.

As Emily saw in the simulated sky the development and changes of the universe, she discovered that the Wonderland where she and David now lived in was almost the ultimate.

The extremes of the matter will be reversed, and the great changes in the universe would soon take place. Athena told her that the sad news must be kept secret from the world, or it would cause fear and frustration among the world people. Emily promised not to let the cat out of the bag after she left the academy.

Athena casually asked Emily if she believed there were aliens. Emily replied, "Absolutely." Then Athena called out. Several men and women came to them. Athena introduced Emily to them. The appearance of these people reminded Emily of Mr.

Gan Ruida at Sanxingdui. These people said that they were aliens from outer space, and they talked to Emily about the alien world. The narrative came alive, making the listeners feel as if they were there. Emily got the impression that aliens were in many ways more advanced and superior to people on earth.

When Athena waved her hand, the few people left. Athena said, "These aliens have long since died. It is artificial intelligence that allows them to speak like real persons. The content of their talks was synthesized through reasoning and artificial intelligence processing. The real information of aliens visiting the earth is stored in the national archives of some big countries, and it is not considered suitable for public disclosure at present. The information about aliens stored in our academy is also required to be kept confidential for social stability."

Emily said, "Don't worry about that. I will not reveal any secret information here. Besides, may I ask if there are any information of historical file for civilians in the academy?"

Athena said, "Yes. But we need to get the person's DNA info before we can find it."

Emily said, "That is DNA ancestor-seeking. It's already widely used."

Athena said, "The DNA ancestor-seeking of our academy can be more detailed and accurate through artificial intelligence. The participant can talk to their ancestors, to learn and understand more historical facts and reasons. Now, we need first to get your DNA data." Emily readily agreed.

As Athena called, two nurses came and collected Emily's test samples. Before long, the DNA test results came out and were sent to the artificial intelligence processing center.

After a while, Athena said, "It's ready, madam. Let's go and watch."

Emily is a little excited. Through DNA ancestor-seeking, she had learned that her ancestors could be pursued to the northern Chinese ethnic groups like Han, Manchu, and Mongolian. The DNA test was more specific, and she was found to have a royal lineage to the Qing Dynasty.

Emily said, "Isn't that a little out of place?"

Athena said, "The academy will not create false information. If you have any questions, you may wish to ask your ancestors personally."

Emily: My ancestors? I don't know much about my earlier ancestors. Can I meet my dead father?

Athena: Of course.

Emily was a little excited, her heart was beating violently. She met her father several times in her dream. Now she really wanted to see her father who had been separated from her for many years.

Athena let Emily enter a room and left herself outside.

As soon as Emily entered the room, she saw her dreamy father sitting there, still dignified, kind, and amiable, just like when he was alive. The father was excited to see his beloved daughter. He came over to hug his daughter, and Emily fell into her father's arms. But she didn't have any feeling of touching at all. Father's image was real, and his words were vivid, but it seemed a bit illusory. Emily felt as if she was hugging a photograph or a shadow. Anyway, Emily finally got to see her long-lost father. Emily, like a child, was happy to see her father with tears in her eyes. She said excitedly, "Dad, I missed you so much these years!" Her father said, "So am I. I've been thinking of you, too, my dear daughter."

Later the father and daughter sat down and started talking.

Emily: Dad, I heard that my ancestors had royal lineage. What was going on? Can you tell me something about it?

Father: I didn't want to mention those things when I was alive. Since you asked me, I'll tell you something about them.

Emily: I only know that we were originally Manchu with the surname of Aisin Juelu, but later changed to Jin.

Father: When Yuan Shikai was in power, he ordered the surname Aisin Juelu to change to Jin. So, most of the Manchu surnamed Aisin Juelu had changed to the surname Jin.

Emily: The surname Jin is not bad.

Father: Not all the people with the surname of Aisin Juelu in the Qing Dynasty were royal. But our ancestors were pure royalty. Emperor Guangxu was named Aisin Juelu Zaichun. Our ancestor at that time was called Aisin Juelu Zaiying who was of the same generation and close relative to Emperor Guangxu.

Emily: I know that Emperor Guangxu was open- minded and supportive of reform. However, the stubborn and conservative Empress Dowager Cixi suppressed and imprisoned the reformers with their reform ending in failure.

Father: Yes. Our ancestor, Aisin Juelu Zaiying, was one of the reformers of the time who had close contacts with Emperor Guangxu. After the failure of the reform, he fled to Japan, and returned to China during the period of the Republic of China, hiding in Yantai, Shandong.

Emily: So, we are the descendants of the royal Aisin Juelu family in Yantai.

Father: That's right.

Emily: I think if the Qing Dynasty had been successful in a reform, China would have kept up with the world trend and not been completely defeated by the world.

Father: The Chinese royal court was stubborn in order to protect their land and authority. The Empress Dowager Cixi used the exclusive Boxers to attack and kill foreigners in China, including diplomats and missionaries, as well as Chinese Christians, and to destroy modern facilities such as railways and power lines.

Emily: It was like the Red Guards during the Cultural Revolution.

Father: Those who are enemies of human civilization will suffer the consequences and be eliminated by the civilized world.

Emily: I heard that after the defeat of the Qing Dynasty, the Qing court was forced to sign a treaty with the eight powers and made compensation of 450 million liang of silver.

Father: The Qing government kept power temporarily, and was overthrown by the tide of democratic revolution within a few years.

Emily: Thank you father for telling history. Now I have a better idea of our family context and many important facts.

Father: I learned that you married an American and now live in the United States.

Emily: Yeah, I'm doing fine and I have a daughter. Father: Knowing my younger generations are doing well,

I'm relieved. With a wider perspective the world should be one family.

Then Emily found that her father's image became a bit faint, and his expression a little abnormal. She shouted, "Daddy, Daddy!"

Father said in a vague voice, "Time's up. Dad has to leave now. Goodbye, Lili."

Emily shouted, "Goodbye, Dad. I will come to see you again in the future."

Father's figure completely disappeared.

Emily went out and saw Athena waiting there.

Athena said, "Emily, You are from the home of the prominent royal family, it is beyond my expectation."

Emily said, "That is the last royal family in China, the object of the revolution. It was overthrown in the early 20th century and replaced by the Republic of China. I have no glory in this identity at present."

Emily also browsed and inspected some other projects at the Academy of Athens. Then she left the Academy.

After some training and cultivation, David also obtained qualification for entering the Athens Academy. He learned from an investigation of his personal history and origins at the Athens Academy that one of his ancestors were Marco Polo, the famous Italian traveler and businessman who wrote The Travels of Marco Polo. David did not expect himself to be a descendent of celebrity. He was passionate about tourism, the nature of adventure, and the love of Eastern culture, which were especially like his ancestor Marco Polo.

*Later generations often have di.Iferent interpretations of their own history. Some people regard history as a little girl who can be dressed up at will. However, the truth is hard to be permanently emasculated and distorted. In time, it will always come out. Little girl's powder ornaments will also be washed away by the rain, showing their true colors.*

# Chapter 16

## THE FASCINATION MONASTERY

David lost his qualifications to study at the Academy of Athens due to his failure to resist the seduction by a beautiful woman at the Beauty Garden. He was determined to cultivate and improve himself.

David discussed with Emily about going to a monastery to make up for his own inadequacy. Emily didn't quite agree to the idea at first. She didn't have much hope for the monastery. But David insisted. Emily had to agree, but told David that he should not stay there for too long.

David went to a new-type monastery called the Fascination Monastery. This monastery was unusual. It did not belong to any religion, but had its own system.

The purpose of this monastery was to transform the monastic students into "saints" like gods. The monastic students listened to the sermons every day, faced the wall to meditate, and removed distractions and evil thoughts, repenting of past mistakes and faults, seeking forgiveness from God, purifying the soul in life, inhibiting the seven human emotions (Joy, Anger, Grief, Worry, Fear, Sentiments, and Affection) and six desires (Lust, Vanity, Dignity, Pleasant Sounds, Good Life/Death, Sensual

Pleasures). At the same time, monastic students in the monastery were required to take regular pills, receive injections, radiation tests, and medical procedures.

At first, David didn't quite adapt to the life there. In order to obtain a pureness of mind, David tried his best to restrain and adjust himself. He firmly bore in mind Mencius' teachings: "When Heaven is about to place a great responsibility on a man, it always first frustrates his spirit and will, exhausts his muscles and bones, exposes him to starvation and poverty, harasses him with troubles and setbacks so as to stimulate his spirit, toughens his nature, and enhances his abilities." David felt that the tribulations of the present were intended for the important task of the future.

Under the guidance and revelation of the elders of the monastery, David and all the monastic students were pursuing a state of deification, completing a transformation from mortal to fairy. What is a god? In ancient Chinese mythology and legends, the gods are the characters of "omnipotent, detached, beyond reincarnation, jumping out of the three worlds (Heaven, earth, and people), immortal." Taoism says: "The immortal is the man of Tao. It is the sage who is true with the avenue, dynamic and invisible, out of nothing, immortal and live forever. The movement is invisible, incompetent, and indestructible." Taoism will have insight into the universe and the origin of life, truly awakening, people of such consciousness are called "Real Persons."

The monastery encourages practitioners to study the limping Taoist's "Song of Freedom of the Immortals" in Dream of Red Mansions:

They all know the freedom of the immortals
But Reward and Fame they cannot forget.
Where are the ministers and generals past and present?
Under the neglected graves overthrown with grass.

They all know the freedom of the immortals
But Gold and Silver they cannot forget.
All life long they save and hoard and wish for more
Then suddenly their eyes are forever closed.
They all know the freedom of the immortals
But their wives they cannot forget.
They speak of love and constancy while you live
They will marry again before your graves are dry.
They all know the freedom of the immortals
But their sons and grandsons they cannot forget.
Doting parents there have been many since ancient
times
But whoever saw filial and obedient offsprings?
From the "Song of Freedom of the Immortals,"

David not only had an insight into the human society's worldly coldness and warmth, fickleness, ethical corruption, and moral decay, but also realized the world's worship and yearning for gods. The general readers of "Dream of Red Mansions" usually can only understand the literal meaning and basic implication of "Song of Freedom of the Immortals," which is profound and thought-provoking, usually unquestionable, and readily agrees. The lyrics repeatedly chant "the world all knows the immortal good" and with the achievements, gold and silver and other vulgar objects to contrast, showing more the sacredness of the gods. With the affiliation of mortals to good wife, children, and grandchildren, to make the gods more refined from vulgarity.

Then the immortal became the highest goal of life, and the days of immortality became the highest realm of life.

David realized more clearly that everything in the world was just a passing sight. The people around you, the things beside you, are fleeting. A person walks in this world, with nothing he can take with him, nothing he can retain for himself. Naked, towards the end of life, and then vanishes. In the eyes of others, he or she is also a wisp of smoke, passing by in front of them. The good people, the benefactors, the wicked, the enemies in the world, the living relatives and close friends, the moments of beauty, the joy of success, the pain of failure, all in all, is just like a passing lantern, fleeting away, also like a soap bubble, will eventually break and disappear.

In the monastery there is a mysterious hall, like the Temple of Heaven in Beijing, called the altar. The immortals sometimes appeared on this altar, and senior students were allowed to enter and talk to the immortals.

When the gods appeared, they assumed the image of the human beings, men or women, but their appearances were solemn and elegant, refined and free from valgarity. According to the gods, they were souls that had been refined and sublimated, whose appearance was just the skin and the virtual object attached to it. The essence of human soul is immortal. Once one became a god, he or she would enter a realm of ecstasy, that was, "a fairyland." completely out of the world, the customs. It was fascinating.

David's practice was commendable, and he was allowed to enter the altar to talk to the gods. He asked the gods and mortals how to get beyond oneself and reach a wonderful state. The gods answered, this matter could only be regarded as unspeakable. What Lao tzu says "The Tao that can be talked about is not the true Tao. The name that can be named is not the eternal name" is similar to this. David felt enlightened and opened his heart to the gods to express his feelings. The gods affirmed and encouraged David's progress, and gently touched David's head, saying: "This young man is awesome and promising." Then he quietly left.

David practiced in the monastery for a considerable period of time. He was studious and inquisitive, thinking day and night, almost obsessively. Later, he suddenly felt that he had somewhat entered the state, and finally understood tacitly, achieved mastery, got through and gradually into a better situation. David's spiritual transcendence was extraordinary and refined, and it was sublimated into a magical wonderland. He seemed to have thrown off all kinds of loads he had been burdened with. The body was simply an unnecessary shell. It was as if he were floating in the clouds.

David's soul was elevated with the approval of the elders of the monastery. He understood the reason why "They all know the freedom of the immortals." Through self- cultivation and discipline David also felt that he possessed a certain divinity. David had been recommended several times to share his experience among practitioners. A few months later, he passed the defense and was awarded the title of "Real Person" by the monastery. He completed his studies and returned to the world.

After returning from the Fascination Monastery, David first went to the office of Professor James to talk with him. Professor James found that David at this time had indeed changed. He had seen the vanity of the world and his ideas were extraordinary. His soul was purified and refined. James discussed the issue of David's admission and visit to the academy with Athena, the director of Academy of Athens. David finally obtained the admission qualification and entered the Academy. David learned a lot at the Academy, where he carefully examined the origins, the evolution and development of the universe, the earth, the living creatures, and human beings. He also found out the origin of his ancestors, made magical contact and communication with his ancestor Marco Polo, and received the tribute of him.

David returned to his home after studying at the Academy of Athens. Emily was overjoyed to see David after a long departure. She blamed David for spending too much time away from home but David only grinned and chuckled. He did not get close to his estranged wife and daughter, but kept silent all the time. All day long, he was taciturn and thoughtful, muttering something in his mouth. Emily found that David had changed, and he seemed to be a different person. He was a little bit cynical and indifferent to everything. The phrase "doesn't matter" became his mantra. His mood was calm and unruffled as if he had no emotions. His state of mind was smooth and steady, pure, and asexual, does not seem to have any ideal or pursuit.

Emily was somewhat disappointed with the changes in David after his training. She felt that David had become somewhat abnormal and unreliable, unlike the David in the past. However, Emily still loved David. She would rather regard David at this time as a husband who was afflicted with minor illnesses.

David claimed himself to have the scriptures and to be near the gods. Every day he exercised his skills in order to soar into space like a true god. Although his practice was effective, it was difficult for him to lose weight significantly, not to say to zero. He could leap to a high platform and jump off a wall with ease, which he was not satisfied with, but was stroving for a higher level.

Once David jumped from a high slope into a deep ravine, thinking that he could fly up gently, but he fell straight to the bottom of the ravine and hurt one arm, one leg and with many bruises in the body.

At this time, David could no longer walk and was in an embarrassing situation. Two young people happened to be passing by and managed to take him to the hospital. It took many days of treatment in the hospital for him to be fully recovered.

David learned that the two young people, named Tony and Laura, were passionate lovers. Emily thanked them for their help to David. The four became good friends.

Emily was worried about David's current state. She went to talk to Professor James for advice. The professor was also surprised and regretted of David's change. He decided to make an investigation into the monastery and find out the reasons for David's change.

Through investigation, Professor James had learned about some of the inside stories about the Fascination Monastery. This monastery claimed to purify the human soul and transform the mortal into an immortal. Some artificial intelligence and other intensive means had been adopted in the monastery. It not only damaged the human nervous system, but also adversely affected people's health. It also violated the basic human rights and dignity of human beings and violated human ethics and jurisprudence. The question now was how to restore David to his normal life.

At Professor James's suggestion, Emily went to see a psychologist with David. David was subjected to a series of tests by a psychologist who determined that his mind was severely distorted, mainly by artificial intelligence. To correct this distortion, a counter-artificial intelligence technology must be applied to restore it. Emily agreed to this treatment. After a period of treatment, David gradually returned to normal.

David's love for his wife Emily and her daughter, Sophia, was rekindled and it was extremely blazing. He had long been gazing at the faces of his beloved wife and loving daughter, and his joy was palpable. He was grateful to Emily for her careful care of him when he was wounded, and comforted and enlightened him when he felt lonely. There was also the cuteness of her daughter, Sophia. David thought, "If I were a god, I would live forever by myself, then my wife and children would pass away before me. I would stay in the world alone, without any relatives and friends, what would be the worth and meaning of it?"

David became as passionate and full of vitality as ever, showing all the desires and pursuits of ordinary people. David continued to study astronomy, biology, and philosophy, while practicing martial arts and clambering. He could turn dozens of somersaults without getting tired. He could climb steep cliffs as if they were flat ground.

David walked alone in the wild and was in a good mood. He lay on the ground and looked up at the sky. He felt that he was more practical and more attached to the ground. He knew that he originally came from the earth and would return to it when he died. The vast expanse of the sky, high and dimly discernible, could be seen but unreachable by people on the ground. It was unrealistic for people born on the ground to dream of becoming immortals.

Moreover, at this time, David began to realize that the immortal was not as beautiful as people think. It was actually rather boring to dwell on the days of the deities. The realm of immortality was transcendent, too holy, too clean, too quiet, too restrained. As an immortal, after some time, it was inevitable to feel a kind of greasy. In people's life experience, there were always emotions such as joy, anger, sadness, and happiness and the tastes of acidity, sweetness, bitterness, and spiciness. Folks on earth were performing plays on the stage of life that were wonderful and lively, far better than the divine and pure but peaceful and indifferent realm of gods.

Emily talked closely with David. Emily thought of the history of Western art from the divine world. She compared the divine world to classicism in painting, which mostly depicted religious subjects. Classicism reached its zenith in the Renaissance. However, with the development of society, paintings had gradually turned to civilians. People were tired of God, Virgins, and Holy babies in classical paintings. The image was lifeless, far removed from, or even irrelevant to, civilian life and images. In classical paintings one cannot find the passion of romantic paintings, the mediocrity of Barbizon paintings, the colorfulness of Impressionist paintings, the whimsy of surrealist paintings, and the ultimate play of modern art from all walks of life.

David greatly appreciates Emily's point of view. He realized that civilian life was the most colorful and vibrant. For "Song of Freedom of the Immortals" in Dream of Red Mansions, his comprehension and insights had been beyond the past, and surpassed everyone. He realized that the limping Taoist's "Song of Freedom of the Immortals" profoundly revealed the true meaning of the world. But being a god was not necessarily good. Co-operated with Emily David composed his own version of "Song of Freedom of the Immortals" with a different tune and some other truth in it.

> They all know the freedom of the immortals
> With pure heart, no desires and toiling.
> But where is the bliss and where the happy song?
> Joy of success is nowhere to be found.
> They all know the freedom of the immortals
> But who knows their boring!
> Less human family happiness for them,
> Love between men and women is gone.
> They all know the freedom of the immortals
> Living in the clover with little trouble!
> Holy and elegant but groundless,
> Perfect with no def ect, who saw?
> They all know the freedom of the immortals
> With no relatives, no friends and intimates
> Noisy clamor is the human world,
> Limpid air and clear water, but no fish in it.

No fish can be found in too clear water, because fish is difficult to survive there. Similarly, it may not be a good thing if a person is placed in a vacuum space where all impurities are removed, only pure oxygen and the most pure distilled water is supplied to nourish him.

Why is the fairy Qixiannu (the Seventh Fairy) willing to descend from Heaven to become a civillian and go hand in hand with a villager, not fearing poverty and cold?

Why is the millennium snake spirit Bai Suzhen (the White Snake) willing to transform into a woman, to get married to a civilian and give birth to a baby, risking herself of being captured and imprisoned? It is because the world is diversified and colorful, there is bitterness as well as amusement there.

David and Emily had revived the ordinary life of the common people. Three meals a day, taking care of their daughter, keeping pets, planting flowers and trees. Life was flat, but full of flavor.

Seeing their toddler daughter fell down, David hurried to help her up and asked, "Are you OK?" Hearing Emily sneezing because of a cold, David used to say "Bless you."

The clock chimed in a low-key, resoundingly at the right time, and the white cat was sound sleeping under the table....

This was life - the daily life of ordinary people.

As for the monastery, which was known as "Fascination Monastery" was ordered by the court to suspend operation for rectification due to alleged violations of regulations. The gods on the altar of the monastery were actually intelligent robots, and some of the drugs used by the practitioners did not meet the hygiene standards.

In fact, there is a world of difference between god and man, and there is no possible transformation between the two. It is ridiculous to deify certain characters among the people. The supreme god is the Creator, before whom man is really insignificant. Also, comparing some people to the sun is also unacceptable and ridiculous. The Supreme God is the Creator, and man is really insignificant before the Creator.

*God and man are quite di.Iferent, and the transfor-
mation between god and man is even more impossible. God is often idealized by people. Mortals dream
of deification and pursuing ideal state. In fact, the
life of a mortal is more natural, vivid, mellow, and
sweet, and full of fun and taste.*

# Chapter 17

## THE EVER-MIGHTY HEAVEN

Due to the rapid development of high technology and artificial intelligence, various miracles had appeared in the land of the Wonderland: automated production had greatly improved production efficiency, production capacity, and product quality; robots, alive and vivid, almost like real, entered people's lives in a grand manner; characters and situations in human history could be restored and reproduced in the way of artificial intelligence, and even could interact with modern people; medical treatment and health care had been greatly improved, all incurable diseases had been eliminated, human organs and blood cultivation and replacement had been popularized, with people's physique generally improved, and greatly raised, and life expectancy significantly extended. All these were bringing endless convenience, comfort, and space for further improvement to people's lives.

All this made the people at that time very excited. Some of them even felt elated and carried away. They were dizzy with victory and success, trying to challenge and subvert some inherent ideas, even the laws of science and nature. Generally speaking, innovation can promote social progress. However, to go against the laws of nature, to disobey the heavens is a little ignorant of the heights of the sky and the depths of the earth, which is tantamount to delusion to ascend to the sky in one step and pick off the stars there.

Some people even put forward the saying that "man will prevail over nature" and "dare to let the sun and the moon to change into a new sky." They pointed their suspicion and challenged at the master of all things - the Creator and God and wanted to transform and rebuild the world created by the creator. This unrealistic dream had given birth to a number of new disciplines, like the project of rejuvenation and resurrection; like the immortality of world and the universe; like gene editing, artificial genetic engineering; like controlling and reengineering time and space, and so on.

The top thinkers, scholars, and scientists with real vision at the time were not very optimistic about these "new explorations" and "new disciplines." They did not drift with the current and did what they thought was unreasonable and infeasible. They always believed that human beings should not deviate from nature and go against the wishes of the Creator.

David and Emily, who were middle-aged, were sober and abided by the inherent ideas formed in their lives. They had been exploring life, the world, and the universe all their lives, pursuing truth. At this time, they did not deliberately pursue and cater to new thinking and new trends. This was because there were God and Heaven in their hearts. They knew that man was a creature of the Creator. Man should have unlimited reverence for God and Heaven, and conform to the will of Heaven and the laws of nature, instead of being whimsical.

David and Emily had a lot of good friends and acquaintances in the Wonderland. Young lovers, Tony and Laura, were among them.

Tony and Laura were students of Professor Robert James. On the knowledge structure of history and archaeology, they turned to philosophy and space-time theory.

Although they were a few years younger than David and Emily, the four of them were as close as brothers and sisters.

These few people often got together in their spare time and indulged themselves in conversation. Sometimes they ate BBQ, drank champagne and beer together. Together, they flew along the coast and over the city in a small plane, enjoying the beautiful scenery.

Tony was a stocky man with Pushkinesque whiskers, rather like an artist or a poet. The young man was cheerful and active. He was smart and quick-witted, he was used to talking and laughing, and sometimes even bragging to make everyone "high." People said they never felt lonely with him.

Laura was a kind, enthusiastic girl. The girl had big eyes, a tall figure, delicate, ruddy skin, and a smooth, graceful figure. Her hairstyle was somewhat unconventional, reminiscent of European women in the 18th century. She was good at singing and dancing, her voice was as clear as spring water, and her dancing was as beautiful as rosy clouds.

Tony and Laura were energetic, romantic, and modern in appearance and behavior.

David and Emily found it a pleasure to be with these two young people, and they seemed to be getting younger themselves. They sometimes indulged in singing to the accompaniment of Sachs, relaxing mentally and emotionally. Sometimes the four of them sing together in a wild mood, with their spirits and emotions greatly relaxed.

Once, at a party at Professor Robert James' house, David, Emily, Tony, and Laura talked casually with the professor about the universe, the world and the theory of time and space. Professor

James said that human beings would eventually die with the destruction of the universe.

This was the general trend.

Tony asked, "Isn't there a way for the human race to escape its doom? In ancient Chinese legends, Nu Wa, a goddess repairing the sky, reformed the deficiency of the world and created a new sky for the benefit of future generations." Laura added, "Yi shooting nine suns, which is another example of changing the world. Although these are myths and folklores, they show the desire of people to change the world. I wonder if today's more intelligent humans can't change the old world?" Laura stared at Professor James in the eye and asked, "Are we right, Professor?"

Professor James smiled and shook his head, indicating that the answer was no.

Tony and Laura were young scientists with fresh ideas. Brilliant and ambitious, they were brewing a plan to defy the current laws of time and space. The project first aimed at the motion of the planets in the solar system. According to their assumptions, appropriate adjustments should be made to the orbits of some planets to make more planets suitable for humans to live on. This made it possible for people on earth to migrate to these planets. Once this plan was realized, it would definitely bring a new look to the solar system and greatly benefit mankind. By extension, it might even turn things around, delaying or avoiding the end of the world.

In order to achieve this goal, they needed to establish a new space-time theory and overturn the traditional space-time concept. They had superseded Einstein's theory of relativity and space-time to create a different kind of space- time theory. In accordance with this theory, they would gradually realize their plans to transform the planet.

As the first step of this project, they would go to space to do some field investigation and have some experience, to collect all kinds of relevant data and information. They asked and discussed with David and Emily many times about their experiences and feelings about space flight and time travel.

They knew that David and Emily were the only people who had experienced time travel in the Wonderland.

Although David and Emily had reservations about their close friends' space-time transformation plan, they still took an adaptive attitude in some specific links, actively cooperated and wished for its success.

Tony and Laura had meticulously designed a spaceship to travel through space without going through a space tunnel. This was a "quasi-space-time crossing" spacecraft.

Their ideas were implemented by various senior engineers with artificial intelligence operation procedures to produce a blueprint for processing. In the highly developed automated manufacturing industry at that time, it was successfully processed into a beautiful space-time traversing spacecraft.

They asked David and Emily to name the spacecraft. David and Emily suggested calling it "the Intrepid" to show the brave spirit of the young couple.

It was a fine, sunny summer day when the Intrepid set sail at its launch base on the coast. In addition to their R & D team, David and Emily were also invited there to see their friends, Tony and Laura, off with their best wishes.

Time to take off, after the countdown signals 5, 4, 3, 2, and 1 were issued, the spaceship soared smoothly into the blue sky, like an eagle flying in the sky. The crowd on the ground burst into cheers. Before long, this eagle disappeared from people's view.

In the main cabin of the spacecraft, Tony and Laura had been in video contact with the ground command center and exchanged information with David and Emily. Their whereabouts in space, and even their every move in the spacecraft, were reflected on the large screen of the Mission Control at any time, as well as on the computer screens at David and Emily's house, and at Professor James's. At the same time, Tony and Laura could also see the staff in front of the ground screen and David and Emily from the screen in their space cabin.

Tony and Laura were doing fine in the ship. They said they felt great. They had delicious meals and drinks, preserved fresh fruit and snacks on board every day. There was a comfortable bedroom and a clean toilet. Beautiful music could be played in the room at any time according to oral instructions. When they were happy and excited, they danced happily, or sang beautiful songs. They did whatever they wished to do and enjoyed it, except that all this was done in weightlessness. The two of them were floating in the space of the cabin, like fish in the water, full of fun. Even more interesting was that Tony and Laura had brought their beloved cat, Wayway, with them in the spaceship. Wayway was floating around in the weightless space, with her tail wagging around, her face full of curiosity.

Tony and Laura's space flight was actually a simulated time travel. This route through time and space traverse was mostly preset, rather than a normal spacecraft that could be controlled at any time. In addition to the solar system, they would also visit several other small galaxies in the Milky Way to understand whether there were more reasonable planetary orbits than the solar system. Through comparison, refering to other celestial body's advantages, they could transform the solar system.

The crossing trip was originally scheduled to be completed in 12 days. On the seventh day of the flight, the spacecraft suddenly had an accident and appeared abnormal. Ground control found that the spacecraft apparently deviated from its original course. Tony, Laura, and their ground team took emergency measures to try to adjust the course. Exhausting all contingency plans, none of them worked.

If the fault could not be removed in time, the consequences would be disastrous.

The engineers in the ground command center of the spaceship, as well as David and Emily in front of the computer screen, were very anxious at this time. People were looking for the cause of the accident in order to determine the solution. Tony and Laura thought of all aspects of the flight plan, including the parameters of space and time. At this time, Tony and Laura suddenly realized something and admitted that in their plan for crossing the orbit they boldly adopted the new space-time model developed by them. The new model was different from the traditional spatiotemporal model in some important parameters.

On hearing this, David and Emily's hearts suddenly sank down and exclaimed, "Oh, no! This new space-time model made Tony and Laura deviate from the right path and go astray, and the spacecraft lost the return mechanism. This was a quasi-space-time travel, not a normal spaceship voyage. Once a mistake was made, it was difficult to remedy it. The traveler would inevitably suffer bad luck, even doomed eternally."

Tony and Laura were aware of the seriousness of the situation and the embarrassment they were in. Their "mischievous" and unruly made them become lost lambs now. Their wrong decisions would result in the destruction of their spaceship and the disappearance of themselves in the boundless space.

The ground crews of Tony and Laura's team, as well as David and Emily, were soberly aware of this, although emotionally reluctant to accept the fact.

On this journey, Tony and Laura tried their new model of space-time theory, which was based on what they called "space-time folding." This kind of space-time folding could give the man-made aircraft a chance to "overtake on the curve" and take a shortcut. But this idea was just a pipe dream. "Curve overtaking" was reminiscent of the idea and trial production of the "perpetual motion machine" at the beginning of the industrial revolution. A "perpetual motion machine" is a delusion that can never be realized because it violates the law of conservation of energy. Similarly, deviating from the normal pattern of time and space, "overtaking on a curve" violates the basic laws of time and space, which is bound to be a kind of unrealistic dream.

Time and space are closely related to the motion of the universe. Man is but a creature on a small planet in the universe. How can man control the operation of the immense universe? If one overreaches oneself and tries to manipulate time and space, one can only reap the consequences. Tony and Laura knew that their traversal ship had been thrown into outer space due to a deviation from its normal orbit. The spacecraft could only fly aimlessly by inertia, like a tiny dust drifting in the vast space. The ship's oxygen, fresh water, and food would soon run out. The ship would eventually go up in smoke, and then the end would come for them.

Tony and Laura wept for the failure of their exploration and the misfortune they had brought about. Fortunately, they were deeply in love and shared weal and woe. They were fortunate to go to the end of their lives hand in hand. For this, they felt great relief.

The people on the ground saw on the screen that the two lovely young people wiped their tears from their faces and smiled innocently and brightly. They told people on the ground that their last wish in this life was to hold their wedding on the spaceship. Friends on the ground applauded for them and invited a priest to marry them.

The people on earth and in the sky were interacting, and the chief minister wished them to love each other all their lives. The two of them also vowed to never abandon under any circumstances until death. Wedding music sounded simultaneously in the spacecraft and the ground base hall, and the two were intoxicated in the beautiful atmosphere of love.

Tony and Laura flew farther and farther with the spaceship, and everyone knew that they were rapidly dying. As expected, with time going by, there was a shortage of oxygen, water and food necessary for human survival in the spaceship, and finally it was completely cut off, because their spacecraft had traveled in space far beyond the original schedule, and the reserved supplies were insufficient. Tony and Laura were seen on the screen with haggard faces and dry lips. Later, their faces turned to vegetable color, and their lips pale and cracked. Laura was unable to speak but only blinked her beautiful eyes Tony said in a weak voice, intermittently: "We are going to Heaven. Before parting, we leave a word of advice to the people on the earth: Don't go against the Heavens. People can never overtake the Heaven. Remember, remember."

After days without food and water, Wayway, the beloved cat, still had some vitality and was meowing. However, she looked terrified and flustered, and seemed to have noticed some ominous signs. Some animals were more prophetic about the impending disaster than human beings.

Professor James also watched Tony and Laura in the spaceship in front of the computer screen. He was muttering to himself" Young people, rest in peace. You're just one step ahead. Sooner or later, people on earth will have this day, too."

David and Emily were full of attachment and sadness when they saw their close friends leaving and were about to say goodbye to them. They regreted that they were unable to persuade their friends to give up the adventure.

People saw that Tony and Laura closed their eyes, stopped breathing, and slept in space. Tears welling up in David's eyes rolled on his cheeks drop by drop. Emily covered her face with her hands, changing from choking and sobbing to crying.

Tony and Laura, the gracious and serene faces of the young lovers were deeply imprinted in people's memory.

The passionate, innocent images of them always lingered in people's minds. Tony's loud and magnetic voice of talking and laughing, and Laura's beautiful singing was always ringing in people's ears.

> *Human wisdom and energy can never surpass that of God, not equal to the minutia of the Creator.*
> *Heaven always acts in a regular way. Human beings should not go beyond the rules of Heaven, act wrong or be naughty in front of God.*

*The inherent feelings and love between peo-
ple from ancient times to the future, from the earth
to the sky, are eternal and unchanged.*

*Slight di.Iferences in people's ideas can
hardly a.Ifect the true feelings between them.*

# Chapter 18

## THE DOOMSDAY

### 3015 AD

David and Emily had lived in the Wonderland for about two years, leading a life of infinite happiness.

But not for long before they unfortunately coincided with the great changes in the universe. The operation of the universe was stagnant at first, then reversed.

Astronomers observed that the speed of ever increasing distances between distant stars was slowing down, and the expansion of the universe caused by the Big Bang seemed to be nearing its end.

The universe was in a depression with gradual weakening vitality. The movement of the universe was in a decline, becoming slow, idle, and weak.

The sun, the moon, and the stars were blurry, fuzzy, and dim and the sky was in a twilight.

There were squeaky noises everywhere, as if large vehicles were screeching and slamming on the brakes.

The operation of the entire universe seemed to be about to halt and stop.

Some animals, such as rats and snakes, were scurrying around, bats and owls flying about in the daytime like headless flies, as if they were harbingers of foreboding.

People realized that mankind would be in trouble. All human beings, living creatures and even highly developed human civilization would not be spared.

At the end of the gradual slowing down of the cosmic tempo, time reached a standstill.

At that moment all activities ceased. Time no longer passed.

The hands of the clocks and watches stopped rotating for no apparent reason.

The water in the river no longer flowed, just like being frozen.

The water curtains of the waterfalls hung there, like crystal artworks, noble and luxurious.

There was no wind in the air, as if in a vacuum. People could not smell anything, nor hear anything.

The surfaces of the sea and the lakes were without a ripple, like pools with stagnant water.

The world was deadly quiet, and the entire universe was in perfect silence.

The originally animated world became utterly unenergetic.

Pedestrians and vehicles in the streets were all stopped there and could not move.

What was more interesting was that in an instant, the flying planes and birds suddenly stopped in the air, like being nailed to the sky.

The falling raindrops also stopped in the air, neither up, nor down, as if crystal clear dewdrops hanging in the air, spectacular and abnormal.

Fish, turtles, shrimps, and crabs in the water also seemed to be mothballed in the ambers, motionless, to be appreciated and played by people.

All people seemed to be fixed in place by some invisible force, like wax figures with various poses, static.

David and Emily, who were walking in the park, were stopped there, unable to move, posing gestures as for taking a photo, even the momentary expressions of the two talking and laughing were fixed like in a picture. The images were rigid.

The expansion of the universe created by the Big Bang was over, followed by a brief stasis, and then a crunch of it, with regression of time, because both time and space were closely related to the material of the universe.

The great contraction of the universe caused the reversal of time. The reversal of time had led to a dramatic change in the world, which had resulted in a reversal of everything everywhere.

At the beginning of the time reverse, people heard the noise of a cheep and a tremendous roar that followed. Then there was the swishing sound. The reverse flow of time throughout the universe began.

What kind of scenario was the time reverse flow?

If one looked at the clock, he would see that the hour hand of the clock was turning counterclockwise, from 12 to 11 to 10...

The days were upside down, from today to yesterday, from yesterday to the day before...

Days in a month from 31st to 30th to 29th...

All in all, it was retreating from the present to the past.

The reversal of time led to the reverse movement. People saw everything unusual, grotesque.

The water in the river was flowing backward, from low to high.

The water of the waterfall gushed up from below. Rain drops rose from the ground to the sky.

The planes and birds flew backwards.

David and Emily, who were walking in the park, once frozen by the stagnant time in a pose, now suddenly started to go backward.

This was truly a veritable retrograde.

The whole world order was chaotic and unsystematic. Amazing things were everywhere.

The pieces of a glass shattered on the ground were gathered together, synthesized into a whole glass, and flew back to the table where it had been placed.

The language discourse of people also appeared disordered, the vowel and consonant positions in the speech flow were exchanged, unable to communicate.

For instance, speak became keeps, own became no, march became charm, card became dark, eat became tea...

The reversed order of the five tones in a song resulted in strange sound oddities.

Colors on a painting canvas were reduced stroke by stroke, and then there was only one blank canvas left. Finally, the blank canvas fell off from the wooden frame supporting it, and such a valuable painting disappeared.

The robot beauty in the Beauty Garden died because there was no electricity for it to get recharged. Complex circuits and chips, as well as artificial bones and muscles, littered here and there after the robot's disintegration, like old household appliances abandoned on one side, with no vitality at all. When David and George saw this, they could not help feeling that they, as living people, had once been fascinated by it, bewitched by it, played round and round by it and had grand romantic affairs with it. That was absolutely ridiculous.

The Athens Academy was completely destroyed, with all the astronomical and historical treasures of the Academy lost. Athena was dead with none of the Academy staff survived.

The altar in the Fascination Monastery collapsed, and the robots that were used as immortals showed their original shapes, only a few broken leather bags, revealing some worn parts, chips, and circuit boards wrapped in them.

Tall and magnificent buildings in the city were dismantled bit by bit from the top and leveled to the ground.

Residential buildings had been reduced to rubble automatically. People lost their homes, becoming homeless.

The roads and streets became uneven grounds and overpasses torn down. The bridges across the rivers had vanished without a trace. Traffic was paralysed completely.

Even more abominable was that the sewage in the sewers and urinals, even the stool in the toilet poured out and splashed around everywhere.

People could not prevent themselves from getting dirty.

Their clothes and faces were stained.

People could not poop, urinate, and the food and soup that were being digested in the abdomen gushed out of their mouths and it was nauseous.

People were discomfited, lost their minimum dignity, and all of them were perplexed, annoyed, disappointed and almost crazy.

The most intolerable thing was that people could not eat and drink. When one ate or drank something, they would spit it out automatically. Many people were dying due to lack of water and nutrition.

First of all, the old and weak, sick and disabled died, and then the strong, young, healthy men and women were not immune from death.

David and Emily learned that their daughter, Sophia, had died with all the children and nurses in the nursery. They felt dizzy as if struck by lightning. They had not even had the chance to see Sophia's dead body due to traffic paralysis.

Human and animal corpses littered the streets. Flowers and trees withered. The Earth was desolate and dreary.

Human beings and other living creatures in the world had been designed according to the positive direction of the time flow. They were completely inconsistent with the reverse direction of the time flow, that was destroying all kinds of living things on Earth.

David and Emily experienced the great change of the time direction. They witnessed two distinct eras, and a terrible reversal scene. The beautiful "Heaven on Earth" instantly turned into a hideous "Hell on Earth."

Emily thought of the Russian famous artist, Carle Brullov, and his masterpiece "Pompeii Doomsday." Pompeii was the ancient Rome city engulfed in 79 BC when the volcano Vesuvius erupted.

The present catastrophe was even more traumatic than the doomsday of Pompeii. Pompeii was just the destruction of a city, but now it was the whole world, and the entire universe was about to collapse and vanish completely.

In the midst of the apocalypse, Professor James, George, David, and Emily's other friends, colleagues, students, and neighbors died.

David, though physically fit, unable to sustain it, died too.

Emily grieved over David's death, but without tears.

Tears welled up in her eyes, then automatically flew in.

Emily dug a pit in the ground to bury David. She covered David with dirt. She planned to pile up a tomb and set up a tombstone for David. However, she did not expect that the dirt that covered David was automatically removed and David's body was thrown out of the pit, then the pit was refilled with excavated dirt and turned into hard ground. Emily lost all her energy in vain.

Emily laid helplessly on the ground, looking at the gloomy sky. Knowing that she would die with the end of the world which was the arrangement of Laotian (the Creator). She should be satisfied that she had had the companion of David, who loved her deeply, and she had had a good time in the Wonderland. No one in the former world except David, Sophia, and herself was lucky enough to enjoy this honor.

Suddenly, Emily felt her body dragged in one direction by an invisible force, and when she reached a place that looked like a pit, she fell head down into it. She cried out in horror.

After a long while, she gradually felt comfortable, and the direction of her whereabouts seemed to be rising, rising, and rising...

Emily knew she was in the time-space tunnel again where she was no stranger. But last time she was traveling with David, and this time she came back alone. She felt sad, like ten thousand arrows piercing her heart.

Emily closed her eyes in pain and fell asleep.

Suddenly, a violent jolt woke her up from her dream. Emily opened her eyes and saw some light before her. She saw the blue sky and the calm sea.

*David and Emily's dreamlike journey through the future world shows that there is no absoluteness, no extremes, no immortality, no ever-living. The universe, the world, and mankind all have doomsdays. The true, the good, and the beautiful may turn to their opposites. Paradise may become hell, positive can become negative. The Earth may topple over and the universe may turn upside down. This is the act of the Creator. The ants-like ordinary populace is helpless. It is better to wait and see, conforming to the Creator's will.*

# Chapter 19

## Return to the Original

**2015 AD**

mily found herself lying on a beach alone, with a faint morning light flooded over her whole body, and the sea breeze drying her up with her wet hair and clothes soaked in the sea water. She asked herself, "Where am I?" Two seagulls skimmed over the sky, shrieked, as if to answer her question, but she was still puzzled.

Emily felt tired and exhausted, the long-term hunger, thirst and torture made her extremely weak physically. She looked up and saw no one around. Struggling to turn over, she slowly rose to her feet on the sand and lingered on the beach. After walking for a while, no one was seen. At last she heard a distant chat and the barking of a dog. She walked in the direction of the sound, and saw two figures approaching. It was an old couple walking a dog. The old couple felt a little surprised to see Emily in her current condition, and the dog came up and sniffed at her. Emily asked the old couple politely, "Good morning. Excuse me, what is this place?" The old man and old lady looked at her with curiosity, eyeing up and down the Oriental woman in her semi-wet clothes, and said enthusiastically, "Good morning! Good morning! It is here Key West." Emily said, "Thank you." She got it. This was the southernmost tip of Florida.

The old lady asked, "You are...?" Emily was a little overwhelmed and made up a story: "I was in a ship in distress at sea, and I fell into the water and was rushed to the beach by the waves." The two seniors thought the woman was so lucky and pitiful, that the old lady said, "Thank God! Where is your home?" "I used to live in Boulder, Colorado," said Emily. "That's a nice place," said the old man, "We have been there. The scenery there is pleasant, skiing in winter and hiking in summer." The old lady asked, "But how could you get home? Do you have any money or credit card with you?" Emily shook her head. The old lady said, "Come on with us. Have breakfast in our house and have a good rest." Emily thanked them with gratitude and felt she had met some good people.

Emily lived in the old couple's home for a day, that was not far from the former villa of Ernest Hemingway, the famous American writer. The old man was named Alexander Brown, and the old lady was Mary Brown. The old man had special worship for Hemingway. He felt that he was like the Old Man in Hemingway's novel The Old Man and the Sea. He had caught fish in the sea, also trained and farmed crocodiles in the marsh. When the old man saw that Emily was penniless, he booked an air ticket for her to go to Denver the following day and gave her some change to use on the way. The next day, Emily bid farewell tearfully to the kind old couple. She took a bus and went to Miami airport, where she boarded a plane to Colorado, and arrived in Denver four hours later.

Emily took a bus to Boulder from Denver airport. Her mind was full of thoughts. She thought of the good times and the little things when she was with David in the past few years and Sophia, their lovely daughter, who was born in Wonderland. Now she was back alone while David and Sophia were gone forever. David and Sophia died in the World's End. There was no sign of them whatsoever. They could no longer be with her. Her heart was aching with tears in her eyes. She thought that she had left David and their daughter on the other side of the time tunnel, and now she came back alone with no face to see the folks here and confront David's relatives in Boulder. She decided not to go to the home of David's parents, although she was eager to see her son Oliver and other relatives there.

In the early evening, Emily found herself in the neighborhood of the house of David's parents, hoping to see in privacy the family members who might occasionally come to the courtyard. How she wanted to see her son, Oliver. She had lost her daughter, but now she had "regained" her son. Oliver should be eight years old by now, and she was eager to see what he looked like at present. Emily waited patiently in the woods outside the courtyard, hoping that the child who she had not seen for more than two years would reappear in front of her eyes, also the affable faces of David's parents and sister, Jessica. She was unaware of how long she had been waiting when Oliver appeared in the yard. He came to the yard to look for the cat, calling the name of the cat, "Mimi, Mimi!" The cat Mimi appeared. He picked up the cat and embraced her. How Emily wished that she could come over to Oliver at once, pick him up, embrace, and kiss him. Maybe the mother he hadn't seen for more than two years was a little strange to him, but normally the child should not forget his mother. Emily suppressed her impulses and her passion for her own child. She gazed at Oliver obsessively. The child had grown and changed a lot. Emily suddenly felt dizzy. When she came to her senses, there was no sign of her son in the yard. Oliver disappeared from Emily's sight.

At dusk, Emily felt homeless. She had a simple supper of some bread, an apple, and a cup of water from a store. If she were in the Wonderland, she would have been offered free accommodation in a comfortable hotel and a free delicious dinner. The environment would be neat and beautiful, refreshing, and pleasant. Coming back to the world today, she really needed to adapt and get used to it.

At night, Emily lay down on the park bench to rest, but could not fall asleep. Looking at the stars in the sky, she remembered an English song and sang it softly.

> Twinkle, twinkle, little star
> How I wonder what you are
> Up above the world so high
> Like a diamond in the sky
> Twinkle, twinkle, little star
> How I wonder what you are
> When the blazing sun is gone
> When he nothing shines upon
> Then you show your little light
> Twinkle, twinkle, all the night

Emily thought, in the vast universe, our Earth was but a twinkle, twinkle, little star, and human beings were just some tiny creatures on that star. How small and insignificant we were relative to the universe!

The following day, Emily was wandering alone in the town of Boulder, in an aimless trance. She went to Boulder Creek, where she was familiar, and watched the churning waves of the river and the wild ducks foraging by the river. A young couple passed by. The young lady noticed that the Oriental woman's dress was a little wield. It looked graceful and elegant. When the young lady's eyes swept over the Oriental woman's face by the river, she felt that it was somewhat familiar. After a walk, she remembered Emily, then turned back and asked the woman directly, "Excuse me, are you Emily?" Emily looked up and saw Audrey. She pretended not to know her and shook her head. She did not want her relatives or friends to know that she had returned to Boulder. She did not want people to know that she was "back from her death." The news that she and David had been killed in the Bermuda adventure two years ago was a well-known event in the United States. How should she explain it? She would rather not tell the terrible nightmare she had experienced, which would cast a shadow of the great calamity on the innocent modern people in the hope of a bright future.

Audrey could not forget her accidental sight of the Oriental woman she encountered by the river. Audrey was very familiar with Emily's face, body shape, and gait. She grew to think that it should be Emily. She talked to her husband Jerry about it. Jerry said, "I think you're probably mistaken. That can't be Emily. Emily and David have been dead for more than two years, and they have no chance of survival. Westerners are often confused about the Oriental faces, and I have made such mistakes in the past."

Once again, at dusk, Audrey met that Oriental woman who resembled Emily so much in a small street west of Broadway in Boulder. They were far apart, and the woman did not see Audrey. Audrey followed her and walked a few blocks. The woman turned south from Pleasant Street and walked along the 9th Street, then disappeared. Audrey remembered that there was a cemetery there called Columbia Cemetery. She was scared and broke into a cold sweat. The woman she saw was clearly the ghost of Emily, for Emily's grave was in the graveyard. Yes, two years ago, David and Emily disappeared in Bermuda. The family decided that they were dead and set up a tombstone in their memory in this cemetery.

After seeing Audrey, Emily felt increasingly reluctant to survive in the world today. She felt that she did not belong to the present world. David's death made her feel that her living alone was meaningless, like a walking dead. Now that people thought David and she were dead, just let it be and she should not force a "rebirth." She wanted to find a suitable place in the cemetery where she could sleep without waking up, as the destination of her life. She often went to the cemetery, where she saw some tombstones lined with flowers presented by their dear ones. Some of the flower bouquets were fresh, indicating that the family members came recently, and some had withered, indicating that their relatives came a long while ago. She glanced at the names of the dead on the gravestones, thinking that David and she should be their companions. Inadvertently, she noticed a tombstone inscribed with the names of David Polo and Emily Polo, and their DOBs too. Awesome! It was just for David and herself. That was a newer tombstone. It ought to have been built by their relatives for David and her. Emily thought, "David is here, and we're together. That's great. This is my home!"

Emily saw several dried flowers scattered beside her tombstone, as well as some bird droppings and a couple of leaping crickets. She thought that she should be buried in the earth and integrate with the nature. Emily stroked the name of David Polo on the gravestone with her hand. She recalled the time bit by bit with David, especially in their deep mountain adventures when she hurt her leg and David himself was also injured, but walked all the way with her on his back in the jungle, also with water in his mouth from the stream, sent to her mouth. Her tears dropped on the tombstone as she thought of these. "My dear David," she said softly, "I will be with you, and we will never be separated."

Then she lay by the tombstone, hugging the cold stone and falling asleep.

As for David, after he had died in the Wonderland, he was miraculously resurrected due to the reversal of time. He was towed back by the reverse time and recovered little by little to his early state and position until reaching the spot of the time-space tunnel through which he had traversed to the Wonderland. He was pulled into the tunnel, and flew to the other end of it. He flew and flew, and came out of the tunnel finally, back to the point where he and Emily had traversed, the devil angle at the sea of Bermuda. When David was floating on the sea, he was picked up by a local patrol helicopter. Rescuers took David to Miami Relief Center, asked the cause of the accident, and learned that he was from Colorado, had the small aircraft crashed at sea. They assisted him boarding an airplane at Miami airport. Then he flew to Denver, Colorado.

So, David returned to Boulder too. Like Emily, he hesitated and decided not to show up. In the Boulder City Library, he found a record of his plane crash in Bermuda Triangle two years ago on the computer. The incident was a great sensation at that time, adding another layer of mystery to Bermuda Triangle. The names of the two youngsters were also recorded as brave explorers.

David found in the Internet, that his relatives had set up a tombstone for him and Emily in the Columbia Cemetery in Boulder. So, he went to the cemetery and saw the tombstone.

He felt dizzy at the sight of Emily's name engraved on the stone. Emily should have died in the Wonderland. If Emily had come back alone, she should have shown up. Emily was dead and was gone forever. He could not believe and accept the fact. David sat down on the ground, stroking Emily's name on the tombstone, falling into the abyss of despair and depression.

David had some relatives and acquaintances in the city of Boulder. He didn't want to meet them in the street and let them recognize him. He disguised himself with a wig and a fake moustache. Yet his shape and gait were hard to disguise, especially for those who knew him well. Once, David's sister, Jessica, noticed him in the hallway of the Boulder Library. Jessica followed the man who looked like David, watching, and pondering with curiosity, "Could there be anyone in the world who walked and

behaved so much like David?" As the man sat in front of a computer searching for something, the mischievous Jessica deliberately walked beside him, pretending to accidentally bump against
his hair. The man's wig slipped, and Jessica recognized that this
was her brother, David. When David saw Jessica, he panicked. He
couldn't hide himself anymore. He took off his fake moustache
and said with trembling lips, "Jessica, I'm David, your brother.
I'm not dead. Did I surprise you? I missed everyone of you these
years!"

Jessica couldn't believe her eyes and ears. She stared straight
at David, stunned for a long while, and murmured, "Really? You
are David? You are not dead! Then where have you been these
years, David?" David was silent and speechless. Jessica continued, "We thought you and Emily were no longer alive, and
we put up a tombstone in the cemetery for you. Then how about
Emily? Where is she?" David remained silent. Jessica grabbed
David's shirt at the front and demanded, "Tell me, David, you've
got to tell me, where's Emily?" David said, "You don't have to
ask again, Jessica. I'm afraid we'll never see her any longer in our
lives." Jessica drooped her head, with tears rolling down her face.
Although she had seen her "resurrected" brother, she could never
see her beloved sister-in-law again. Jessica asked, "What have
you been doing these years? Why didn't you go home? Don't
you miss Mom, Dad, and Oliver? The child is eight years old and
looks very cute. He always asks when Dad and Mom will come
home."

David was deeply moved and hung his head. After a moment
of silence, he looked into Jessica's eyes and said, "I and your sister-in-law had a magical experience. You'll know the truth later.
I beg you to keep a secret about our meeting today. Don't tell it
to mom, dad, and the child for the time being. I'm in trouble now
and will come home later. Will you promise me, my dear sis-

ter?" Jessica said, "I promise you, brother." "Thanks." David said softly. He gave Jessica a loving hug and hurried away.

Jessica had been in a state of daze ever since she met her brother, David, in the Boulder Library. She kept wondering if the unexpected meeting with her brother the other day was a dream. Was the David that she met a ghost? Two years ago, David and Emily were killed in a plane crash in Bermuda. Were they saved by chance and headed off a danger? But where did they go during this period of time? Why was there no news whatsoever about it? It was even more puzzling that David mentioned that they had a magical experience and was reluctant to speak out the whole matter. Jessica went to the City Library frequently, hoping to meet David there again. But David never showed up ever since their last meeting.

Jessica was now 31 years old and had her own family. She used to be a lively, cheerful girl, but now she became care-laden, heavy-hearted as if with difficulties hard to solve. Her husband, Steve Dodge, noticed her recent changes but could't read her mind.

Steve accompanied Jessica to the psychiatrist for consultation. After the doctor repeatedly questioned her, she told the truth. But the doctor did not believe her story. How could there be such a thing in the world? The doctor thought it was Jessica's psychosis, and said that she should have some psychological shadow in the deeper layers of her mind.

Jessica's parents learned about Jessica's story, but would rather believe that it was true. They talked closely with Jessica. When Jessica mentioned that David and Emily had "a magical experience," she asked her dad what that meant. Dad thought it was abnormal. Bermuda Triangle was an enigma with many mysteries that often exceeded people's imagination. Jessica asked, "Could it be that David and Emily had been hijacked by some Aliens who turned them to Superman and Superwoman who participated in the Star Wars, and lost a battle so they had no face to meet their relatives and friends?" Dad laughed and said, "You, girl, are really imaginative."

David climbed alone up the hills on the west of Boulder City, overlooking the city from the high, steep cliffs. He saw the university buildings and campus that he knew so well. Looming out in the gaps between the lush trees and bushes he could barely see the house of his parents. He recalled his first encounter with Emily on the campus lawn and her first visit to his parents' house. Their lovely son, Oliver, the crystallization of their love, was living in that house now. A sense of loss suddenly came to his mind, accompanied by intense pain in his heart.

In the mind of David often appeared Emily's beautiful face, her generous and decent behavior, her blinking eyes when she was pondering, her good-looking mouth when she spoke. From time to time, he seemed to hear Emily's hearty laughter, good speech with a magnetic voice. David had never seen any other woman with such extraordinary foresight, intelligence, and breadth of mind as Emily. No other woman can replace Emily's position in his heart.

David is extremely unused to the life without Emily. Emily had become an integral part of his life. Without Emily, he got lost, like a sleepwalker. He loved life, but now he lost the courage to live, even thought of death. Only death could allow him to escape from the boundless sea of misery that overwhelmed him day and night and to reunite with Emily in Heaven.

At this time, David seemed to be in a situation in which Hamlet was to determine "to be or not to be."

As for Emily, she lay on the lawn in a park and looked up at the sky. She saw that clusters of white clouds in the sky assuming different shapes that were constantly changing. She saw a young man in white riding a white horse across the sea of clouds, looming. The man on the horse looked like David. Emily called out loudly: "David! David!" But the horse-riding man did not seem to hear it. He rode straight ahead and disappeared into the misty clouds.

Emily recalled her first meeting with David. At that time, she was sitting on a meadow on the campus. David was like a Prince Charming who descended from the sky. Since then, they loved and got along well with each other, leading a sweet and happy life. But after a few years, David first traversed alone to the prehistoric era, then they both crossed to the Wonderland, lost their angelic son. Now their son was back, while their lovely daughter was buried in the World End, having disappeared without a trace. Emily asked the Laotian (Heaven), "Hey my lord, you have generously sent David, the Prince Charming to my side. And now you suddenly and grudgingly took him back? Why, why? This joke is too big. It's not humorous at all, it's too cruel!" Emily thought again. "Maybe I shouldn't blame Laotian, the Creator only determines the "innate," not the later "acquired." It should be my fate that is teasing me."

Emily felt that the days without David were boring and bitter. She felt that her soul was connected to David. Without David, she had simply lost her mind.

Emily couldn't extricate herself from the extreme inner pain, and her spirit almost collapsed.

Both David and Emily were in Boulder now, but they hadn't had the chance to meet each other, each thinking that the other was no longer in the world. Their hearts which beat in unison seemed to be linked. Both of them were ready to die, yearning to reunite with their partner in another world.

They knew that they would become nothing after death, but they wished that there should be another world for them.

David bought a pistol and Emily prepared a bottle of sleeping pills.

That evening Emily came to her grave. She put a lethal dose of sleeping pills piece by piece into her mouth, washed them down with bottled water, then lay on the lawn next to the gravestone, and gradually fell asleep. Emily lay quietly on the grass, assuming a beautiful and plaintive image, just like Ophelia in the play Hamlet, in which there was a scene that Ophelia was lying peacefully on a stream's surface and was floating away with the water. John Millais's famous painting Ophelia had provided a vivid portrayal of the scene.

Later, David came to the cemetery. As he walked towards his gravestone, he found a woman lying there, and when looking closer, he recognized that it was Emily! He looked over and over, and found that Emily was dead, but there was some warmth in her body. It seemed that she had not been dead for long. David lifted Emily's head with both his hands and felt that Emily's hair was still so soft. He kissed her repeatedly on her cheeks. David thought that Emily had just died, he blamed his misjudgment that Emily had passed away long ago, but it was beyond redemption anyway. David was determined to die. He would go with Emily and stay with her forever. David took a pistol from his pocket and pointed it at his right temple. What a tragedy! Just like Shakespeare's play Romeo and Juliet.

David was going to pull the trigger when someone shouted from afar, "Stop it! Stop!" Then came a breathless woman, followed by her husband. She snatched the pistol from the man's hand and growled: "What are you doing, young man?" At this moment, she noticed that this young man was David Polo, who had been known as already dead in Bermuda! David also recognized that the woman was his ex-girlfriend, Audrey. Audrey saw that the woman lying on her back there was Emily, dead. Greatly terrified, she asked in a trembling voice, "Are you people or ghosts?" David looked at Audrey and Jerry and said, "I am not dead. Emily has just died. I'll talk about it later."

"Then why are you going to die today?" cried Audrey, "Do you want to be Romeo and Juliet? You are crazy!"

Audrey saw Emily clutching a bottle of medicine in her hand. She took it and looked at it and said, "Emily took some sleeping pills. I am familiar with these pills. I used them when I was depressed. Let's call an ambulance to rescue Emily. Maybe she can be saved." Jerry dialled 911 on his cell phone.

Before that, Audrey told her husband, Jerry, that she had seen the ghost of Emily. Jerry did not believe it but agreed to go to the cemetery with Audrey to see it. They came to the cemetery, and saw a woman lying in front of a tombstone, while next to the woman a man was holding his gun committing suicide. Audrey recklessly let out a loud cry and stopped the man. As she approached, she found that it was David who was sitting next to the dead Emily.

After a timely rescue, Emily slowly recovered from a deep coma. She found herself lying in a hospital ward, next to David who was accompanying her. She asked David, "Am I in a dream?" David said, "No, you are not in a dream, Emily. We're not dead." Emily said, "I obviously saw that you were already dead at the World End, and I buried you myself." David said, "But the time had gone backwards. I had not only survived, but through that wonderful passage back to Bermuda in the Caribbean. It was incredible. But that night if it were not for Audrey and Jerry to arrive in time, I am afraid we would have already turned into ghosts." Emily's eyes welled up with tears of happiness and excitement.

Emily thought of a difficult problem for both of them, and that was how to explain their terrible experiences to the world. After some discussions, the two of them decided to hide all that from the world, and not to mention the absurd experience to any-one. David and Emily felt that even if they told the truth, others would not believe it, and they might say that the two of them were seducing.

But how to explain the experience in those two years?

They had made up a story: After their plane crashed, they were rescued at sea by a Greek cargo ship. The freighter took them to Naples, Italy. With no money on hand to return to the United States, they were in a dilemma. It coincided with a Chinese freighter that was going to Yantai. The freighter promised to take them to Yantai for free. They boarded the freighter and set sail for China through the Mediterranean Sea, the Red Sea, and Indian Ocean. Then the freighter was unfortunately attacked by some Somali pirates on the way to China. Four people on board, includ-ing David and Emily, were taken hostage in Somalia. They were detained separately in Somalia for two years. After a series of negotiations, they were released when the shipowner paid most amount of the ransom. The two had been missing each other and mistakenly believing that the other was dead. Because of their deep affection and unwillingness to accept the reality of living alone, they chose to reunite in another world by suicide. So there was the type of tragedy as Romeo and Juliet in the graveyard, and the comedy that they were later rescued by Audrey and Jerry. Whether or not the world could fully believe the story they had coined, it could at least avoid the endless heckling of journalists and the constant pursuit by the curious people.

So, David and Emily finally reunited with their relatives and friends in Boulder, including David's parents, sister, brother-in-law, their son, and friends. Everyone was delighted to see David and Emily back "from their deaths." David's parents were in high spirits, Jessica held Emily's hand and could't bear to let go. Their son, Oliver, ran to and fro, kept calling Daddy and Mommy. Emily embraced her son, Oliver, and stared at the little angel in her arms, with joy and happiness in her heart.

David and Emily regarded Jerry and Audrey as their saviors. Since then, the two families had become close friends, not only had frequent contacts, but also talked freely and frankly with each other.

Once Jerry and Audrey bluntly criticized David and Emily.

Jerry: With all due respect, your attempt to commit suicide should be a lack of respect for life. It was an unwise act.

Audrey: Even a blasphemy against the Creator, a stupid and absurd act.

David: You're right. We also regret our impulses.

Emily: Because we loved each other so deeply that we couldn't be relieved for the time being.

Jerry: I can understand that. The touching plot of love and lyricism described in literary and artistic works are actually misleading. The notion "Life is dear, and love is even more precious" is actually a value not worth pursuing.

David: I know that life is the most precious thing of mankind, given by the Creator and one's parents.

Audrey: A person's life, from conception to birth, to upbringing, to growth, contains immense efforts, love and expectations of one's parents and all their dear ones.

Emily: I know that very well. It wasn't easy for my parents to bring me up. I was worried about my son all the time. I missed him every single day when I was away from him.

Jerry: Do you know how sad your relatives would be if they knew you killed yourself?

David: Imaginable.

Audrey: Suppose your son Oliver dies for love when he grows up, what do you think?

Emily: I can not bear it. I will blame him for being stupid, unwise, unfilial, and selfish. Similarly, if I die with some excuse, my son will never forgive me.

David: We almost made an absurdity, and I really repent about it. Hope to get everyone's forgiveness.

Jerry: It's over anyway. It's a good thing you two missed the chance to become "the modern Romeo and Juliet."

Everyone laughed.

*Heaven and the world are far apart, but human nature is interlinked. The a.Ifection between husband and wife, relatives and friends is deeply rooted and hard to be separated.*

*The lives of people and other living things are precious. It's treacherous to deprive the lives of others or oneself. The love tragedy is vivid and touching. But dying for love is not worth advocating or praising.*

# Chapter 20

## SUPREME ENLIGHTENMENT

David and Emily returned to the peaceful life before their traverses. But their experiences at the Wonderland and the World End, their memories of the scenes there, were like fond dreams and nightmares that mingled and lingered around in their minds.

And at the same time, they were thinking about the meaning of life, the world, and the universe.

Emily discovered that the book Tao Te Ching (Moral Scriptures) written by the ancient Chinese philosopher and thinker, Lao Zhu, was very reasonable in many ways and fit well her experiences and ideas.

Lao Tzu says, "Everything under heaven is born of Something and Something comes out of Nothing." "Something" and "Nothing" of the universe supersede each other. This is what Lao Tzu says "Nothing and Something alternate."

Our universe is actually "Something" born out of "Nothing." Its demise is a return from "Something" to "Nothing."

After the destruction of the old world, the new world will regenerate.

This speaks to the creation and demise of the whole universe, which is simple and profound.

This is a great insight, great wisdom.

The universe grows from Nothing, expands from small to large, and is constantly dilating.

That is the reality that today's Big Bang theory reveals.

The expansion of the universe is not infinite. "Young and strong will turn to old and weak," "An extreme will turn to its opposite." The universe will halt when extending to a limit. And then it will give way to contraction, from large to small, from "Something" to "Nothing," and reduce to zero.

That is "the Big Crunch" of the universe. From the Big Bang to the Big Crunch is a life and death process of the universe.

Time and space are interrelated and inseparable from the material. Time and space are virtually the existing forms of the material. So, the contraction of the universe must be accompanied by the reduction of space and the reversal of time. This is the starting point for the universe to come to an end. When David and Emily were at the future world, they had the misfortune to encounter a sudden change in the universe from boom to bust. This kind of disaster is actually the natural prospect and inevitable destination of the universe, the world and mankind.

Emily shared these thoughts with David, who felt the same way and began to study the book of Tao Te Ching. David found that the book by Lao Tzu, the Oriental sage was a great treasure-house of human philosophy, and the wisdom contained in it was comparable to that of the Western philosophers Plato and Aristotle who were ancestors of idealism and materialism.

Whether the world and human beings are created and governed by natural or supernatural force is a crucial issue. Materialism or idealism, which theory is more reasonable, closer to the truth?

David and Emily felt that to interpret everything in the world simply by nature and substance a lot of things could not be well explained. However, if just by supernatural and divine elucidations it was also inconsistent with the facts, and hardly convincing.

David and Emily thought that matter and spirit were inseparable and complement each other. Both materialism and idealism were unavoidably biased. The fusion of the two was the root of Heaven and Earth, the source of all things and the essence of the universe.

David and Emily initiated a theory of "Spirit" and "Matter." It can be summarized as "Unity of Spirit and Matter." Most scientific achievements in the study and exploration of the universe are not contradictory to this theory. Many of them can be incorporated into this theoretical system to support the core value of it. For example, the explosion theory of the universe, the discovery and application of the biological gene (DNA), (Einstein and Hawking's theories of time and the universe, etc., have provided some insights for the theory of Spirit-Matter Unity. Various religions are actually different interpretations of the creation of the world by the Creator in the spiritual aspect, some interesting stories with different plots. Yet, these stories are full of artifacts and superstitions.

The universe and everything in the world are material, visible, and palpable. Whether their formation, operation, and development are completely disordered, directionless, uncontrolled, at random "let it be," "incidentally obtained," or orderly, directional, controlled, tracked, predictable?

The views of David and Emily lean towards the latter. In fact, humans have discovered and recognized many laws of nature.

How then could the universe and everything in the world be controlled?

There ought to be a master or a controller of everything, which should be a supernatural power. It is like an invisible master, manipulating the form and working of the universe. David and Emily called it the Spirit. The "Spirit" is somewhat similar to Lao Tzu's "Tao." Lao Tzu says, "The Tao is the source of all things." "The Tao pours out everything into life. It is a cornucopia that never runs dry, it is immense and boundless, like the origin of all things."

Lao Tzu also says, "The sky and the Earth cannot last long, not to say people." Here he makes it clear that the universe and human beings will not live forever and will eventually die. This is what Lao Tzu refers to as "born to die." People are doomed from the moment they are born, sooner or later. It is the law of nature and is perfectly justified.

Zhuangzi has inherited the thoughts of Lao Tzu. He believes that the origin of the world is "Tao." He says, "There is no start and end for the Tao but life and death for everything else." The "Spirit" that David and Emily refer to is different. "Spirit" does not exist in the state of "nothing" or "zero." Once the universe is gone and returned to zero, the Spirit of the Universe ceases to exist. In their eyes, "Spirit" and "Matter" are interdependent, inseparable, and integrated. David and Emily have not fully embraced the Taoist theory but have abandoned the eternal concept of the Tao.

Taoism believes that the Tao precedes Everything, and gives birth to Everything, the Tao lives forever while Everything else has its life. David and Emily believe that Spirit and Matter form one unity. They coexist, rather than that Spirit comes first and Matter later, and that Spirit lasts forever while Matter will extinct.

Living creatures and life are a particularly wonderful kind of existence in the universe, a combination of Matter and Spirit. It has births and deaths, and also inheritance and mutations formed and restricted by DNA and external influences. It needs nutrients to maintain itself, like a fire that requires constant fuel addition for maintenance.

The human brain can think, it is like a smart machine, but also like the "hardware" in the computer, to carry out various thinking procedures according to instructions. What commands the brain is an invisible piece of "software." It is the human "Soul."

Each person has a Soul and a Body, like a small universe.

The Soul and the Body are inseparable. When a person dies, his (or her) Soul disappears. This is different from Lao Tzu's doctrine and those of some religions.

The body and life of a living creature are one spiritual entity.

Inorganic objects like inanimate stars, mountains, stones, drops of water are all inanimate. They are not spirit- matter unities. They are governed directly by the spirit of the universe.

David and Emily noticed that the Spirit was spiritual.

There are various levels of spirituality. The spiritual paramount in the universe is the Spirit of the Universe that leads the universe, including humans and other living creatures.

The spirituality of human beings is far superior to that of other living creatures, but it is incomparable to the spirituality of the Creator.

Other living creatures have varying degrees of spirituality. Apes, for example, have relatively higher spirituality, and plants have relatively lower spirituality.

David and Emily found that the Spirit of the Universe designed and controlled the universe and life, which under different conditions would display a certain degree of autonomous behavior and free expression, going its own way, far from being mechanical, largely manipulable, and predictable. This was actually a function of the Spirit of the Universe. The irregular operation of some stars in the universe that collided with each other was not necessary and predictable. People's environment, destiny, ability, and achievements were different. They performed life dramas of various features on the stage of life.

Each person has its own independent "Soul." The Soul determines a person's character, behavior, integrity, and even the destiny of a lifetime.

Human performance is to a considerable extent autonomous. This is different from artificial intelligence, intelligent chess games, or GPS positioning system. The artificial intelligence, intelligent chess games, or GPS positioning system stipulates the optimal strain mode adopted under various conditions, which is programmed, or prescriptive.

Today, robots and other intelligent products designed by humans are increasingly ingenious and intelligent. However, compared with the universe, the human beings and other creatures designed by the Spirit of the Universe, the human design works are naive and inferior, and cannot reach the level of "elementary."

Some people say that the life of the human beings is a vicissitude. In fact, the same is true of the world and the universe. Rapid changes are at hand. Time flies. All creatures on Earth are born and die, like a river with water never stops flowing, wave upon wave. People see their parents grow old, get sick, and die. One also notices that a person grows from childhood to juvenile, youth, middle aged, and elderly. One's children and grandchildren are growing day by day. The changes are dizzying.

It is often said that time flies like an arrow. Not only the rapid passage of the past, but every minute, every day, every month, every year passes on in a twinkling of an eye. We are like riding on a high-speed train, no, on a spacecraft that is even faster than the speed of light. All things around it sweep by like the lightning, instantly left behind.

The motion of the universe is even more remarkable.

There is a cycle for the emergence and extinction of the universe, cycle after cycle, just like the pendulum swinging back and forth, or the beacon with light on and off. On the macro level, the birth and death of the universe is but in the blink of an eye.

What does a man's life count, even if the centenarian age?

David and Emily see all of this, at this time their views and comprehension of everything are grand and magnificent as if overlooking from a commanding height.

David and Emily have witnessed and suffered the pain of purgatory of the World End, David also had a fantastic experience in prehistoric primitive society. Emily saw through the life of people on the sky canopy. In addition to their special experiences in the future world, they diligently think about the macro world over and over again, being inspired by the wisdom of the Western and Eastern philosophers, have formed a comprehensive view about the universe and life. Now they have been greatly discerning and apprehending by a supreme enlightenment.

> *The universe is vast, the land is wide, while the life of a living creature is brief. Everything changes from time to time. Who governs all the ups and downs? What is the source? The integration of the spirit and the matter is the answer and the truth. Materialism and idealism are both biased. Human intelligence is constantly improving, but it is no match to the creation by the Spirit of the Universe. From macroscopic to microscopic, celestial bodies and individuals are all rising and falling, being born and dying, constantly changing, circulating and reversing. This is the eternal path, the normal state of the universe.*

# Chapter 21

## CREATED BY HEAVEN AND EARTH

avid and Emily had a deep and comprehensive understanding of the universe and human life. But their explorations did not stop there.

How the universe, the planets in the universe, and the creatures on the planets, are born out of nothing? How do they assume their special forms?

Emily was thinking that after the big bang, matter formed numerous spheres in the sky. Would they flow off like a series of soap bubbles moving in the air, or would they follow some rules, forming large and small galaxies, according to the preset organization with stars that follow a pattern?

The biological world is more mysterious. Does an animal, or plant, grow a certain way, by accident or chance, or by following a predetermined blueprint?

Is everything in the universe pre-designed? This is a crucial issue. The design of everything in the world, especially man, is extremely mysterious. This kind of design cannot be accomplished by the human brain, the wisdom of human beings, even with advanced artificial intelligence. The level of human design is very naive. In this sense, there should be certain superb pre-design, not "natural generation." The so- called natural generation is actually no direction, no target, and grows randomly and accidently. This kind of statement cannot explain the current regular movement of the earth and sky, neither everything in the world.

If the universe and the world and the creatures on earth are pre-designed, who is this superb designer? These questions always lingered in Emily's mind. She was meditating about them and the answers were hard to find. One night, "the Heavenly Wise Man" appeared in her dream to guide her.

The Heavenly Wise Man said, "Madam, considering your eager to learn and your sincerity to Heaven, I would like to give you a little guidance. You and your husband are smart enough, knowledgeable, and have experienced the rise and fall of the future together. Your husband traversed alone to the distant ancient times. You had once watched the celestial visions with me. You should be able to comprehend the meaning of what I will convey to you with a little hint." Emily rejoiced and said, "I would like to hear your valuable advice, Sir."

The Heavenly Wise Man left Emily a few words in her dream, which benefited Emily a lot.

Emily recorded His remarks as follows:

Thinking back to the beginning of all, the origin was nothing and empty. The Heaven and Earth were zero, vacant, silent, and quiet. One day, chaos was suddenly dispersed, the sky was full of twinkling stars, the earth covered with countless creatures. It was a scene of prosperity.

The sun, the moon, and the stars were running regularly. The living creatures on earth are active, constantly proliferating, emerging, and perishing.

Who made all of them and how? How did they assume different shapes?

Here's the answer: "Created by Heaven and molded by Earth, actively and conditionally."

Emily thanked the Heavenly Wise Man repeatedly.

The Heavenly Wise Man bid farewell to Emily and flew away by riding on a cloud.

Emily was overjoyed as if she had acquired the authentic scripture. She repeatedly pondered on the meaning of "Created by Heaven and molded by Earth, actively and conditionaly," and suddenly, a light dawned on her. The Heavenly Wise Man was right.

In the doctrine of a certain religion, it is said that humans are created by the Almighty God according to his own appearance, which is obviously unreasonable. Human appearance is not randomly generated. Their body shape, facial features, bones, internal organs, etc., are all functional and adapted to the ground environment, just like the body shape of a fish is suitable for living in water and the body shape of a bird is suitable for flying in the air. The appearance of God should adapt to the environment of heaven and should not be the same as that of people on earth.

The shape and variety of things were neither arbitrarily nor naturally formed. Neither were they kneaded by the omnipotence deity with His subjective imagination, out of clay, one by one, within a week, nor were they carved by external strength, like the water scouring the stones in the river to form round pebbles in a span of a thousand years.

After all, the external environment was an external force. It would not create lively animals by wind and sunshine out of thin air. The Monkey King jumping out of the stone was just a figment of the novel writer.

Creation is done by the combination and synergy of internal and external forces. This is the so-called "created by Heaven and molded by Earth, actively and conditionally."

The Creator creates and governs all things, including not only the galaxies and stars in the universe, but also the people and all kinds of creatures on some planets. Its design is subtle and magical, incomparable, but not random and disorderly. Just take living creatures for example, first of all, they can only appear and survive on a planet with the right conditions.

There is water, air, sunlight, the right temperature, ultraviolet rays, and pressure on the earth, so there are living things on the earth. In addition, the internal structure and external morphology of a species depend on its environmental conditions. For example, birds have streamlined wings and bodies, which are suitable for flying in the sky. Wolves have four legs and a coat of fur, suitable for survival on land. Fish in the water is streamlined, with water-foiled fins, which draws water. It does not need to breathe constantly in the air, suitable for living in the water. In addition, the internal organs of birds, beasts, fish, and shrimps also have their own structure to adapt to different environments.

The biological gene DNA works mainly internally, but also bear outside force on certain level and show some kind of mutation.

The most common example is the transformation of dogs from wolves. As a result of long-term breeding and variety selection, some wolves have gradually lost their wildness and become tame and friendly dogs. They are differentiated from other wolves, and their genes were affected, but they have not transformed into other species. Other examples are feral cats turning into domestic cats, cattle, horses, pigs, and sheep being domesticated in captivity, and differentiated from their wild counterparts.

"Created by Heaven" is the design and creation of the universe and all living things by the Creator actively.

"Molded by Earth" is the external restrictions, constraints on the created things, to make them adapt to the external environment, hence "conditionally."

Creationism focuses on supernatural creation, ignoring the limitations imposed by external conditions on biological appearance. Evolutionism focuses on natural conditions, ignoring the internal motivation of bioforming. The theory of spirit – matter unity integrates creationism and evolutionism and reveals the origin of biological species comprehensively and objectively.

Why should all things in the world be such a riot of colors, such a feast for the eyes?

Each species in the universe usually has to adapt to its living environment and conditions, it is reasonable and diverse, and there are numerous kinds of species. There are hawks, crows, swallows, pigeons, etc., in the sky. There are cows, horses, pigs, dogs, etc., on the ground. There are fish, shrimps, clams, crabs, etc., in the water. And so on, and so forth.

Individuals in the same species are not identical, like copies from a photocopier. It is difficult for the human eye to distinguish each of the sparrows in a flock, and it is hard to tell the differences of each piece of the grasse in a patch. But it does not mean that they can be confused, no distinction between each other.

There are billions of people in the world today. Their appearances look alike, but they are different and rarely confused. Nowadays, facial recognition technology is used to identify people, which is widely applied, such as in security inspection, mobile phone, credit card, ticket purchase, paying bills, and so on. It is inconceivable that there should be such a great variety of the human images. The designing ability of the Creator is far beyond human imagination.

It has been found that the diversity of living species in the world and the distinction between individual organisms in each species rely on a wonderful life code — gene. Genes support the basic elements and properties of life, storing all the information about life processes. The number of living creatures in the world are endless, as vast as the sea. Yet all are distinguishable. Just look at the fingerprints of people, thousands of patterns for thousands of people, absolutely not identical. The creation of the Creator is incredible and magical.

The Creator differentiates the creatures by their genetic mechanism, which enables each biological species and individual to maintain its basic characteristics. Heredity and variation go together. Environment is one of the factors contributing to the variation. The mutual dependence of environment and heredity deduces the reproduction of life and vitality.

Emily introduced the idea of "Created by Heaven and molded by Earth" to David. David agreed to it readily. He believed that human, this superior animal, was a perfect example of the concept Created by Heaven and molded by Earth. The human body and limbs, in particular, the clever brain makes a person extraordinarily competent, being able to command the wind and clouds, to develop their abilities to the fullest, to excel in the environment of the earth. Almost every part of the human body is designed to be reasonable and useful. For example, the four fingers of the human hand are separated from the thumb, which is convenient for manual labor, and the nails have a good protection effect on the fingertips. Each finger in three sections, flex and extend freely. If human hands were like human feet, or like the bear's paw or the chicken's claw, it would be impossible for human beings to perform a variety of delicate and meticulous work.

Isn't it funny if an elephant or an ostrich trying to use a computer or mobile phone like a human?

The idea of the creation by Heaven and Earth combines the thinking streams of idealism and materialism, as well as the human origin theories of creation and evolution while rejecting their own insularities.

Of all the living things on earth, why can mankind enjoy the privilege of His Creator and stand out as a superior animal far more capable than any other creatures? Humans rule, enslave, and consume other living creatures. With its constant development of intelligence, science and technology, and social progress, mankind seems to have the potential to dominate the entire universe.

What advantages and qualifications do humans have? What virtues do they possess to be the favorite of Heaven? Emily thought hard, always missing the point.

It was the Heavenly Wise Man again who appeared in Emily's dream and tackled the maze for her.

The Heavenly Wise Man left her a motto of "Unceasing, No Full," and asked her to ponder it over.

Emily was so smart that she quickly realized the connotation of the wise man.

"Unceasing" means the continuous progress of mankind, not satisfied with the status quo. "No Full" means that human beings are not proud of their progress and keep trying to take it to a higher level.

People have the need to engage in a variety of complex work, as well as the interest in scientific research, culture, and entertainment, so their brain is developed, along with the flexible hands and fcct. Whcn the Creator designs a creature, He must adapt to its needs. The basic needs of other animals are foraging, survival, mating, and reproduction. Besides, they seem to have no extravagant aspirations while being satisfied with their status quo. Therefore, the endless demand of mankind has caused its internal and external plastic interaction, so that human beings stand prominently among the living creatures, being the greatest and most gorgeous species on earth.

*Things in the world are complicated and move orderly. They are created by Heaven and molded by Earth. Heaven refers to internal forces and Earth refers to external forces. The internal and external forces cooperate and interact, then there are the world and things on it.*

# Chapter 22

## THE POLO CONJECTURE

David and Emily had a sober view of the universe and life, which also aroused a greater interest in heaven and Earth in their conversations. That day they inadvertently touched the topic of heaven and Earth in a daily chat.

Emily: We live in a universe that contains numerous large galaxies, each of them contains countless small galaxies, each small galaxy contains millions of stars, each star contains various chemical elements of substance, each chemical element is composed of molecules, the molecule can be further divided into smaller particles called atoms, an atom is divided into nuclei and electrons, and so on. This is a series of entities, ranging from large to small.

David: Acording to the principle of quantum mechanics, the material can be infinitely divided.

Emily: In that case, is the size of the universe the absolute maximum? Can humans only stop here in their exploration in the macroscopic direction?

David: Oh. That's an interesting question. Some people have proposed the theory of multiple cosmos that the universe in which we live in is not unique, and there are other universes in parallel. Stephen William Hawking, the outstanding British physicist and cosmologist, asserts that the number of universes is more than tens of trillions.

Emily: Large entity like the universe can be inexhaustibly divided into small ones. Among them are always that a larger entity contains and governs a number of smaller ones. Layer upon layer. So there should be a large entity that contains and governs the many universes. Then what is it?

David: Yeah, we can't help questioning about it with this kind of big-to-small inclusiveness and governance.

Emily: I'm thinking that our universe, in the macroscopic view, is just a small entity, like a molecule or a cell, and maybe there's a larger entity over it. That entity contains an infinite number of universes, and our universe is just one of them. Furthermore, there may be even larger entities on top of those large entities, and so forth.

David: Super! What a wonderful idea! I think it should be possible. Since there is infinitely small, then there should be infinitely large. This is not fanciful.

Emily: If we regard our universe as the largest, we are limiting our vision. At present, we are only limited to the range that the Harbert telescope or the high power electronic telescopes can reach. We think that our universe is so big, and in fact we are probably as short-sighted as the mice that can only see inches before their eyes.

David: Emily, You're telling a wonderful story. According to your story, there may be a larger entity on top of our universe. The idea of going in the macroscopic direction is likely to have an infinite number of layers. Viewing at a higher level, the creation and extinction of a universe is as normal as the emergence and death of a cell in a human tissue. Cells need to be constantly updated.

Emily: I think there should be life on many planets in the universe, and the universe we live in should be organic. Let's say that it is just a small cell in the internal organs of a huge human body, inside the skin, or inside the nostrils, even in the toe. It could also be in the eyes of a giant cat, in the teeth of a giant python, in the wings of a giant fly in the upper universe. All of this is possible, not a fantasy.

David: So, our sacred universe could be in the cheek or lips of an elegant and beautiful girl in the upper universe, or on the butt or tail of an ugly and nasty hyena. Interesting! Emily, you have such a rich imagination, it is really impressive.

Emily: This idea has broadened our horizons. We were like frogs in a well that are suddenly brought to a vast expanse of an ocean.

David: I think it's a reasonable inference or assumption.

The idea is valuable, but it requires tangible evidence and systematic theory to prove it, support it, and improve it.

Emily: Yes. This is a philosophical derivation. Human understanding of nature is often guided by hypotheses and inferences, and then gradually verified, refined and deepened.

David: Correct. In quantum mechanics, the concept of negative ions was first derived theoretically from the concept of positive ions, and negative ions were discovered and confirmed later. The mathematical world had a Goldbach's Conjecture, which was cracked by Chen Jingrun, a prominent Chinese mathematician. Here we might call our idea "the Jin Li Conjecture."

Emily: No. This is the idea that we both share. It should be called "the Polo Conjecture." Polo represents both of us. Don't forget, my name is Emily Polo (An American woman changes her last name to her husband's after getting married).

David: OK. "The Polo Conjecture" is actually an initiative and a proposal to explore the macro realm in the study of the universe. There may be larger layers of entities above our universe that we have to explore.

Emily: So, the universe we are in is the smallest of the layers of the universes. There are no smaller universes under our universe?

David: It is reasonable to say that there should be. Perhaps an electron could contain countless small universes. There is a smaller universe under a small universe. Layer upon layer, infinitesimal.

Emily: Wow! Fantastic! We have infinity up here and infinitesimal down there.

David: That's possible.

If we refer to the first cosmic entity above our universe as Upper Universe 1, the cosmic entity above the Upper Universe 1 as Upper Universe 2, and so on, we have Upper Universe 3, Upper Universe 4, etc., to form the Upper Universe N Series.

Also under our universe there will be a "Lower Universe N Series."

ll these entities up and down our universe add up to form an infinite series of entities, which we can call Superuniverse or Super Cosmos).

Emily: Now we have a complete model. To me, it's a bit like the Russian matryoshka, with layers upon layers.

David: It's a bit like that. But the number of layers in the Superuniverse is infinite.

Emily: So, do you think this idea conflicts with our theory of "Spirit-Matter unity?"

David: I think it is consistent with the theory of Spirit-Matter unity. The supreme being should still be the "Creator." In the past, we limited the scope of the Creator's command to our universe, and in fact we underestimated him, not justified to its talents.

The super universe is the largest Spirit-Matter Unity. Emily: So, the super universe is the largest Spirit-Matter Unity. It consists of layers of universe controlled by the Creator. Each cosmic layer contains countless lower layers of universes. Each universe holds countless galaxies and planets.

David: Yes. Every universe has its birth and death, like the cells in the human body. So, does the Creator also have life and death? Will it be as the Taoism advocates that the Tao (Spirit) will last forever, while things (Matter) will die?

Emily: Spirit and Matter should be a unity. Both should live and die together.

David: That's right. In addition to the life and death of the individual universe, the huge super universe and the supreme Creator should also have life and death, in a super macro cycle. That is, "something" is born of "nothing," and it boils down to "nothing."

Emily: The spirituality of the Creator is supreme in the super universe, higher than the spirituality of all universes, not to mention the spirituality of human beings. Human beings are just a kind of intelligent creature on certain planets in certain universes.

David: The spirituality of human beings on Earth cannot be compared to that of the Superuniverse. There is a world of difference between the two. This is why there are always puzzles in the universe that people on Earth are hard to crack and there are always designs and arrangements in the world that are infinitely awesome.

Emily: Aliens' visits to our globe is one of the wonders and mysteries to be explained. I think Aliens on other planets are perfectly possible.

David: Mr. Gan Ruida whom we met at Sanxingdui is a descendant of Aliens. Although his blood is not pure and his Alien genes are very weak, there are no signs of the ugly, mythical Aliens of the legendary Alien image in him. Alien are also humans.

Emily: Alien civilization is not necessarily inferior to human civilization on Earth. Aliens can come to Earth, and can work miracles on it, which shows that the development level of Aliens is not lower than that of the Earth people. It is said that some Alien civilizations have surpassed our planet for at least 10,000 years.

David: We saw many achievements of human civilization in our last global tour, such as the towering spectacular buildings, the bustling metropolis, the convenient transportation, the highly developed literature, fine art, and music. It seems that this is not unique to our Earth people. There might be human civilizations and cultural achievements on other planets, which may even be more glorious and resplendent and colorful.

Emily: With the development of science and technology, humans can also travel by UFO or spacecraft to explore and roam on other human planets. It appears to the local people there that we are the amazing "Aliens."

David: Interesting!

Emily: I'm also thinking, people on the planets in our universe cannot only travel and communicate with each other through spaceships, they can also communicate with humans on planets of other universes, or even other layers of universe

David: Ah, that's a bit out of line. The distance is so far away that it's almost impossible and inaccessible.

Emily: However, humans on Earth can get there in another way.

David: Are you talking about time and space crossing?

Emily: Exactly. The Superuniverse has even more expansion of time and space, among which there must be a larger span and more types of time and space tunnels.

David: But as far as we know, the current crossings are accidental and passive, and there is no controllable, active crossing.

Emily: I think there are a lot of existing tunnels in the universe. People can take the initiative to traverse through them as long as they find them and learn the destinations of them.

David: Humans will eventually find all kinds of tunnels to traverse through. People can come and go between the stars in the universe, between the past and the future.

Emily: What a fascinating sight!

David: But from a macro perspective, it's not beyond the realm of the "Super Universe."

Emily: Sun Wukong (the Monkey King) turns over a somersault covering a million miles, but he finds himself still in the palm of the Buddha.

David: Well. The more we talk the more we seem to be apart from the topic.

*The original model of a series of universes organized in layers seems absurd, but it shows the infinity in macro and micro scopes. This idea is ingenious and seemingly nonsense, but it is derived by logical reasoning, and is rational in phylosophy. It opens up people's minds and visions, and it shows them a new paradigm for understanding the universe, the world, and humanity.*

*Humans have made great achievements in the scientific exploration of the universe, but there are limitations. The empiricism and calculus of materialism is facing a bottleneck. The unraveling of the mysteries of the universe and life seems impossible without the aid of philosophical reasoning. Some new perspective might as well be added to the too deadlocked way, from the limit into the infinite, in order to browse the broader space.*

# Chapter 23

## SURVIVORS OF A DISASTER

t had been two years since David and Emily returned from the distant horizon. Both of them devoted to researches in cosmology and philosophy. This was a bit of a departure from their original majors, but it brought them endless pleasure and satisfaction. They published jointly a number of important papers and books. In particular, their unique views and insights about "spirit-matter unity" "created by Heaven and Earth" and "multilayer universe " had an important impact in the relevant academic fields.

Occasionally, they would inevitably fall into contemplation, recalling their magical experiences of the past.

David and Emily thought they were lucky enough to have seen and experienced the perfection of "the Wonderland," and fortunately escaped the disaster of the Doomsday of the world and returned to the current world through a time-space tunnel. They were about to merge with the future humanity to perish, dying out with the future world and universe in the demise to zero. They were actually lucky enough to survive the rest of their lives.

At the End of the World, all the people there were killed, why should only they two have survived? They studied and discussed this question seriously. They concluded that they had passed through the tunnel of time and space from the past, for they were the only people in the Wonderland who could return to the distant past by reverse-crossing through the time tunnel. Their daughter, Sophia, who was born in the Wonderland, had no chance to cross back to the origin of her parents.

One afternoon, Emily received a call from a hotel saying that a guest was coming to visit them and that they would know who he was when they saw the guest. Emily was a bit puzzled. The doorbell rang in less than an hour. The visitor was a Chinese man, accompanied by his wife and a boy. As soon as he saw Emily and David, he shook hands warmly with them. "Do you still remember me, David, Emily?" the man asked. Emily was stunned and looked at him for a while. Then she blurted out: "Hey, you are Fang Hua! You guy, I almost couldn't recognize you!" Fang Hua was now dressed neatly and elegantly in an elated air. He looked like a different person as when they met him in Yantai last time.

David also recognized Fang Hua and said, "It's you, Mr. Fang. Sorry that I offended you in Yantai last time, I hope that Mr. Fang will bear with it." Fang Hua said, "Oh, not at  all. I need to thank you both. Otherwise, I will get deeper and deeper in the quagmire, and the consequences will be disastrous." Emily brought each of them a cup of coffee.

Everyone began to talk freely. Fang Hua said that he was released from jail ahead of time in just one year and two months because of his good performance in prison. After several years of hard work, he set up an audio-visual products company in Yantai. The company was doing well. He was well-off, and then he had a warm home with a wife and a son.

Emily said, "Mrs. Fang is so young." "Fang Hua is eight years older than me." said, Madam Fang, " I think that's OK. I like him because he is good and talented. He sings well. I was so fascinated by his singing that I walked along with him."

Emily asked, "Are you traveling in the United States this time?" Fang Hua said: "Yeah. We first went to California and toured there for a few days. I learned in China that you two were killed in a Bermuda expedition a few years ago, but we didn't really believe it. With that in mind, when we were in California we asked the online tracing agency to help us find your current address and phone number. Then we came to Colorado." Fang Hua's son, Xiaohua, was already four years old. He knew some English, and was now talking with Oliver.

In their conversation, Fang Hua also mentioned Ding Zhiyang and Anna, who had opened a café in Yantai. Fang Hua said, "This couple is well-known in Yantai and is now running a Western restaurant. Sometimes, we went to their restaurant to have our dinner. The girl Beilei whom you rescued learned from the media that both of you had died in a Bermuda adventure. She was so grieved that she set up a memorial tablet for you, placed it at home, and worshiped you on important occasions."

David and Emily were very excited to learn about Ding Zhiyang, Anna, and their daughter, Beilei, as if they had suddenly gotten news of their long-lost relatives. Fang Hua said, "The first thing after we return to Yantai is to bring a message to Zhiyang, Anna, and Beilei and tell them about our meeting with you here. If the Ding family learn that you are still alive, you cannot imagine how happy they will be."

David and Emily proposed to let Fang Hua sing a song. Fang Hua sang "Yesterday Once More" in English:

> When I was young
> I'd listened to the radio
> Waiting for my favorite songs
> When they played I'd sing along
> It makes me smile.
> !ose were such happy times
> And not so long ago
> How I wondered where they'd gone
> But they're back again
> Just like a long lost friend

All the songs I loved so well.Fang Hua presented David and Emily with some high- end audio and video products, including his own songs.

David and Emily entertained the guests with Western food. Then they drove around Boulder City with them and toured in the nearby mountains. The Fang family admired the environment here very much. Fang's family bid farewell to David and Emily and went on traveling to the east of the US.

It was some time since David and Emily returned from the distant horizon. Unable to bear loneliness, they took their son, Oliver, to Las Vegas for a tour.

The three of them took a plane to Las Vegas, planning to stay there for a few days and have fun.

They stayed in the luxurious Wynn Hotel. Although the conditions here were already quite high-end, luxurious, and almost top-notch in the world today, they were still not as comfortable and pleasant living environment of Wonderland. In those days, they toured the casinos one by one. Each of these luxurious buildings had its own characteristics. There was a casino called The Venetian, which showed the style of Italian Renaissance in the 16th century and the water city of Venice, with small bridge across the water, and boating on the river. Oliver cried out to take a boat, so they bought tickets to board the long and narrow wooden boat, rippling in the river. The sailor was singing while rowing, which was poetic. The whole family enjoyed the fantastic scenery of Venice along the coast, looking up at the artificial blue sky.

After landing, they stepped into the casino hall. They saw that there were Renaissance works of art all around, such as classical zenith paintings, classical sculptures, and large- scale imitations of Michelangelo's famous sculpture David.

The family took a group photo in front of the sculpture.

One by one they saw luxury casinos in the gambling city with different appearances and characteristics. The interior decoration was even more dazzling, magnificent, and extremely luxurious. They wondered how much money these buildings had cost. It seemed that various casinos were fighting for the game, competing who could throw more money in it without the blink of an eye. It was said that the total investment of the Venetian Hotel in Las Vegas was nearly $1.8 billion.

Oliver was dazzled and asked innocently, "Why are the people here so rich?" "The owners of the casinos make a lot of money from gamblers." aid father David, "They set aside a small portion to decorate the casinos and attract gamblers in order to make more money." Emily said, "People know the truth of "Ten bets and nine losses," but gamblers try their luck with the psychology of winning by luck. Most of them come here to deliver money to the casino owner." Oliver said, "These people are really stupid!"

In the evening they went to the street to watch the fountain on the roadside. The spouting water splashed into the sky, wave after wave, rumbling when falling down, accompanied by beautiful music, very spectacular. As they made their way through the crowd, Oliver saw that some one was handing out a small card with a picture of a pretty girl on it, he asked, "What's that? Let's have one too." David told Oliver, "No, No. don't ask for that." Oliver asked, "Why?" Emily said, "Kids don't understand. Don't ask." It turned out that it was to solicit business for the porn business. Oliver had to give up.

Once, when they were walking along the road, they saw a tramp begging from passers-by. The tramp was dressed in rags and dirty, holding a paper board with handwriting words "HOMELESS Need Your Help." He had a dog with him, and the dog lay beside him. Emily searched her pockets for some cash to give it to him. Then David approached the man and looked carefully at him. He asked the man, "Excuse me Sir, are you Uncle Hank? I'm David Polo. Do you still remember me?" David recognized this man as his uncle Timothy Polo's former sexual partner. He remembered that Hank was more than ten years younger than his uncle Timothy. He used to be a handsome young man. Now it seemed that this guy was at his sixties. The man looked at

David and said, "Yes. I'm your Uncle Hank, David. Ain't you in trouble in Bermuda?" David said, "Reason let me go.

I'm back in Colorado. Let's talk about it later. How did you end up like this?" Hank smiled and said, "Like this? What's wrong with this?" David was a little puzzled and frowned. Hank said casually, "I'm completely free, come and go naked, with no worries and cares. It's cool! Chic!" "I've heard about the state-run homeless shelter," said Emily "where you can always live a more stable life if you go there." Hank didn't seem to hear it, humming a song in Spanish, "Quizas, quizas, quizas…. (Perhaps, perhaps, perhaps)." Emily handed him two twenty-dollar bills. Hank took the bills over, laughed, and thanked Emily and David again and again. "Wow! Forty bucks! It's enough for me to have a good meal! With some beer!" David asked. "You've been with my uncle for years, I heard that he had left you some legacy before he died." "I threw all of it in there." He pointed his finger at the casinos in front. "I have no children. What do I want so much money for?"

During the stay of David's family in Las Vegas, one of the largest shootings in the United States occurred overnight. While people were holding a music festival in the plaza near the Mandalay Bay Hotel, the crowd was suddenly pelted with gunfire from a window on the 32nd floor of the hotel. The shooter used a burst of automatic guns to fire at the crowd. Later it was ascertained that the murderer was a man named Stephen Paddock, at the age of sixty-four. He possessed multiple automatic firearms and a large number of bullets and committed suicide after the shooting.

David and Emily fortunately didn't go to the music festival that night because the child needed to go to bed on time in the evening and couldn't stay too late.

The next day, there was a lot of talk about the shooting. It was said that 58 people were killed and 413 injured in the shooting. There was also a tramp among the dead, and his dog had been guarding his body. David said, "Oh. The dead tramp must be Uncle Hank." Emily looked sad and dropped her head. Uncle Hank was alone most of his life and had been pursuing a free and dissolute life. Now he disappeared in this world.

Emily: Let's pay tribute to Uncle Hank and the victims of the shooting.

David: This savage and brutal event should not have happened in today's society. In recent years, there have been numerous shootings in various places. In Colorado alone, there have been Columbine High School massacre and Aurora cinema shootings.

Emily: Life is the most precious thing for a person. No one has the right to deprive others of their lives. Even with a felony, the death penalty should be applied with caution. The death penalty has been abolished in more than one hundred countries in the world.

David: The United States ranks first in mass shootings in the world. On average, more than 5,000 people are killed in mass shootings each year.

Emily: Private ownership of guns is a big problem. Strict control of private gun ownership is imperative.

David: According to the constitution of the United States, citizens have the right to own guns. The government has also called for a ban on guns, but more than half of the citizens surveyed in the country disagree. Citizens of the United States have a strong support for private guns.

Emily: Imagine how many civilian casualties would have been avoided without a private grab of guns.

David: But with guns people can defend themselves and oppose the government in some cases. The number of people who want to buy guns in Colorado has increased dramatically since the cinema shooting. Private ownership of guns is part of American culture.

Emily: It's hard for me to accept such a culture.

David: The United States is seeking some proper ways to control the private guns.

Emily: Not only the shooting, but also the terrorist attacks, suicide bombings and so on in the world are barbaric acts against civilization and humanity.

David: More than 3,000 people died in the September 11 terrorist attacks in New York 11 years ago. Terrorists claimed the lives of countless innocent people at the expense of their own lives. This is a paralysis of the precious life and a violation of human civilization.

Emily: Moreover, human wars cause massive casualties among soldiers and civilians. It's a barbaric practice with tens of millions of people died in each world war. Besides, there were wars between nations and civil wars within countries.

Even man-made disasters in peaceful times could cause millions of people lose their lives. I hope everyone in the world should cherish one's own life as well as the lives of others.

David and Emily had seen what human life should be like a thousand years later. Returning to the world before crossing, they noticed more clearly the shortcomings and deficiencies of today's society. Although the United States was strong in national strength, leading the world in politics, economy, science and technology, and was the most ideal immigration country in the world, there were actually many disadvantages, such as the frequent shootings, the unnecessary wrestle for their own power, the irrational wastage of resourses and time in struggle between the political parties are beyond mutual supervision and benign interaction. Society in America today is generally harmonious, but the gap between rich and poor is large, and it is still growing. People in the Wonderland are generally prosperous, and there is almost no gap between the rich and the Poor. Gambling and pornography are extinct (The aforementioned Beauty Garden is a laboratory, not a place of pornography). People don't know what beggars and tramps are. No guns, no shooting.

David and Emily were leading a happy and meaningful life in their middle age.

The fact about what happened in the two years when David and Emily were missing remained unknown. Those things, they carefully concealed mentioning even to their son as a taboo.

However, over time, such a big secret was hard to keep forever, and it would eventually leak out in some way.

That fall, David and Emily were invited to an international symposium on cosmology and Hawking theories at the University of Cambridge, England, for the outstanding achievements in their research.

At the symposium, they presented their latest paper on cosmic black holes and space-time crossing. There was a heated discussion at the meeting about the possibility of human crossing the time tunnel. David and Emily's views were strongly disputed. For the first time in a desperate situation, they revealed to the world the experience of their personal journey to the future world. Their adventures opened the eyes of the participants. Many still remained skeptical, asking them to show some solid evidence, otherwise, their presentation would be treated as academic fraud.

David and Emily were prepared for it. They showed the clothes they wore when they came back from the future world. These clothes were not only different in style, but also in texture and craftsmanship. Besides, the material could not be traced to any textile ever produced in the current world. Yet a few people still had doubts, saying that different clothes were not evidential enough.

David and Emily took out their "killer mace." It was a pocket card that was lighter and more versatile with more features than today's smartphones. It contained the holder's ID and various information, as well as numerous photographs taken in the Wonderland. It had been unintelligible and couldn't be read when it was first brought to the present world. It only applied to the future world. David and Emily asked high-tech companies like Intel, Apple, and Google for help. After some complex process of system conversion and information recovery, it was decoded with the information inside obtained. It was only then when the participants of the symposium saw their ID cards with the year indicated on it in the future world and the large number of photos taken there that they were convinced.

At the symposium, David and Emily also met their friend, Mr. Gan Ruida, a descendant of the Sanxingdui Alien clan, who was over eighty now but was still hale and hearty and talkative. He presented his article about the issue of Alien descendants on Earth, which aroused great interest among the participants.

After returning home, David and Emily told their son for the first time about the fact of their disappearance for two years. At this time, Oliver was eleven years old. The fantastic experience of his parents sounded like a science fiction to him. When he learned that he had a sister who had died there, Oliver blinked and said, "if only she were alive!" Emily said, "Yeah, we want Sophia to be with you, too.

However, we're already fortunate enough for your dad and me to come back alive. We should not demand too much." Oliver said, "When I grow up, I will go to the World End to find my sister." David said, "Now the end of the world has become a utopia, that no longer exists. Where to find her?" Oliver lowered his head in frustration.

## 2019 AD

More than half a year later, David and Emily were invited by a charity agency in Orlando Florida for an interview, saying that there was an important news for them, and that they should arrive as soon as possible. During the interview, Ellen, head of the agency, asked them if they had a girl who had been lost a few years ago. David and Emily were puzzled, saying that they had indeed had a daughter, but she was dead about four years ago. Ellen took out some photos of a girl and showed them to David and Emily. When David and Emily saw the pictures, they were shocked.

It was their daughter, Sophia! There was a photo of her when she was about one and a half years old, and also pictures of her growing up until she was about six. Especially the one when she was a toddler that David and Emily remembered more vividly, when she was still wearing the unique clothing from the Wonderland. Absolutely, it was true that this was their daughter, Sophia.

"Sophia is still alive? Oh, my God! No, no. That's impossible!" Emily was excited and nervous, her eyes glistened with tears.

David and Emily anxiously asked Ellen about the matter. Ellen told the story of this child. Four years ago, a violent hurricane blew a little child floating on the sea by Cocoa Beach, east of Orlando. Because the child's clothing material was special, fluffy, and impervious to water, like a life jacket, so the child was safe. The child was picked up by a good samaritan and taken to an orphanage run by the Orlando charity agency. The charity agency had been looking for children's parents through DNA information. After searching the national DNA database for four years, the results were finally found.

The girl's DNA information showed a strong match with David and Emily who now resided in Boulder, Colorado. (David and Emily had done DNA tests recently, and their DNA information could be available on line) . So the charity agency contacted them.

David and Emily met their long-lost love, Sophia, with feelings of sadness and happiness interwoven.

The child was a little restrained at first when she saw her parents and soon became excited, like a stray lamb back to its mother's warm embrace. David and Emily went home with Sophia. Oliver did not feel strange to see his sister, Sophia.

The two were so intimate that they immediately played and teased together. Blood relationship tied them up.

David and Emily always felt puzzled about this matter. How could Sophia suddenly return to them after she had died at the End of the World? They thought hard and finally had the answer. It turned out that Emily was pregnant when they crossed the time tunnel from Bermuda to the Wonderland. Although the child's life was only two months then, she passed with their parents through the tunnel. At that time, Emily didn't care to tell David about her pregnancy due to the great changes they had gone through. The baby was born in the Wonderland, but her DNA was of a different type from the people there. She could still go through reverse crossing like her parents, back to the original point. The children in the nursery in the Wonderland were known to have died, but Sophia's dead body was never seen. Actually, she wasn't dead.

The reverse time pulled her into the time tunnel, and like her parents, she was back to Bermuda in a reverse crossing.

At this point, our story has come to an end for the time being.

The most fantastic and high-pitched part of the story took place at the distant horizon, and the wonders at the distant horizon had been reached by traversing from Bermuda Triangle. So, the story is entitled World End and Sea Angle.

> *The end of the Earth is connected to the sea angle. The future is linked to the present. David and Emily's traverse spanned a thousand years. This unequalled wonder of the world is amazing and shocking, and also aroused some suspicion. Their adventure and experiences had revealed the mystery of the expansion and contraction of the universe, and demonstrated the magical power of time and space tunnels.*
>
> *The story is illusory and misty, somewhat far-fetched. The plot is plausible and paradoxical, but it tells some profound philosophy in its absurdity.*

# World's End and the Sea Angle

*Revised Version 2024*
*Sequel*


# Yank Shi

# Foreword

The main part of the book has concluded, and the stories before the year 2020 have already been told.

The following part is related to the main part and can be regarded as a sequel of it. These stories have a certain color of reasoning, seemingly true, but actually illusory.

This sequel is composed of three stories.

The first story takes place in the year 2020 AD with both the actual situation at the beginning of the year and the subsequent reasoning evolution of the year.

The second story happens around the year 2035 AD, fifteen years later from now.

The third story is set in an unknown year. It could be any year after 2020.

# Chapter 24

## PANDORA'S BOX

Hubei Province situated in the middle of China and the middle reaches of the Yangtze river is an important location called the Jingzhou and Xiangyang fortress in the history of China. Hubei once had historical celebrities such as Qu Yuan, Wang Zhaojun, Li Shizhen, etc., and is one of the cradles of Chinese civilization.

Hubei people are both smart and strong, both hearty and cautious. As the saying goes "Nine head birds in the sky, Hubei guys on the ground."

Wuhan, the capital of Hubei Province, is composed of three cities: Wuchang, Hankou, and Hanyang, with a population of nearly 10 million.

Wuhan is the birthplace of the famous Wuchang Uprising in the 1911 Revolution, which is a milestone from feudal to republican society in China.

As an important industrial base in China, Wuhan is known as the "Oriental Chicago." It is also an important scientific and educational base in China. It ranks the third among cities in the number of universities and scientific research institutions in China.

Wuhan is an important transportation hub in the country. There is the Beijing-Guangzhou railway, which runs from north to south, and the Yangtze River inland navigation across the east and the west.

The following story is taking place in Wuhan City, Hubei Province.

In the fall of 2019, Ding Beilei (Deborah), a mixed-race girl from Yantai, left her parents Ding Zhiyang and Anna for Wuhan, Hubei Province. She had been selected by Hubei Film Studio as the main actress in the new movie Magic Box and was busy filming. She played the beautiful Pandora in the play. Both her image and acting were in place.

As mentioned earlier, Ding Beilei's mother, Anna Marino, was an native Italian, and her father, Ding Zhiyang, was a common farmer in Yantai, Shandong province. Bei Lei's face and figure absorbed the advantages of both her parents, a typical and perfect combination of Chinese and Western features. When she first arrived in China, she was a lively and cute elementary school student who loved singing. A beautiful long hair set off her naturally smiling face. Her temperament and demeanor were quite graceful and decent. She was spontaneous and unrestrained in her manner.

The actor, Gan Yunfeng, known as Xiao (young) Gan was big and burly, measuring 1.82 meters in height. He was very strong and powerful. He had a look that appeared a little out of the ordinary. His face was chiseled and firm. It was later discovered that he had a few alien genes in his blood. Xiao Gan had a natural masculinity, commonly known as "a pure man." He behaved with great demeanor.

Xiao Gan, chatted well with Beilei. Talking about their family histories, Beilei learned that Xiao Gan was the only grandson of Mr. Gan Ruida, a descendant of the Star clan of Sanxingdui in Sichuan Province. Xiao Gan had participated in the filming of

Star Love based on the love tales of Gan Sanlang and Du Lanzi in the Song Dynasty. Gan Sanlang was an ancestor of the Gan family. Xiao Gan played Gan Sanlang in the play. Ding Beilei was the protagonist in this new film The Magic Box, in which Xiao Gan played Prometheus, the god of the world who saves mankind.

Xiao Gan usually spoke with a slight Sichuan accent, and Beilei occasionally revealed a little Jiaodong dialect. But when they spoke in the play, they could speak pure Mandarin. The two often study plots and performances together, and they were becoming more and more familiar with each other.

Xiao Gan was deeply in love with Beilei. He regarded her as his ideal lifelong companion at first sight of her. He boldly expressed his love for her. Beilei said that she was still young, just 19 years old, and did not want to fall in love too early.

Although Xiao Gan was not immediately accepted, he was not discouraged. He even firmly believed that they should be a natural pair. Beilei was not averse to Xiao Gan's love, she just had no thoughts in advance and felt a little bit caught off guard. They worked together every day, all the time. Neither was a star or celebrity, but they were new buds in the movie world and colleagues of a performance team. They treated each other equally, just like a brother and a sister. In life, Xiao Gan was tender and considerate of her, and emotionally he was more affectionate towards her. All of these were caught in her eyes and stored in her heart. Love will come in time, Beilei felt more and more that she couldn't do without Xiao Gan.

Xiao Gan and Beilei were not pure Han people. Their exotic qualities made them more attractive and compatible to each other. Xiao Gan was seven years older than Beilei. Beilei always felt that Xiao Gan was like an elder brother who was always attentive and caring for her, and sheltering her everywhere like a guardian spirit.

Mr. Xue, director of the film The Magic Box was strict with the actors and actresses, warning them not to fall in love during the shooting. However, he himself was sometimes frivolous and flippant towards Beilei and even implied to implement the "hidden rules" (director sleeps with the actress to make her more attractive in exchange. He promised to help Beilei to become a star, but Beilei declined it. Xiao Gan showed Xue a color for this and warned him not to be silly, otherwise, he would be impolite. Mr. Xue was shocked by Xiao Gan's suppressing aura.

## The Beginning of 2020 AD

The year 2020 was an unusual year for Wuhan and Hubei.

Immediately after the Lunar New Year, Beilei who returned to Yantai to reunite with her parents for the Chinese New Year, hurried back to Wuhan and continued to engage in intense shooting.

One evening, Xiao Gan and Beilei were walking in the riverside park. They talked about Pandora's Box. Beilei believed that most of the disasters and sins of human beings came from that magic box. Pandora, out of curiosity, released the evil poison from the box, which was a big blunder. Xiao Gan said that Pandora's Box was just a myth of the West. When people come to this world, they will inevitably make mistakes and even commit crimes. Pandora is not to blame.

However, Beilei was a little too deeply involved in the play, and the experience of Pandora's sin made her depressed and even unable to get rid of her self-reproach. She felt that people around the world were blaming Pandora and regarded Pandora as the root of all evils.

One night, when Beilei was half asleep, the terrible magic box appeared in front of her eyes. When the lid of the magic box was opened, a wisp of smoke came out of the box.

A strong odor suddenly filled the air. A large number of mosquitoes, flies, cockroaches, bats, sick mice, poisonous fruits, miasma, acid rain, germs, and viruses gushed out of the box, with all kinds of ugly creatures in the world, one after another. This toxic flow was as strong as a spring and totally unstoppable. Beilei's head swelled with fear, and she was cold all over. She kept shouting, "Stop! Stop!" But to no avail. The box was still gushing. Beilei screamed and cried. She picked up the box and slammed it to the ground. The box flipped around on the ground and continued spraying. Beilei stamped on the box with her feet, trying to crush it.

Unexpectedly, the box was very sturdy and never deformed. The innocent girl wailed so loudly that she woke herself up. Beilei touched her forehead and found it covered with cold sweat. Looking around, there was no magic box in front of her. It was a false alarm.

The next day, when she was still fearing about her nightmares last night, she saw a nightmare-like reality in broad daylight. Wuhan, a metropolis of ten million people, was in the doom. The deadly neocoronavirus was raging in the city. People's health and lives were under great threat. For several consecutive days, the number of infections and deaths skyrocketed. The whole city of Wuhan was sealed off. People in the city could not get out, and people outside the city could not come into the city. The whole city was shrouded in terror, misery, despair, and darkness.

Beilei saw in her nightmare the neocoronavirus mixed in with the filth from the magic box. After zooming in, it appeared round, with some small antennae around it, a bit like a sea mine. It was said that it could spread quickly from person to person and was far more deadly than SARS or Ebola when it entered the human body. It would damage the lungs, kidneys, and other organs of the human body in a short period of time, making them as porous as a sponge.

Beilei was disgusted at the sight of these terrible viruses. Human life is precious. These little viruses gang up to do evil and take away human life in a hurry. Some people said that the virus came from some wild animals, while others said that it was syn-thesized in a genetic recombination, a product of gene editing. In any case, at present, people must overcome them, otherwise they would bring endless disaster to all mankind.

The neocoronavirus had spread rapidly in the country. Within a few weeks, the infected people had spread all over the cities, provinces, and autonomous regions of China, and also extended to many countries in the world. To prevent the virus from China, those countries stopped airtraffic with China. They still remembered the plague of SARS and Ebola before that, fear-ing the terrible plague would come back. With the spread of the epidemic, more and more countries cut off from China, forming a seal of the country. Because there was no specific medicines or vaccine against the virus, the persistent disease would run ram-pant around the world. Some scientists predict it could eventu-ally infect two-hirds of the world's population if not controlled effectively.

Due to the outbreak of severe epidemic in Wuhan, the film The Magic Box, being shot by Hubei Film Studio, was suspended. Ding Beilei and everyone in the crew were trapped in the city, unable to go out. Everyone wore a mask being on alert every day.

Director Chen of the studio was modest and dedicated to his work. Unexpectedly, his father first contracted the coronavirus and he contacted all the hospitals, which had no beds available. So, his father had to recuperate at home. It was just a few days before he died. Then the grieving mother became infected and died following his father. Director Chen and his wife were also infected while taking care of their parents and died one after the other.

One family, with two generations and four members, all died of coronavirus, while only a son in France survived. In his last words, director Chen said to the world sadly, "Farewell to those who I love and those who love me."

All the people in the studio were very sad for the fate of the Chen family. At the same time, they felt that their fate was at stake, being in danger. Ding Beilei was even more nervous. As soon as she closed her eyes, there was always a terrible magic box with evil poison spewing out. She was haggard and seldom at peace. She had suffered from leukaemia in her early years, and had a narrow escape from death with the help of a noble man who gave her a second life. Now faced with the second visit of the god of Death, could she still survive miraculously this time? She dared not think further.

This lively and cheerful girl was now quiet and worried.

After the outbreak of the new coronavirus epidemic in Wuhan and the closure of the city, countless medical personnel spared no effort to rescue patients. They work long hours and suffer from extreme fatigue, hunger, and inconvenience in using the toilet (to save on protective clothing). Many medical workers fell ill themselves and even lost their own lives while rescuing patients.

Medical personnel out of Wuhan had rushed to the critical area, one team after another. With too many patients, the medical staff was exhausted and overworked. In one video, a young female nurse was seen crying loudly and helplessly. Her voice was bitter and piercing.

At the same time, Ding Beilei noticed a kind of virulent poison in the venom sprayed from the magic box, which was more terrible and harmful than the new coronavirus. This evil poison specially eroded people's mind, depriving them of human conscience, moral bottom line, and minimum civilization consciousness, making them lose their human due compassion, sympathy, redemption, helping others for pleasure and self sacrifice, and giving way to the worst selfish, cold-blood, greedy, jealous, hypocritical, defamatory, abusive and other bad featuress in human nature.

Some ugly phenomena had appeared in the society, which were disgusting. Some people from Wuhan and Hubei who stayed in other provinces had been discriminated against. They were treated as savage beasts, relentlessly driven away, chased, and beaten. Their residence was sealed, nailed with wooden bars, and welded with iron rods. Hotels and restaurants forbade them to enter, and they had to be wandering in the streets. They were already victims of the virus. What was their crime? They were a vulnerable group, but they were abused by their compatriots.

The pandemic was spreading and the disaster was taking the lead. Xiao Gan and Beilei were even more sympathetic to each other. The situation of suffering made them more dependent and understanding of each other. Their hearts were tightly bound up.

Xiao Gan and Beilei lived in their own rooms and were not allowed to go out for shopping or doing business, as if they were in prison. They sometimes got together to talk, exchange information, and encourage each other. They had fun in suffering. They played musical instruments and sang songs together. They were seeking light in the dark night, hoping for the dawn.

Xiao Gan sometimes spoke over the phone to his grand-father, Gan Ruida, in Langzhong, Sichuan province, to tell him about the pandemic breakout in Hubei. Mr. Gan Ruida encouraged him to live on persistently, saying that the descendants of the Star clan of the Gan family were as sparse as the morning stars. They must pass down anyway; their roots should not be broken. Beilei often communicated with her parents in Yantai by WeChat and online videos. Zhiyang and Anna were very concerned about their daughter. Beilei comforted her parents, assuring them that their daughter was safe and sound. After the epidemic, she would return to Yantai to be with them as soon as possible.

The pandemic situation in Wuhan was still worsening.

The number of confirmed cases and deaths continued to rise.

The funeral crematoriums in several funeral homes in Wuhan ran continuously 24 hours a day, which were still struggling to cope with a large number of dead patients. They had to add some mobile cremator vehicles for emergency.

There were also a number of confirmed cases among employees in Hubei Film Studio. Due to the shortage of hospital beds, many patients had to recuperate at home, in fact waiting for the the arrival of death. Grim Reaper moved quickly, taking away the patients one by one, and they were hurriedly burned in the crematorium. Thick smoke floated from the cremators into the sky, and a pungent smell spread out. In this way, these once lively people had ascended to the sky one by one and disappeared.

Mr. Xue, the director of the production group, contracted the disease unfortunately, and was seriously ill. Knowing that that he was doomed to no hope of improvement, he even thought of dragging Xiao Gan to go with him. Xiao Gan had once warned that he should not have any improper thought about Beilei.

He bore a grudge against Xiao Gan, thinking that Xiao Gan had destroyed his good affair and wanted to wait for an opportunity to retaliate. He spat his saliva on Xiao Gan's doorknob at night and went away with a triumphant hum. And so it worked well. Gan accidentally touched the saliva with the virus, also infected, and became another confirmed case. Xue died of illness and was sent to the funeral home for cremation. Gan was still recovering in his room. He was puzzled and could not find the cause of his disease. He never thought of being insinuated or harmed by others, nor the sinisterness of the human heart.

Xiao Gan called Beilei to inform her about his illness, and asked Beilei never to visit him. Beilei cried. She said that she must go to see him and die together with him. Xiao Gan scolded Beilei badly and said that he wanted to break up with her in that case. Beilei was afraid of losing Xiao Gan, who had been integrated into her soul and had become an integral part of her life.

Without Xiao Gan, she would lose her Optimus Prime, everything would collapse, and she would not know how to live on by herself. Without Xiao Gan, her feelings would lose the destination, the support, like a dry river, no longer flowing.

Beilei spent two days and two nights alone in pain, with tears as her companion, but she decided to take a chance to visit Xiao Gan. On the third day, when she came to the door of Xiao Gan's room, she found that it was empty. The residence manager told her that Xiao Gan was taken to the hospital yesterday with serious illness. Being incurable he died. He was already incinerated by a cremator vehicle.

Beilei slumped on the ground, with eyes straight, and no tears in her eyes that had gone dry. Her expression was numb, her mind seemed to have stopped working, with no thoughts, no emotions, she didn't even know who she was and what was around her.

Tired legs carried the numb Beilei back to her room. Day or night Beilei was half asleep, and half awake, being groggy. In front of her eyes was always the dreadful Pandora's box, out of which, the evil poison kept pouring, the once vivid image of Xiao Gan and the flickering apparition of him, the piles of corpses in the funeral parlor and the billows of thick smoke floating above the incinerators.

About a month later.

It was said that Ding Beilei gradually woke up from a semi-coma and returned to normal.

It was said that she managed to escape from Wuhan and Hubei with the help of her best friend, Jin Qing'er, and came to Yantai to live with her parents.

Because Ding Beilei was young, healthy, energetic, and resistant to viruses, she was safe from the epidemic. However, she actually carried some virus with her. After returning to Yantai, she got along with his parents day and night, being intimate. So, her parents contracted the epidemic one after another. Also, due to the untimely rescue, both her parents died in a hurry. Jin Qing'er, Bei Lei's best friend, was killed by the virus, mostly caused by the virus she carried. Beilei was in agony and extremely self regretting.

Ding Beilei, alone and unaccompanied, drifted around like a duckweed.

A few more months later,

The pandemic spread rapidly around the world, endangering almost all countries and every corner of the world, and claiming the precious lives of hundreds of thousands of innocent people. These small mine-like viruses raged wildly in the world. If not well controlled, they were no less dangerous to mankind than nuclear weapons. The number of diseases and deaths caused by this plague was increasing day by day. People were evading at home, unemployment soared, all businesses slumped, and the economy collapsed.

At this time there was no traces of Beilei. People said she had gone abroad. Some said that she had originally planned to go to her grandmother's (her mother's mother) home in Italy. But the epidemic in Italy was severe and her grandmother had died of coronavirus unfortunately. Other people believed that she might have gone to the United States, where there were her "reborn parents" David and Emily who had saved her life. She did have the idea but was never able to do so because she had learned in advance that the outbreak of pandemic in the United States was also severe, so she failed to realize the plan.

Another statement about Beilei's whereabout was even more bizarre.

Ding Beilei was said to be the incarnation of Pandora. Her original name, Deborah, was somewhat similar to Pandora. Ding

Beilei was not a mortal, which was perhaps the main reason why she was sludge-free, and the coronavirus that was ravaging the world was hard to harm her body of deity.

People remembered the story of Pandora: In Greek mythology, Pandora was the first woman brought to the world by Zeus, the king of the gods, as a punishment for Prometheus' creation of man and theft of fire. Pandora's box was donated by Prometheus who had repeatedly told her that the box could not be opened. Out of curiosity, Pandora quietly opened the box when people were unprepared. As a result, numerous pests and calamities poured out of the box and spread rapidly to the earth and the human world. However, there was only one good thing hidden underneath the box, that was "Hope." Pandora, according to Zeus' admonition, closed the lid quickly before it flew out, so the "Hope" placed at the bottom of the box by Athena to save mankind was always locked in the box. Since then, all kinds of disasters filled the earth. Disease was widespread, rampant, and silent among humans. A variety of plagues ravaged the earth, and the God of death was galloping on the earth.

It was believed that Pandora, who was transformed into Ding Beilei, being cornered in the world with no way out had already left the world at this time and ascended to heaven again. Seeing the sufferings of the world, she was more regretful for her early curiosity and recklessness, which led the devil out of the cage and brought endless suffering to the world. However, she did not release "hope" from the box. She's going to do it now. She wanted to bring hope to the world to make up for her early mistakes.

*The plague caused by virus threatens human health*
*and life. What's more terrible is the erosion of evil*

# Chapter 25

## A GIGANTIC FRAUD

### Around 2035AD

About 15 years later, it is said that around the year, David and Emily, the protagonists of this book, are already in their fifties. Their son, Oliver, has grown into a young man of twenty-eight years old, handsome, and good-natured. His girlfriend, Alice, is naive, gentle, and affectionate. David and Emily's daughter, Sophia, is nearly twenty-two years old, a tall and graceful young girl. Her boyfriend, Frank, was the grandson of a Chinese American (Ye Qiuming) from Yantai, China. He is generous and well-mannered. Oliver and Sophia are both intelligent and talented, excellent in character. Oliver has a Ph.D. in genetics specializing in human gene studies. Sophia like astronomy and music. She often talks with her parents about the Earth and the universe, plays piano, and sings songs with her boyfriend.

Oliver, much like his parents, was naturally brave and challenging. He had the courage to innovate and explore academically. Especially he admired and worshipped the physicist and astronomer, Stephen William Hawking. He had obtained outstanding achievements in gene theory and related medical techniques, for which he was regarded as a small authority on human genes.

He was conceiving an experiment with "gene editing," a taboo area of medical ethics. He regarded this restricted area as the devil's Triangle of Bermuda in the medical world. Although the gene theory and technology at this time had been relatively advanced, and gene editing on humans was completely possible, yet no one dared to set foot in this troubled and dangerous area. Once, someone proposed or tried it, he was immediately condemned and criticized by the public. Oliver knew that this experiment was unusual. If acting rashly it would not only be against the will of Heaven, but also violate the human relations, and even cause a great catastrophe in the world.

Genetic editing was extremely risky. The subsequent changes in people who had been genetically edited were unpredictable. It might even be compared to the opening of Pandora's box, with all devils rushing out, and the entire world would be out of control. Hawking had spoken of the possibility that gene editing could "create super-strong humans with today's human beings eliminated and obsolete." It could be a catastrophe for modern people.

After many years of development, gene medical technology had reached the level that gene editing surgery could be performed on adults and even on the operator himself. Oliver didn't want to experiment on babies or other people. He would operate on himself and bear all the consequences. His success could benefit mankind, and his failure would be his self-sacrifice, for people to learn a lesson, and to warn future generations. It will be the so called "succeed or die."

Oliver pondered about it over and over, weighing the pros and cons. Inspired by his parents' spirit of daring to challenge the devil's Burmuda Triangle, attracted by Hawking's goal of "super-human," he thought, once successful, all mankind would become "omnipotent-human," all the people would be super strong and healthy, long-lived, super-intelligent for generations to come, and mankind and the world would definitely be changed completely.

Oliver was unable to obtain the consent of his parents, girlfriend, colleagues, and friends for his plan and the support for him. He persisted in going his own way, being duty-bound, without turning back, he rushed to the storm and danger.

Oliver conducted gene editing in his own cells with exquisite technology.

The operation was carried out in extreme secrecy. After the operation he kept his mouth shut to everybody.

At first he had no apparent feeling of anything different, as if nothing had happened.

Gradually, he began to feel himself stronger, more energetic, more agile, and working long.

Gradually, he felt that his mind was more intelligent, his IQ enhanced, with difficulties overcome smoothly in his work, and problems and puzzles resolved easily in his research.

Oliver was very excited and happy, thinking that his adventure was successful and victorious. He proudly announced the exciting news to the world.

When people learned about this, they were naturally happy for Oliver for some time. But when pondering about it, in an afterthought, they began to think that things were not that simple. After all, the act of gene editing to alter the code of life had touched the "Dragon Vein" of human beings.

The consequences had not yet fully manifested. Everyone was inevitably worried about it and sweated in fear for what this brave and reckless youth did.

As feared, some negative signs were trickling down on Oliver.

It was discovered that this boy, although having become physically and intellectually superior, had changed his normally gentle, humble, friendly, and tolerant nature, and had become rude, arrogant, jealous, and ruthless towards people. He seemed to have changed into another person completely different from what he used to be. As time went by, Oliver was no longer admired or liked by all, and people gradually distanced themselves from him. His family members and relatives were disappointed and distressed. Could this be their Oliver? That was simply an unwelcome stranger, a fully-fledged freak.

Now, Oliver was ruthless, reminiscent of the hero in the German movie A Cool Heart, in which the hero's heart was replaced by the Dutch ghost, with a cold stone in his chest.

When Oliver's girlfriend, Alice, met him, he was cold- faced with a cold tongue, and even arrogantly ridiculed her, so that the two of them quarreled for it. However, Alice had a deep affection for him, and after a while she took the initiative to apologize to him, hoping to break the stalemate. Oliver was as cold as ice. He turned his back on Alice and said with a blank expression, "Alice, let's break up." Alice was shocked. She thought that her close boyfriend wasn't serious, so she hugged Oliver hard and said, "No, no. Oliver. I can't leave you!" Oliver mercilessly brushed the girl's hands off. When the girl still wanted to hold him, he pushed her to the ground and said, "Hate" He walked away without looking back. From then on, he never paid any attention to his once beloved girlfriend Alice.

Oliver made rapid progress in academic research and medical practice. He was recognized as the leader in this field and the perfect candidate for the Nobel Prize in physics and medicine of the year. His analysis of human genes was deep and thorough and continued to make breakthroughs, with more and more extensive coverage, involving all aspects of human individual traits, such as individual form, temperament, ability, emotion, morality, even life trajectory, destiny, and so on. He roamed the realm of human genes with irresistible force, as freely as if he were working with the Creator. The patterns of the genetic codes seemed to him like combinations of musical scales in the ear of a composer, or the keyboard for a pianist, operating freely and skillfully.

Oliver was called a "ghost genius." He was almost omnipotent. In terms of high-tech and artificial intelligence, he helped the technology elites develop more advanced chips, which made the high technology take a big step forward on the basis of the present. He improved the operating platform of the Internet to make it ten times more efficient. In the field of art, he was able to determine whether a person with lofty ideals was promising through genetic analysis and to make effective directions to guide one for improvements and success.

For example, under his inspiration and guidance, the spirituality and talent of his sister, Sophia, had greatly improved, and her vocal music ability had soared so that Sophia was becoming a new star in the music circle.

The talented Oliver was brilliant, famous, romantic, and debonair, having naturally won the hearts of many young girls. Pursuers were numerous, among whom there were no lack of girls who were outstanding in appearance, elegant in temperament, enthusiastic, and gentle in manner. However, Oliver was not impressed and tempted. He either refused or ignored them. In fact, he had become so indifferent to people that he almost lost any affection for others. There was no love—the most beautiful feeling of mankind in his heart. His affection for his relatives and friends was as thin as the water. He was like an extremely intelligent robot, wise and ruthless. It seemed that during his gene editing, the emotional string in his gene pattern was accidentally broken.

Oliver maintained his own integrity and lived a happy single life. He did not look for a girlfriend, did not fall in love with a girl, did not want to set up a family, to marry a wife, to have children, and to enjoy the family life. He said that to do such things would be like asking for troubles and seeking sufferings, and simply equal to grabbing a louse to put it on his own head.

His fun lay in his personal accomplishments and illustrious fame. He was enchanted by the admiration, praise, and cheers of his followers in the world, and he was addicted to his continuous academic triumphs.

Oliver's mother, Emily, was reluctant to believe that her son would ever have a complete loss of conscience. She felt she knew him best. She had a heart-to-heart talk with Oliver about what was going on inside him now, but found that they shared less and less thoughts and feelings in common. When talking about the past, Emily mentioned that when Oliver was a child, just seven or eight years old, his parents traveled outside and traversed far, far away. He was not able to see mom and dad for years. Emily could imagine how he wished to see his parents back at home. Emily also talked about the scene that she had peeped at the courtyard when she had just returned from the horizon. In speaking of this, Emily was inevitably bitter and shed tears. Oliver said coldly, "What are you nagging about with this old stuff?" In fact, at this time, although Oliver had great changes, he had not become an ironhearted man without a slight trace of human nature. There was still a little bit of humanity and human feelings in him. At least he could not completely forget his mother's love. He could not deny the fact that his parents gave him his life. This might be a remaining trace of affection and humanity in his genetic editing.

Mom advised Oliver to return to his girlfriend Alice and resume their relationship, to get along well with her, and to cherish the pure love between them. Oliver said, "Where is the pure love? If there is no sex, can there be love? If either a man or a woman has no sexual ability and sexual desire, do they still have love? Love between men and women is but a mischievous prank directed by God, that hateful old guy. He chants an incantation and drags men and women together so as to let them have children and breed offspring. Come on, can love get away from the genitalia thing? Melons, apples, pears, and peaches are beautiful and delicious, so they attract people and other animals to eat the fruit, throw the stones far away, so that they can sprout everywhere, grow up, and then bear fruit all over the world. Everything in the world is played and fooled by God, and the people being played with do not realize it." Oliver's view of love really shocked his mother, Emily.

Not content with his current success, Oliver operated a second gene editing on himself. His intelligence and ability were improved greatly again after the operation. He was far ahead in related academic fields. He could also give guidance to non-related fields, and produce fruitful results.

Oliver was secretly researching a personal stealth technology. The reason why a viewer can see the object before him (or her) is that the shape and color of the object are reflected into his (or her) eyes, forming an image in his (or her) vision. Then the optic nerve passes it to the brain, and the person can see the object. Using this principle, Oliver wanted to develop a mechanism to block the reflection of an object into the human eyes and attached it to himself, so that he could not be seen, to achieve the effect of invisibility.

After repeated experiments, Oliver succeeded in achieving a stealth technology. He turned on the invisibility mechanism on himself and tried to walk through the crowd in the street. Passers-by sometimes bump into him with a shock because they couldn't see him. While he was eating food and drinking water, the food and water disappeared as soon as they entered his mouth.

Oliver was very excited. With this stealth technology, he could go to a lot of places where he usually couldn't go, and do a lot of things that he usually couldn't do, which greatly expanded his freedom of action.

In stealth mode, he could spy on anyone's secrets, and could assist the judiciary to collect evidence of the suspects' crimes. In wartime, he could also penetrate into the enemy's headquarters and spy on the Enemy's top secret military information and serve for his own side.

His invention had been affirmed by people for its judicial and military applications for some time. However, some people believed that stealth was an immoral and improper behavior and should not be advocated and promoted. Furthermore, obtaining evidence in this way is difficult to have legal effect. Once stealth technology was popularized, it would be easy to cause social chaos. The wicked took the opportunity to commit crimes and were difficult to trace.

Oliver did not think so. After his second gene editing, he lost his moral compass. There was no difference between good and evil in his view and he would do anything if he wished to.

Oliver openly laughed at all the moral principles. He said: "Chinese people like to talk about loyalty, filial piety, chastity, righteousness, also benevolence, justice, propriety, wisdom, and faith. For me, they are all man-made hoops, sheer nonsense, fussiness, bullshit"

Oliver felt that he had entered a whole new realm. He wanted to challenge the existing social order, human civilization, ethics and humility. Oliver's wild thoughts and actions were like a flood that rushed out of an open floodgates, dashing straight and flooding everywhere. He began to be unscrupulous and mischievous.

With invisibility, Oliver acted tyrannically, leisurely, and unhurried. He acted wantonly everywhere, unimpeded. He always ate the best meals in high-end restaurants, took first class seat in the airplanes, stayed in most luxurious hotels, and never paid, he went away without a trace.

Oliver gained some notables' dirty privacy in a hidden way, posted it on the Internet, so that they lost their faces, with no place to hide themselves for shame. Although he was not short of money, he robbed a great deal of wealth by concealing himself. Many bigwigs suffered big losses and were heavily in debt. Some of the wealthy plutocrats had shrunk their assets overnight and were in poverty. Oliver only thought it was fun for him.

Oliver had no love for women, but he could be extravagant and promiscuous, having "read" countless women. He always chose the prettiest and sexiest young ladies and went straight into their bedrooms at night without being noticed. He had sex with women by stimulating their libido with sex hormones. Women who were sexually assaulted did not see their abusers. Some were willing, some were depressed afterwards but helpless. There were women who reported the cases, and the police knew that it should be Oliver who did it. But Oliver was nowhere to be found , and it was difficult to pursue.

Oliver seized and leaked stock and bond information, causing chaos in the stock and bond markets. He manipulated the gambling devices and tricks in casinos and let the gamblers won tons of money and the casino owners lost their shirts.

He managed to release prisoners in prisons at night, allowing them to enjoy the air of freedom and continue to do evil in society.

Oliver also used his cover to play all sorts of pranks. He danced on the big dining table of the grand banquet of dignitaries and corrupt officials and urinated in their plates and glasses. He cut off the genitals of the giant bosses and their rich sons who indulged in philandering with countless mistresses and threw them on the streets for public display, despite his own sexual indiscretions.

For Oliver, all that he had done was to show to the world his omnipotence, omnipresence, fearlessness, unlimited freedom, and the cynicism with which he despised, ridiculed, and mocked everything he disliked. He declared that he no longer cared about human values, conscience, and dignity. His wildness and arbitrariness made him enjoy great excitement and endless pleasure.

Even more absurd and dangerous was that Oliver recruited a group of young cowboys who flouted all the rules and regulations and pursued unlimited freedom. They had developed into a gang of eight under Oliver's command, known as the "Eight Warriors." Oliver applied invisibility on them, allowing them to take Oliver as the chief of the gang. Oliver firmly controlled the stealth switch in his own hands and switch them on and off at will, no matter wherever they were.

These gangsters were more rampant and ferocious than Oliver. They went their own way in the society, lawless, doing a variety of things out of line, absurd and damaging.

They robbed banks, destroyed cultural relics, insulted social celebrities, and cultural elites. They took whatever they need in the shops, ate, and drank for free in restaurants, and had fun in erotic places. They amounted a myriad of sexual assaults against beautiful women including celebrities. They hurt and killed people for pleasure, seriously disrupting public order.

They destroyed the original ecology, slaughtered pets, set fire on the forests, attempted to blow up the dams on the rivers, let the surging flood drown the huge crowds of people, which they called "flooding ants." They even tried to detonate the nuclear bombs of the nuclear-armed countries, ruining the Earth's civilization by half, which they called "lighting firecrackers." They sneaked into the government buildings, presidential suites, to search for keys or codes to activate nuclear weapons. Although they did not succeed, they made people extremely fearful and the world into a mess.

They were doing evil everywhere, but could be traced nowhere. They were sometimes in South America, sometimes in East Asia. New York today, Las Vegas tomorrow. They wreaked havoc in Shanghai, Paris, and Vienna in one week and created chaos in Hong Kong, Melbourne, and Vancouver the week after. Their evil acts and misdeeds caused great panic throughout the world. It was simply a group of invisible villains and devils. People were uneasy, with a constant fear and threat that the Oliver gang would attack at any moment and their privacy would be revealed, their property looted, their wives and children violated, and their reputations destroyed.

It was the common wish of mankind to remove Oliver and his gang. The police systems of all countries in the world had joined forces to bring these black sheep to justice, to eliminate the evil for the safety of civilians.

It was no easy job to catch these invisible criminals. First of all, the mechanism of their stealth should be broken. Their invisibility was given and controlled by Oliver. To catch the thieves, they must first catch their chief. This was the key to keys. However, the traces of Oliver were elusive and faint.

The demon Oliver became the focus of the world's attention, which was exactly what he was pursuing. Oliver was very proud. He danced cheerfully and sang merrily for his success.

It was known that the boy's only visible interaction with the world was his irregular meetings with his mother, Emily. He still had some kinship with his mother. The occasional meeting counted as an accommodation in his life.

The police hoped that Emily would help them to catch Oliver. Emily said she was willing to cooperate, but she did not want Oliver to be executed, although she knew that her son was guilty of grave crimes that he deserved death penality. She still hoped that his son could abandon the darkness and make a change.

She believed that Oliver should first remove the mechanism of invisibility and be an open and bright man.

The most important thing was to restore his previous state before the gene editing. She hoped to have a gene restoration technology that would recover her son's former genes.

Oliver met with his mother again. This time Emily talked to him for a long time, she wanted to make one last effort to save her son's life. Emily coaxed her son into changing his mind. Oliver, unmoved, said that he was used to this unrestrained life and could not return to the past. Emily asked Oliver if someone else or he himself could perform gene editing surgery to restore the original gene pattern. Oliver said it was impossible to conduct that. Gene editing was irreversible. Gene was the design code of the Creator, editing it without the Creator's authorization was already bold and unscrupulous, very perverse, if bothering repeatedly, it would inevitably irritate the Creator, and incur some catastrophe.

Emily was in a keen agony that she was destined to lose her son. She talked to David about it. David was also very sad. The once lovely angel had turned into a terrible devil. He entered the forbidden zone of gene editing by mistake, went astray and was sinful. They had no choice but to do justice to their son, with tears.

By the time when Oliver visited again, David and Emily were ready to say goodbye to him. David and Emily gave Oliver an ultimatum, and let him change his course completely or die. At this time, police snipers were everywhere around the house, with all muzzles aiming at Oliver. Even if he wanted to be invisible, it was too late to turn on the stealth mechanism. If he resisted, the bullets would hit him all over in a tenth of a second. Oliver agreed to submit. "To prove your integrity," David said, "You must immediately remove your stealth mechanism and those of your fellows." Oliver operated the system to turn off the invisibility mechanism of his cowboys and deactivated that of his own—abolished his own "martial art." The outlaws who appeared in sight fled everywhere, but could not escape the supervision of the people and the police's legal network.

With this act as an exchange Oliver won people's trust in him for his intention to rehabilitate. But he remained under house arrest. He was given a reprieve by the court. During this period, if he could restore the original genetic model by genetic editing surgery, he would be exempted from death. He promised to perform his own surgery.

Thus, Oliver went down to the operating room under tight police supervision for a third gene editing operation to restore his original gene form. The operation took a long time. Despite his wonderful skill, he was always unsuccessful this time, and his gene was hard to repair. In fact, he understood well that this would definitely be futile. Shrewdly, he took advantage of this opportunity to turn the gene operation in the other direction. The first two editing operations made him lose his humanity and kinship as well as human conscience and moral bottom line while he became physically and intellectually strong. He knew that another editing could make him still stronger, maybe even become a "superman," while at the same time causing more negative aftereffects, becoming worse, and even a "demon." At this moment, he had a flash in his mind that he would burn his bridges and would act as a "demonic superman" rather than return to the world where he was regarded as a criminal and controlled by society everywhere.

Sure enough, Oliver turned himself into a superman and a demon through another gene editing. His extraordinary ability enabled him not only to be invisible, but also be able to shrink and fly. He shrank his body, like the chip widely used in high technology, to smaller sizes. Small as it was, it carried a lot of information and functions. His body shrank to almost nothing. Furthermore, it could be either shrinkable and extendable. He could resume to his original size if he wished to. Moreover he obtained the ability to fly up with his reduced body, soaring and swimming in the air. In this way, under the close surveillance of the police, the giant criminal Oliver turned into a wisp of blue smoke, evaporated in the world.

Oliver's third gene editing gave him a leap in intelligence and ability. The world's current high-tech elites were, in his eyes, "small hills by a glance from above," and he stood out from the crowd like a crane standing among chickens, being disdainful of these idiots. He single-handedly took down one by one the targets in gene theory and practice. He claimed that smart computers and mobile phones that he would develop could be hundreds of times more advanced than their predecessors. His mobile phone could be used for many consecutive years without battery charging, and did not require WiFi anywhere. The satellites could be more versatile in function, and the spaceship could travel faster and fly farther. He declared he had even discovered how to find the way to the existing time-space tunnels, so that humans had the possibility of actively traversing into distant time and space.

However, due to the loss of morality, it was difficult for him to distinguish between good and evil, merit and harm, beauty and ugliness. He was building and destroying at the same time. He destroyed numerous satellites in the sky, like swatting flies and mosquitoes flying overhead. He paralyzed countless GPS and radar systems. He used sophisticated hackers to steal information, disrupt the Internet and electronic communications. To destroy large passenger planes, heavy bombers, advanced fighters in the sky, aircraft carrier battle groups and nuclear submarines at sea was a piece of cake for him.

Oliver's escape caused great social panic. People realized that this Oliver, a combination of superman and demon would be more dangerous and do more evil in the world, fearing that disaster would come to them at any time.

This demon was more unscrupulous, running amok, and unstoppable.

It was recognized that to arrest and completely destroy Oliver was of top priority to the fate of mankind. At the same time of reconnaissance and capture, the influence and legacy of the devil Oliver were being cleared everywhere. It was well known that once this demon's horrible gene flew into the human gene pool, the consequences would be unimaginable. It was like a drown fly that spoiled the whole pot of soup.

The consequences of genetic contamination were endless.

The police conducted a general investigation of the women who were sexually assaulted by Oliver, especially those who had given birth to and those who were pregnant with Oliver's children, were asked to surrender their born and to-be-born children after birth. The children would be concentrated and wait for treatment. If there were no better solutions, the children would face euthanasia with their bodies destroyed.

This was a security measure concerning the future destiny of all mankind, somewhat like slaughtering chickens that might carry the bird flu virus. At the same time, all adult and underage women were required to be accompanied or armed at night to prevent the devil from entering their rooms.

The capture of Oliver was in full swing. Oliver's parents, David and Emily, were told to stay on alert. They had private guns, that turned out to be useful now. At present they realized the benefit of private ownership of guns. Last time David and Emily cooperated with the police to catch Oliver. The devil was likely to hold a grudge against his parents. David and Emily were armed at all times to defend themselves in times of crisis.

One night, Oliver appeared in front of David and Emily. He said, "I know you don't like me, and you're going to put me to death. But I won't harm you. After all, you are my biological parents who gave me my life, and the chance for me to have fun in this world. To tell you the truth, I've played all the games in the world, had enough addiction.

That's enough. This time I'm here to say goodbye, to bid my final farewell to you. I will leave this little globe to play on other planets and universes, and never come back again." Emily said, "Oliver, you'd better stay. expressionless in his face, "If I stay, the people of the world will kill me and chop me to pieces, ground me to jam. They hate me so much." David said, "if you go to another planet to do evil, will the people there forgive you?" Oliver's spirits rose and he replied, "Oh! Yeah. Thanks for reminding me, Dad. You are right. I will do more evil. I want to make a scene in the universe, turn it upside down! Like the Monkey King, like the Spiderman. No, what is the Monkey King? a fart! What is the Spiderman! a shit! I'm the Superman! Superman! Do you know? I'm going to touch the head of the Taisui (God), I am going to pull the teeth in God's mouth. It's so exciting!

That's great! So much fun! I won't ask for forgiveness. I won't care about the consequences. Ha, ha, ha, ha... !" Oliver was overjoyed, leaning foreward and backward. When he didn't notice, David and Emily pulled out their pistols, fired two bullets at Oliver at the same time, and killed their son. They would never allow this heinous demon to harm humans any more on Earth before they harm the Alien humans.

Oliver fell to the ground at the shot, his blood oozed from his chest and trickled down to the ground. The color of the blood was crimson. Emily covered her own head with both her hands and closed her eyes, not willing to see the sight. David closed his son's half-opened eyes with his fingers. He stared at his son's face, silent.

Oliver's body was specially treated by a biochemical company to completely eliminate all cells in the body, in order to prevent the devil gene from contaminating that of the human beings. Oliver's body was reduced to zero. He was gone without a trace.

David and Emily were praised by the world for their righteous act above kinship and devotion to the benefit of the people. David and Emily, on a second thought, concluded that they should not entirely blame their son. The child had originally not been so bad. It was gene editing that killed him. Isn't it?

## *Epilogue*

In a wooded mountain area near the city of Boulder, an inconspicuous boulder was found inscribed with a line of words: "Oliver Polo 2007-2034 a soul who intended to devote himself to mankind but went astray."

Due to the deceased's grave sins in his life, he had no chance to rest in the cemetery, and had to stay in the wilderness. His life was cut short by his biological parents, with no remains of him whatsoever. Therefore, "a soul" is indicated. His parents set up a stone here as a reminder, indicating to actually an empty site.

Family members of the dead paid occasional visits to show that they still remembered someone of their family in their mind.

On a gloomy autumn day, Oliver's aged grandfather and grandmother were led here by their granddaughter, Sophia. Sophia picked some wild flowers in the field and put them on the edge of the stone. Grandpa and grandma read the slanting line of words on the stone, silent. After a long while, the old man coughed a few times, mumbling, "This child used to be so good, how could he have changed so much, and in the end with no place to bury himself." Then the old woman said, "My child, come to us when we die."

A couple of large crows flew overhead and made several loud cries.

It started to drizzle. A chilly wind was blowing. The old man shuddered at the gust of wind. Sophia said, "Grandpa, Grandma, let's go." The old couple and the young girl left, walking slowly and unsteadily. They looked back at the stone from time to time.

## *Wakening from a Nightmare*

## 2020 AD

The time had returned to the spring of 2020 AD. That year Emily was 38 years old. Oliver was 13. That was, 15 years before Oliver's supposed death.

It was snowing that day. Spring snow is common in Colorado. Often in spring, when the flowers are in bloom, an unexpected cold current brings heavy snow that destroys the new shootings and tender buds on the trees.

Deep at night, David heard Emily's painful sobs. He turned on the bedside light and saw that Emily's face was full of tears. He gave Emily a push and she woke up suddenly. She gasped and repeated, "We killed Oliver! We killed our son! The child is dead." David said, "Emily, what are you talking about? Are you dreaming? Our son is fine." "No, no," said Emily, "Oliver is gone, gone forever, without a trace." Emily embraced David tightly and cried loudly. David said, "Oliver is not dead. You can go to his bedroom and have a look if you don't believe it." Emily rose and got out of bed. She gently pushed open the door of Oliver's bedroom. Oliver was sound asleep in his bed. Emily stared at him over and over, and listened to his soft breathing. Then he gently closed the door of his son's room. When she was back at her own room, Emily kept murmuring, "Our son is not dead, he is still alive. Oliver is alive, alive......." David said gently," "You must have had some nightmare?" Emily detailed her nightmare to David. She said the child had a genetic editing surgery and had gone bad, becoming a superman and a devil. We two killed him. David said, "It's absolutely impossible. Oliver is always our angel. We have not passed to him any bad genes." Emily said, "But he changed his genes by himself in an operation and turned into a stranger." "He is just a child of twelve." said David, "How could he conduct an operation? Well, well, nothing of the sort. Please go on sleeping." David soon slept sound, while Emily couldn't fall asleep.

After his son got up the next day, Emily kept staring at him. Oliver felt a little weird, and asked his mother, "What happened to you today, Mom?" Emily looked closely at the innocent face of the child and muttered, "Still the original Oliver, still the same little angel." Oliver, puzzled, kept crying, "Mom! Mom!" Emily asked her son, "What are you going to do in the future, son? Do you have a wish?" Oliver answered, "Well, I haven't decided yet." Emily said, "Whatever you do, remember, don't do anything related to human genes." Oliver blinked his eyes and asked, "Human genes? It's innate. Why bother?" Emily said, "It's related to your Dad's major and profession." Olivier said, "I do not like that kind of stuff. I prefer drawing pictures like you." Emily smiled, hugged the boy in excitement, saying, "That's great, great! Remember, child, don't forget what your Mom says." Oliver said, "I will remember it, Mom."

Emily calmed down and looked out of the window, watching the swaying and fluttering snow with interest. The snow was growing heavier and heavier. Snowflakes danced in the wind, covering the ground, trees, and all objects with a layer of white velvet.

Human genes are the specific codes that determine their growth and shape their souls. Artificial editing of human genes is an improper act of stealing the sky and changing the day.

> *Genes are assigned by the Creator. It is sheer reckless, naive, stupid, and arrogant for any person who dares to touch it. The spirituality of the Creator is far superior to that of the mankind. To alter the gene without the Creator's authorization is really overrating oneself, not knowing how high the sky and how thick the Earth. The gene is the God's secret, it cannot be vented, and disturbed. Genes are destined. Destiny cannot be distorted and fooled. Those rash violaters can not escape bad luck.*

# Chapter 26

## THE DAMOCLES SWORD

### Some Year After 2020AD

On a certain day in a certain year after the year of 2020, a small country illegally possessing nuclear weapons had some military friction with another small country. Being doomed to failure in the war, its dictator was desperate to reverse the tide, with no sense of reason, had fired several nuclear bombs to the enemy side. The other country was not a nuclear power and suffered heavy losses, which led to the intervention of some major nuclear powers in the world.

The participation of great powers in the war evolved into a nuclear war on a world scale. The warring powers were trying to destroy each other with nuclear weapons. As a result, it had become a bloody catastrophe leading to suicide of human beings and destruction of human civilization.

It is said that the nuclear weapons that human beings have currently manufactured and stored are enough to destroy the Earth several times. Einstein once said: "I don't know what weapons will be used in World War III, but I know that the weapons that will be used in World War IV should be stones." That is to say, after World War III that might be a nuclear war, the surviving humans will return to the primitive Stone Age.

At present, the power of nuclear bombs far exceeds the two nuclear bombs used by the United States against Japan during World War II. Launched by missiles, they cover most of the land and sea islands on Earth. The consequences of nuclear war can be imagined. It can only be that all sides of the war will be hurt badly and perish together.

At that time, in addition to the United States, the big nuclear powers included two authoritarian powers in the East.

They already had a large number of nuclear and hydrogen bombs in their hands. Besides, the advanced technology and fast speed of carrier rockets make interception more difficult.

During the war, the mainland of the United States and its affiliated islands were fully exposed and attacked by nuclear bombs on a scale far larger than that of the Pearl Harbor Incident during World War II. The United States also launched missile interceptors and nuclear bombs in response. The battle was too close to call.

In the war, the first targets of the nuclear bombing were strategic locations such as missile bases, military airports, military camps, military seaports, and arms factories. There were also national capital, the capital of every state (or province) and the most prosperous and densely populated metropolis. As the saying goes, "When the city gate catches fire the fish in the moat come to grief." Civilian casualties were far much heavier than the military.

In the first round of the enemy's nuclear bombing Washington DC, New York on the east side were becoming seas of fire. Los Angeles, San Francisco, San Diego on the west side were ablaze.

New Mexico was also the focus of attacks because it was said that it had U.S. nuclear sites and facilities there.

Colorado in the mid-west of the US was also an important target for nuclear attacks. The enemy knew that there were air bases, an air force academy, nuclear plants, and suspected missile sites in the state.

On that day, the vast and beautiful land of Colorado was especially sunny and bright, and the flowers were in full bloom, when suddenly people saw some white smoke rolling like a huge mushroom, commonly known as the "mushroom cloud," which was the shape of the nuclear bomb explosion. When the nuclear bomb erupted, the mushroom-like smoke rose from the bottom and rolled up at the top, like a canopy.

The mushroom cloud was glowing and scorching. Nuclear radiation penetrated everything around it like a sword, which was extremely lethal.

The nuclear bombs fired by the enemy missiles rained down on the state of Colorado. Mushroom clouds rose one after another and the ground was boiling. The rows of towering buildings, shops, bustling crowds in busy streets were swallowed up by the rolling clouds. The power of the mushroom clouds was like the autumn wind that swept the fallen leaves, ruined everything in a second wherever it reached. After the mushroom clouds, one saw only a piece of scorched ground, with nothing left at all. Most of the burnt human bodies turned into smoke, and the residual human flesh, human bones, and animal corpses issued a pungent burnt smell, which was a bit like the over-charred BBQ.

The panicked crowd instinctively fled for their lives. As the main airports were destroyed all international and domestic flights in the US were grounded. Fleeing people could only take buses or drive their own cars from home.

The eastbound US-70 and northbound I-25 highways were packed with fleeing vehicles. All the roads leading east and north were also full of cars. People thought that the central and northern parts of the United States should be safer, to escape the bomb-hit states of Colorado and New Mexico. Yet, many of the vehicles that escaped from California poured into Colorado from the west. They got to know that Colorado was not safe either when they arrived. Residents of the northern states fled to Canada and of the southern states to Mexico. Highways across the United States were jammed with vehicles, forming a rare and big nuclear war escape in the world.

Ye Qiuming and Shen Huijuan's two sons were also among these fugitive vehicles. Their whereabouts were never known ever since.

There were often traffic jams on the road. During the congestion, people got out of their cars to breathe the fresh air, to chat and smoke on the roadside. Someone played the guitar. With the wonderful "Spanish dance music" someone danced gracefully. A guy even presented a comic talk, to imitate the warring tyrant, ridiculing the clown of war criminal who attacked America with nuclear bombs, that roused a big laughter.

The war was getting worse. The scope of enemy's nuclear strikes expanded. In addition, the scope of each nuclear bomb was wide, and the speed of the explosion was astonishing. Most of these fugitive vehicles were destroyed.

The nuclear war was escalating, affecting all states in the US, and even every corner of the world. People stopped fleeing because there was nowhere to escape.

As more nuclear powers joined, the world's partial nuclear war had evolved into the Third World War, which was larger and more devastating than the previous two world wars.

Billions of people on the earth, countless kinds of animals and plants, that had been full of vitality and thriving, were inadvertently involved in this disaster. The whole world had become a horrible abattoir, and some people exclaimed, "This is the world end!"

Several rounds of nuclear bombs dropped. All the major, medium-sized, and even small cities in the world were razed to the ground, and none of them survived. The splendid civilization created by mankind for thousands of years was destroyed in an instant. This sudden change was like a bolt from the blue, making people stunning and dumbstruck.

Somebody started to blame why should the Creator create intelligent human beings, and then let them self-mutilate with their own wisdom, almost extinct. It's simply that "the same Xiao He that helps one to win and then makes him lose." The Creator had actually made a big joke on humans.

Since ancient times, wars and man-made injuries have continued. The number of people who died of their own injuries is staggering. Humans themselves are to blame. It is not the original intention of the Creator that some people, for a certain purpose, a certain goal, for the sake of power and profit, destroy their fellow creatures and injure the innocent.

At this time, the familiar deep voice came back to Emily: "Humans beings are crazy! It is an absurd, stupid, tragic, self-destructive catastrophe. How could intelligent human beings come to this point? What a sin!" Emily recognized that it was the voice of the Heavenly Wise Man . "You are right, Sir," replied Emily. "I wonder if there is a good way to save mankind?" The Heavenly Wise Man said: "Up to now, at this stage, the end game has been irretrievable, and human beings have suffered for themselves. God can't help it. Let it be. Take care, young people! Go all the way!"

David and Emily knew very well that they were in great trouble and could not be spared. They were facing the disaster in their home and preparing for death. They had experienced the tragic scene at the End of the World and the reduction of the universe to zero while they were in the Wonderland. The e current disaster appeared familiar to them. They knew that it would be difficult for them to escape this time. People's life and death were the law of nature. They were especially calm in face of death – the destination of everybody.

David said to Emily: Recalling our life, it can be said to be rich and colorful.

Emily: Yeah, we were born in distant and different countries, but we met by chance. Together, we had experienced the perfection of the Wonderland and the tragic end of the world. You traveled alone to prehistoric times and experienced wonderful adventures there. I observed and had a better knowledge of the real life of the world people from the sky canopy. I am content to have such a life.

David: In particular, our exploration and understanding of the universe, the world and mankind have broadened our horizons.

Emily: We've seen through the world. We've seen through life. It's a pity that our lives are so short. I wish we could stay together for more years.

David: I hope so too. But life always has an end, and a fond dream never lasts forever.

Emily: We have been fully cared for by the god of destiny, we should not demand too much.

The two of them leaned close to each other, in the realm of profound love to end their precious lives together. Emily was lying in the arms of David. She said, "I have long dreamed that one day I could close my eyes in your arms and die, which would be a great happiness in my life." David said, "With you in my arms, we will die together, and this is the dream end of my life, too."

The loud bang and glaring flash of a nuclear explosion outside the window was no surprise to them. They had been in keen love for many years, the hot love burned like a flame.

At their middle-age there was still no reduction. The two looked at each other's faces affectionately. Each should be particularly familiar with the other, but suddenly they felt particularly fresh, even a little strange about the other. The feeling of their first love a few decades ago was back. David gently touched Emily's pretty face with his hand while Emily tightly grabbed David's massive torso. They stared at each other for a long time, kissing and hugging. Emily's eyes glistened with happy tears while David gently hummed a lyrictune.

In this way, the two lovers ended their ordinary, short, colorful, and legendary lives in the nuclear explosion. They were swallowed up by the flames of the nuclear bomb. Their bodies and souls went to zero, and they ceased to exist in the world and in the universe.

Ye Qiuming and Shen Huijuan, who also lived in Colorado at this time, had reached their old age.

They knew that a big disaster was imminent. They had a lot of thoughts. They were thinking of their bumpy life experiences. Their family had suffered all the hardships, made a lot of efforts, were now leading a normal and sweet life. They were happy with their children and grandchildren around them. Now they had no other desires and no regret in their hearts.

The roar, glare, and radiation outside deterred the earth and the mountains, people, and all animals. dogs and cats at home were close to people because of terror. The birds in the sky were chirping away in a random way.

Ye Qiuming and Shen Huijuan realized the situation in their own home. They knew that this human catastrophe was not circumvented. They had experienced man-made havoc in the past, and now they had to undergo another greater human destruction. It was still man-made.

They realized that man-made disasters were often more harmful to mankind than natural disasters. Throughout history, the number of people killed by war, massacre, and persecution had exceeded the number of deaths caused by natural disasters such as floods, droughts, and earthquakes.

The current man-made nuclear war was the catastrophe for all mankind.

The Qiuming couple couldn't help but recall the unfortunate lives of their parents. Now they were going to follow their parents to the underworld, perhaps to meet them there, too. They felt calm thinking like this.

This time, they wanted to go to death generously in the disaster, to maintain their dignity as human beings. They put on festive costumes, with high spirit, in the sound of music, to the end of their lives.

Due to the power cut, indoor lights, telephones, refrigerators, air conditioners, and electric horology had been stopped working. The music was unable to play through the stereo.

They played a Chinese song that they liked with an iPad: Why are the flowers so red, so red ah, red as a burning fire?

It symbolizes pure friendship and love Why are flowers so fresh, so fresh?

Ah, fresh to make people, to make people reluctant to leave It is watered with the blood of youth outside the window, the strong blast from the nuclear explosion hit the windows and doors heavily, shaking the walls. Suddenly, there was a loud crash. The window panes were shattered with pieces of glass scattered all over the floor.

Then the roof was slammed down and the whole house collapsed. The old couple were weighed down in the ruins of the house and stopped breathing. The flames came, burned and cremated their remains.

Qiuming and Huijuan's two sons with their wives, a grandson, were also missing. At this time their children and grandchildren did not know that their dear ones of the old generation had been buried in flames, having left the world forever.

The nuclear war in the world was indeed a catastrophe that mankind had never experienced before. In a nuclear war, people felt like that countless volcanoes were erupting all around at the same time, their brightness, heat, and lethality were no less than volcanoes, a larger scale of "Pompeii apocalypse" was being staged on the earth. Its tragic extent was tens of thousands of times worser than the end of Pompeii.

People had a sense of the heaven felling and earth rending, and the forthcoming of the world end. The nuclear bomb was so powerful that it was fierce and the speed was like lightning and thunder. Wherever it went, it was crushing and smashing. The eyes could not take it all in. People saw ugly mushroom clouds rose into the sky, shielding the beautiful sunshine, blue sky and white clouds. In a nuclear war birds do not fly in the sky and grass does not grow on the ground. Numerous fresh lives on the nuclear battlefield were being smeared, killed. They were struggling and dying in pain, like ants in the flames.

In the current nuclear war, the mushroom clouds once covered most of the earth and spread out like a carpet covering all the continents. The whole earth surface was burning and boiling, with dense smog of smoke as if to burn out this beautiful planet that had existed for billions of years with countless living creatures on it.

However, in the vast universe, even in the solar system, all that happened on earth is insignificant. At most, on the moon, one can occasionally catch glimpses of the earth's tiny glimmering sparks with an astronomical telescope.

The war maniacs were clamoring for the destruction of the entire globe. Indeed, it was just like a lunatic raving. The elements of a nuclear bomb come from earth's material and are artificially extracted to make nuclear weapons. It would be whimsical to use it to destroy the earth itself. Moreover, most of the earth is the ocean. No number of nuclear bombs can make the ocean burn.

Once the nuclear war breaks out in the world, there will be no winner. Nuclear war is tantamount to a suicide bombing attack in which the perpetrator and the belligerent are both victims.

Nuclear weapons are so powerful that they can destroy large number of living things and Human beings on the earth and damage human civilization created in thousands of years. But it cannot eliminate all mankind, and exterminate the whole of original ecology on earth.

As the US military fought back, the enemies' homelands were also a sea of fire, their nuclear stockpiles were not depleted before their missile sites were destroyed, preventing further launches. The nuclear war had to end there.

The mushroom clouds which descended like an avalanche was rampant for a while, but in the end, they were just passing clouds of smoke, and eventually had vanished into thin air, nor would radiation be ever lasting.

The earth had restored its former calmness, with mild sunshine and light breeze.

A few people who survived the bombing gradually woke up in the ruins, slowly climbed up from the thick dust, each person's face was covered with a layer of dust. Everybody was "gray-faced." They stared at each other, swearing, "Fuck! Damn it!" They shook off the dust on their bodies, looked around, saw the ruins, and felt as if they had come to a desolate land, a prehistorical cra. Thcy fclt cndlessly curious and unavoidably sad. The original world, the original environment, the original folks, everything they knew was gone. Even the flowers and trees on the earth, the birds in the sky, the animals on the earth, the small mosquitoes and flies, insects, beetles were almost extinct. They were beginning to realize the seriousness of the situation. They were now in a worse situation than the primitive hominids. The primitive hominids's ecological environment was full of vitality, but now before their eyes were just chaotic and bare.

These young modern people were gradually recovering their spirituality, just like the prairie grass that could not be destroyed by the wildfire, was growing again when the spring breeze blew. The human beings and the living creatures on earth had a tenacious vitality. After the disaster, they were still overflowing with vigour. No forcc could destroy them all.

They hummed a merry tune, took light dance steps, and couldn't help cheering, "I'm still alive! I'm alive!" "We are living pretty well." "Go to hell, damn the nuclear bomb! Damn the nuclear war!"

They started a new life, like angels that were floating in the air, roaming and swimming.

They were phoenix nirvana and reborn in the fire.

Someone exclaimed at this time, "Look, guys! What is it in the sky?" Everyone looked up and saw that an eagle was flying. It flew from afar, getting closer and closer, the outline was gradually clear, and the image was extraordinarily majestic. The crowd cheered and jumped up. The eagle was the symbol of the United States. It was clear to everyone that the United States had not been defeated, nor had it been totally destroyed. Some even shed tears of emotion.

The United States were hit hard during the world nuclear war. The capital, Washington, including the White House and the Pentagon, were razed to the ground. The bustling city of New York, along with its tall buildings, was reduced to rubble. Surprisingly, the towering Statue of Liberty though a little tilted, did not fall, and it had resisted the powerful nuclear shock wave in the nuclear explosion. It was said that the huge busts of the four presidents in Mount Rushmore in South Dakota had not suffered any damage, their faces had been covered with a layer of nuclear dust, and they were still the same after the rain, still solemn and stalwart. With sharp eyes, they were watching what was happening in the world today.

The Rocky Mountains running through the United States and Canada remained as strong as ever.

There came news about the whereabouts of David and Emily's son, Oliver and daughter, Sophia, and Oliver's girl friend, Alice. Also, Ye Qiuming and Shen Huijuan's grandson Frank.

During the war, these young people were touring in Yellowstone National Park in Wyoming. They hid in a valley jungle and avoided the threat of nuclear bombs. It was heard that the enemy had planned a massive nuclear attack on Yellowstone. Yellowstone Park was in a large active volcanic zone. It erupted 15,000 years ago, on a huge scale. A heavy nuclear bomb could trigger a major earthquake in the area followed by a tremendous volcanic eruption, endangering the vast areas of the northern, central and western United States, being equivalent to detonating a powerful nuclear minefield. This terrible plan was foiled before the American counterattack paralyzed the enemy's nuclear bomb base. The enemy deliberately relaxed the area during the initial nuclear bombardment, as they had a greater conspiracy to target Yellowstone with a heavy nuclear bombing. These lucky young people had thus escaped a great misfortune while their parents and many of their relatives were killed in the disaster.

After the war, these young people returned to Colorado.

They were deeply saddened and grieved to learn that their parents had been killed in the war. The unique insights, academic achievements and personal experiences of their parents David and Emily about the world, human beings and the universe were precious assets of mankind. The world would always remember them.

Oliver and Alice were married and held a unique wedding ceremony on the ruins of the nuclear war.

Frank and Sophia escaped the catastrophe together. The common experience had enhanced their friendship and love.

The two of them were like-minded and heart-to-heart and had become keen lovers. In this way, the Polo and Ye families were closely linked by kin relationship.

However, these survivors were facing dilapidated remains of a battlefield, and it was really like having returned to the Stone Age. Should they start from scratch and repeat the historical process of human development for millions of years? Oliver and Sophia's father, David, once traversed alone to the primitive human society and described to them about the life of primitive people in the Stone Age. The tools at that time were all made of stone. The low efficiency could be well imagined.

These surviving young people were not, after all, primitive people of millions of years ago. There was an infinite amount of wisdom accumulation of human beings in their mind. They had modern human genes in their blood. When they rebuilt their homes on earth, they could avoid a lot of exploration, research and development, save a lot of cost and time. There were always some corners on the earth that were beyond the reach of nuclear bombs, where a small amount of industrial facilities and raw materials being preserved. There were much useful information stored in the remaining books, documents and USB flash drives, which became useful info for the reconstruction of modern civilization. The reconstruction of Germany and Japan after the Second World War was impressive and convincing and could be used for reference.

The survivors were rebuilding their homes on the rubble, and the urban planning was re-arranged, being more tidy, more reasonable and more beautifull than in the past. There were innovations in industry, agriculture, and services. Technology was making great strides. Everything was started all over again, although laboriously, yet it was convenient to be completely renewed. A cicada chrysalis shed a layer of skin to become a flying cicada.

Nuclear war is a human catastrophe. From another perspective, it promotes the "transmutation" of human civilization.

But nuclear war is not the midwife of a new era. Human beings are always making progress and going up every day. Despite the detours, the general direction will not alter. Nuclear warfare should be and can be avoided.

The occurrence of nuclear war was a painful lesson for mankind to learn. The new international order was constantly improving. The development and stockpiling of nuclear weapons were strictly prohibited in the new era. The possibility of nuclear war was completely eliminated.

The world had changed. The environment was more beautiful and the world population was growing. The shortage of manpower promoted the development of automation and artificial intelligence. All kinds of robots had replaced the manual operation in the past.

The world was gradually recovering its original appearance. It was a pity that people's family members, relatives and compatriots killed in the catastrophe could not be revived, and the ruined tangible achievements of civilizations and cultural relics could not be reproduced. There had been a huge gap in the history of human civilization.

In this new world, the political landscape had undergone some changes. However, the United States and China were still world powers.

The political system of the United States before the nuclear war was superior, but far from perfect. A new generation of people was exploring and building a more complete and rational social system on the basis of the original.

The United States of America was stronger, greater, and more beautiful.

The song "Beautiful America" was heard all over America.
O beautiful for spacious skies,
For amber waves of grain,
For purple mountain majesties
Above the fruited plain!
America! Amcrica!

God shed his grace on thee
And crown thy good with brotherhood
From sea to shining sea!

China, with its great rivers and mountains, was hit hard in the nuclear war. Tall buildings were razed to the ground.

The once bustling city and beautiful countryside had become a stretch of scorched earth.

The land of China was devastated. The little remains of civilization after a decade of devastation in mid 20th century had been plundered by the far greater scourge of nuclear war.

In the desolate ruins of nuclear war, the Great Wall, a symbol of the Chinese culture, had been partly damaged, but the basic outline and main parts still stood proudly, full of national sentiments. The Kunlun Mountains, China's sacred mountains, were impenetrable and majestic. Rolling waves of the Yangtze River and Yellow River were still running through the land of China. These mother rivers, which bred the Chinese nations, continued to push forward the waves and flow eastward to the sea and ocean, integrating with the world trend.

The former Tiananmen Square was quiet. The magnificent buildings around it had disappeared. The places (the palace and the government buildings) where the monarchs and leaders ruled the people for centuries had turned into rubble and ashes. The square was surrounded by an endless open area, which made people feel lost and sad, but at the same time, they felt open-minded and relaxed. The old place was still there, which inevitably aroused people's many memories and associations of the past.

This place had witnessed many political vicissitudes: the end of feudal dynasties for thousands of years, the disasters of tyranny and the heroic struggles of reformists. This land was infiltrated with the tears and blood, despair and hope of the people.

Bulldozers rumbled in. They were burying the decay of the world, washing away the pain of the people in the past, ushering in light and hope.

The stinky skin of the eternal tyrant and murderous maniac displayed in the square was crushed and smashed by bulldozers and turned into the dust of history.

China, an ancient country, had experienced thousands of years of feudal autocratic rule. After the country was transformed into a republic in modern times, the suffering Chinese people were deceived, poisoned, and imposed by the Marxist Leninist heresy that came from the West. They were ridden by the modern tyrants of the heretical mafia and subjected to cruel bullying and exploitation.

The image of the country had been distorted and vilified by the current rulers, becoming the center of international evil forces. It was incompatible with and even sharply opposed to the modern world.

Some Chinese people had been brainwashed and misled by autocratic dictators, becoming abnormal and difficult to communicate and integrate with people from the civilized world.

However, most Chinese people inside and outside the Firewall were sober-minded, pursuing human civilization and political enlightenment. Today's world was beginning to understand that it was right to distinguish between China's authoritarian rulers and the Chinese people.

The old world had been shattered.

The new generation of Chinese people had completely thrown off their fetters and shackles.

They ended the world of unified rulers, completely disintegrated the original "big country."

Many regions in China with their own ethnic and cultural characteristics had become independent countries.

The original Great China no longer existed. It was replaced by a loose, powerful confederation of states, or dozens of vibrant states of varying sizes. These countries had adopted advanced democratic political systems and had abandoned all feudal traditions and Western heresies.

The Chinese nation was once again full of vitality. Those who had survived were busy again.

They were rebuilding their homes with intelligent minds, tenacious will and industrious hands.

The Chinese people were creating still more splendid civilization and splendor on the ruins of the old world.

China had once again become a rich and beautiful country with profound cultural tradition and charming cultural heritage.

At this time, the favorite song of Chinese people was "I Love You China."

> The lark flies through the blue sky
> I love you, China I love you, China, I love you,
> China
> I love you, the flourishing rice seedling in the spring
> I love you, the golden abundant fruits in the autumn.
> I love you, the temperament as the pine.
> I love you, the character of the red plum.
> I love you, the sweet sugarcane in our hometown,
> Which moistens my heart like milk from breast.
> I love you, China, I love you, China
> I want devote my beautiful youth
> To you, my mother, and my motherland.

Frank and Sophia also fell in love with the present China and decided to develop in China after finishing their schools.

Please look!

The young couple, Frank and Sophia, were walking hand in hand, gradually disappearing from the horizon.

The nuclear warfare site, where once no birds flying in the sky and no grass growing on the ground, was now lush and beautiful. The birds in the sky were flying around, the green grass covered the ground, dotted with beautiful blooming flowers. The charming sunshine and rosy clouds dyed the sky and was infinitely fascinating and pleasing.

If modern people can rationally and properly handle the nuclear weapons in their hands and focus on human well- beings, to completely destroy nuclear weapons, the above stories are undoubtedly illusory and fictitious. Otherwise, it will be true and real.

*Mankind has invented, manufactured, and stored a large number of nuclear weapons of mass destruction. This is the Damocles sword which hangs over the human head may fall at any moment. If a world nuclear war were to break out, its destruction would be unprecedented, and human and human civilization would sustain huge losses. This is entirely the sin of human beings themselves. The Creator originally created mankind and endowed them with superb wisdom. However, if this wisdom is not properly applied, it will severely damage mankind itself. However, the chance of nuclear war is slim.*

*Even if it breaks out it will not destroy the entire earth and cause the extinction of all mankind.*

*After a possible world nuclear war, the abused human race would be reborn and start all over again, assuming a complete new look.*

worldatlas
Atlantic Ocean
Bermuda
Miami
Bermuda Triangle
Gulf of Mexiico
San Juan Puerto Rico
Caribbean Sea
©GraphicMaps.com

www.ingramcontent.com/pod-product-compliance
Lightning Source LLC
Chambersburg PA
CBHW041747310726
48978CB00011BB/352